Christmas Lights
and
Cat Fights

Robyn,
Happy Reading!
Heather McKidu

Christmas Lights and Cat Fights

A
**JULES KEENE
GLAMPING MYSTERY**

Heather Weidner

LEVEL
BEST BOOKS

To Stan, Mom, and Dad,
thanks for all the love and support!

Praise for Vintage Trailers and Blackmailers

"In *Vintage Trailers and Blackmailers*, the calm of Jules Keene's Blue Ridge Mountain camper resort is disturbed when a man's lifeless body is found in the woods. What follows is a cozy mystery full of blackmail, secrets, mysterious strangers—and handsome security guy, Jake Evans. Jules and her loyal pup Bijou are in for a suspense-filled adventure. I love the warm and friendly characters and the twists and turns in this new down-home, mutt-loving series."—Susan Van Kirk, author of The Endurance Mysteries and *A Death at Tippitt Pond*

"Jules Keene is focused on her vintage trailer camping resort, but when a dead guest is discovered in the woods and her aunt is questioned, Jules decides to help catch the killer. She must stop the culprit, keep her guests satisfied, grow her business, run for president of the town's business council, and stay alive when the bad guys come after her. This book is a joy to read."—Jackie Layton, author of the Low Country Dog Walker Mysteries

"Packed with action and filled with "Oh, man, I didn't see THAT coming" moments, this first installment in the Jules Keene Glamping Mysteries series will not disappoint. And Weidner made glamping sound so glamorous that I think I'll take my husband up on his suggestion to go camping...but only if it's Fern Valley Camping Resort style!"—Jayne Ormerod, author of *Goin' Coastal*

"Smart and persistent businesswoman Jules Keene puts on her amateur sleuth hat to track down murderers at the upscale Fern Valley Camping Resort, set in the beautiful Blue Ridge mountains. The bad guys have met their match in this fast-paced mystery."—Frances Aylor, author of *Money Grab*

"Heather Weidner's *Vintage Trailers and Blackmailers* is an exciting addition to this year's cozy mystery line-up. Fern Valley Camping Resort, with its refurbished vintage trailers and tiny houses, is as enjoyable as can be, but don't be fooled, this book is all excitement. I don't know how she combines charm with a fast-paced story but I'm so glad she did."—Lane Stone, author of the Pet Palace Mysteries and the Tiara Investigations Mysteries

"Heather Weidner writes a fun and intriguing mystery that's full of twists and turns. Jules Keene, the owner of the posh Fern Valley Camping Resort in the Blue Ridge Mountains, brings sass and adventure as she works to figure out what's happening in her glamping get-away. The other characters are also well defined and add romance, humor, and hair-raising antics! Hard to put down once you start!!"—R. Lambertson, Amazon Reviewer

"Jules, the current owner and operator of a luxury campground of vintage trailers, loved what she did. She enjoyed the campers who came to have a week of relaxation in her collection of small vintage camping trailers. One visitor, in particular, Mr. Perkins, had paid 8 months in advance for the solitude of finishing the book he was writing. Jules was excited about having an almost-author in her campground, although he seemed eternally grumpy. For the most part, families loved coming there and enjoying the quiet and activities for the park's guests, until a murdered Mr. Perkins was found on the property. The local sheriff immediately started an investigation and strange things were discovered in the trailer he was occupying. Twists and turns pursued until the murderer was finally found. Even the reason for the murder was a big surprise. I really enjoyed this fun read and would highly recommend it for anyone. I especially liked the idea of the vintage trailers. What a great idea for a campground!"—Sandra Fehr, Amazon Reviewer

"Jules and her glamping resort are the scene of murder when one of the guests turns up dead. With an appealing cast of characters and a smart amateur sleuth, this series kicks off with a bang. I recommend this to readers who like their mysteries with plenty of red herrings before the satisfying end. Five stars!"—K. M. Rich, Amazon Reviewer

"This is the first book by this author that I have read. The first book in A Jules Keene Glamping Mystery. Jules owns a camping resort "glamping" that she runs with her Aunt Roxanne. Love Aunt Roxanne's personality. The resort is more upscale and is quite busy with bookings. Well, Jules' camper resort gets turned upside down when Ira Perkins is found dead in the woods. A mystery with humor, full of secrets, one very handsome security guy, Bijou the dog, blackmail, and some interesting strangers. A fun mystery and look forward to what happens next."—Amy, Goodreads Reviewer

"This was a great cozy mystery starter. I love the idea of Jules's campground. I think the whole "glamping" would be really fun and unique. Heather Weidner wrote a really great storyline with great characters. I think Jules's dog, Bijou, will be everyone's favorite character. The town of Fern Valley seems like the ideal spot for tourists, but it has that warm familiarity to it that could easily make it home for anyone. I'm so excited to see what Heather will come up with next for Jules and Bijou."—Valerie Blankenship, Valerie Blankenship Book Reviews

"Vintage Trailers and Blackmailers by Heather Weidner is a fantastic start to a new series for Ms. Weidner. I can't wait to read the next book in this series to find out what else Jules can get into when it comes to solving a mystery. Jules, Roxanne, Jake, and Emily are all great characters, and I can't wait to see what else can happen with them. I am giving Vintage Trailers and Blackmailers by Heather Weidner five stars and recommending it to everyone that likes to read cozy mysteries."—Karen Baron, The Baroness Book Reviews

"This is my first book by this author, but it definitely won't be my last! I was hooked from the very first page!"—Tonya S., BookBub Reviewer

"The unique setting at a campground pulled me in and gave me a vicarious "glamping" escape. Memorable characters, unique setting and twisty-turny plotting made this a great weekend read. Waiting (not so patiently) for the second installment in the Jules Keene Glamping mysteries."—Mystery Loving Mom, Amazon Reviewer

"Take a break from routine with a visit to a charming mountain resort that features vintage trailers and other whimsical lodging options. While there, get caught up in a puzzling death of a guest. Resort owner Jules investigates murder with the help of an interesting cast of characters. A satisfying and enjoyable read."—S. E Warwick

"Jules Keene runs a family-friendly campground filled with restored and luxurious vintage trailers in the small town of Fern Valley. But when two of her guests stumble upon a dead body, it could spell trouble for this small town resident. Does the dead man have secrets to hide beyond what he's shared with Jules? Overall, I really enjoyed this series starter. All the characters were likeable, and the setting was superb. I found the writing flowed well and was easy to read and digest. The story focuses not only on the mystery but on small town life and Jules's journey in life. The book was a light, fun, quirky read with interesting characters. It sets up for a unique series. I found it very entertaining and enjoyable to read this clean, fun cozy mystery! I highly recommend this book and series!"—Nellie's Book Nook

"Now, this is my idea of camping! Cute, upcycled vintage trailers are so much better than tents! (Not that I have camped in a tent in the last 30 years…..) If Fern Valley Camping Resort was real, you can bet I'd be vacationing there. As owner of this resort, Jules Keene has got a great thing going. The campers are full, and people are happy. One reason they might be happy too is the delicious breakfasts that they can get in the lodge. I'd fill up on cinnamon rolls. *Vintage Trailers and Blackmailers* is a fantastic start to what I'm sure will be a wonderful series! Heather Weidner paints us a vivid picture, and it's easy to feel as if you're in Fern Valley. She describes not only the camping resort but also the town. You're going to get hungry since Jules visits several trendy restaurants in Fern Valley. So, get some cookies or carrots (or better yet, cinnamon rolls) for your book reading snack. I also love the fact that she doesn't tell us about many of the trailers because that leaves more surprises for the next book. And, speaking of more surprises, I can't wait to see how the tiny house village that they're planning comes along. The characters are very well-written, and I feel like, for a first book in a series, I got to know them fairly well. I'm looking forward to seeing how they grow through the series. There were just enough side characters to not overwhelm us. Everybody plays an important role in the book. I won't tell you who my favorites were from Vintage Trailers and Blackmailers. You never know; I might change my mind later! The mystery is well-plotted, and the pacing works perfectly. I never felt like things were dragging along or moving too quickly. I'm really looking forward to reading more books in the series. Add Vintage Trailers and Blackmailers to your to be read piles today!"—Christy's Cozy Corners

"Jules Keene runs a family-friendly campground filled with restored and luxurious vintage trailers in the small town of Fern Valley. But when two of her guests stumble upon a dead body, it could spell trouble for this small town resident. Does the dead man have secrets to hide beyond what he's shared with Jules? Overall, I really enjoyed this series starter. All the characters were likeable, and the setting was superb. I found the writing flowed well and was easy to read and digest. The story focuses not only on the mystery but on small town life and Jules's journey in life. The book was a light, fun, quirky read with interesting characters. It sets up for a unique series. I found it very entertaining and enjoyable to read this clean, fun cozy mystery! I highly recommend this book and series!"—Nellie Steele, Nellie's Book Nook

"I love the premise of this well-written and light-hearted whodunit where we meet Jules Keene, who owns a camping resort where murder does not mix with vintage trailers, but alas a guest fell victim and it was up to Jules to figure out the who, the what, and the why this person was murdered and to protect her business. From the introduction of the characters to the small-town atmosphere to the vintage trailer camp to the victim to the events leading up to his death and the killer's identity and apprehension, the author did a great job in presenting this well-crafted mystery that kept me immersed in all aspects. The suspect pool was short, but it was the follow-ups that kept me in the guessing game. The author knows how to tell a story that was both intriguing and suspenseful with visually descriptive narrative and engaging dialogue. The pacing was on par with how well this story was being told. Overall, this was fun book and I look forward to more adventures with Jules and her friend in this delightfully entertaining series."—Dru Ann Love, Dru's Book Musings

"*Vintage Trailers and Blackmailers*: A Jules Keene Glamping Mystery is the first book in a new series. The story takes place in Fern Valley, a small town located in the Blue Ridge Mountains of Virginia. Jules and her aunt run the family-owned business, a fifty-acre Fern Valley Luxury Camping Resort. The company specializes in retro-inspired trailers. When a guest at the campground is murdered, Jules becomes worried about the effect on the resort's business. Even though enforcement officers are actively working on the case, Jules takes it upon herself to try and solve the mystery of who killed the guest and why. Any information pertinent to the murder case, Jules passes on to law enforcement personnel. However, she keeps a copy of everything to aid in her quest to discover the truth. The murder is only the beginning of criminal behavior by an unknown assailant(s). Will the culprit(s) behind the unlawful acts be identified and arrested? Heather Weidner has done an outstanding job with this engaging and enjoyable debut novel that features Jules Keene. The story introduces a group of realistic characters. Jules is likable and believable in the central role, and the supporting characters are an interesting mix of personalities. The story is not just about a mystery to be solved. It also encompasses secretive behavior, interpersonal relationships, perseverance, political aspirations, business undertakings, the close connection between a pet and its owner, and a juggling act between amateur sleuthing and fulfilling job-related duties. The author brings the story alive with dialogue that fits compelling characters and well-crafted scenes that use imagery and figurative language. Twists and turns, along with criminal actions that escalate as the story progresses, keep readers invested and make them want to keep reading. At the end are recipes of foods enjoyed by characters in the book. Vintage Trailers and Blackmailers is an appealing mystery that will entertain readers, and I look forward to reading about more adventures of Jules Keene and how her character continues to develop in future books."—Diane Woodman, Amazon Review

"Vintage Trailers and Blackmailers" is the first book in a new series, but doesn't read like one. I mean that in the best possible way. Often, first books tend to spend a lot of time setting the scene and introducing the characters, with the murder almost taking a backseat to the series background. This book launches right in with the mystery element, and does an excellent job of introducing characters, relationships, and the location as part of the narrative. I liked main character Jules. She is a sensible businesswoman who approaches the murder at her glampground in a logical, methodical way. I appreciated that she kept some of her focus on her business instead of devoting every waking minute to solving the mystery, as some cozy heroines tend to do. I also liked the way she worked with her tech-support friend and law enforcement instead of trying to do everything herself. Other characters, especially Roxanne, Jake, and Bijou (her terrier) were well-written, detailed, and added a lot to the story. The mystery itself was also well-written. There were plenty of clues to follow, and I enjoyed watching Jules try to track down answers, both online and in person. I liked the way more was gradually revealed, both about the crime and the motive behind it. One thing that made this mystery stand out was that the main suspect was obvious early on. The real questions to be resolved were WHO exactly this person was, what motivated him, and how to actually apprehend him. I always enjoy it when a cozy offers me something a little different, and this one definitely hit the mark! While the romance aspect was on the back-burner in this book, there is plenty of potential for an interesting love triangle to develop for Jules. I need to learn more to decide which man I'm rooting for. Roxanne's budding romance is also intriguing, and could have some entertaining developments in future books. I very much enjoyed the setting at a glamping-style campground near real-life Charlottesville, Virginia. I liked reading about the different themes of some of the refurbished campers, and the tiny houses. I look forward to seeing more featured in the next book in this series. Five out of five slices of perfect Provolone!"—Chewie the Mouse Amazon Review

Chapter One

Wednesday

"Jules. Hey, Whoohoo, Jules!" A shrill voice echoed above all the noise in the town square. A svelte woman in a leopard-print ski jacket waved her arms and ran in heels toward Jules Keene.

Jules paused with her setup preparations and pushed a red curl that had escaped from her ponytail off of her face. "Hi, Tabbi. What can I do for you?"

"Your partner for this town holiday festival thingy is so unreasonable. In fact, she's arbitrary and capricious. I paid my vendor fees, and I shouldn't be treated like this." Tabbi put both hands on her hips, planted her feet, and shook her long brown curls that framed her face like a lion's mane. Her puffy parka and black stiletto suede boots projected a hipster vibe, but the tiny parentheses surrounding her mouth gave away her true age.

"I'm sorry. What are you talking about?" Jules closed the three-ring binder that had the assigned locations for all the vendors for Fern Valley's Christmas extravaganza.

Tabbi Morris made a harrumphing sound and let out a deep breath. "That woman – Elaine is impossible. I paid to have four trailers here, and I've committed to having workers staff them for the entire weekend. And now, she's telling me that I can't use the sidewalk. She put me on the edge of the square where there's virtually no traffic. She's policing the grass and sidewalks. She doesn't like my extension cords either. I told her I had to have electricity to create the right ambiance for my gear."

1

Before Jules Keene, owner of the Fern Valley Luxury Camping Resort and president of the town's business council, could answer, Elaine James waddled up to the pair. Her poofy blond bouffant added about four inches to her height. Jules smiled when she thought of Elaine's motto: *the taller the hair, the closer to God.*

Elaine paused and took a deep breath. "There you are. I asked your worker, the guy who looks like a young Fabio, only with curly black hair, to start moving your trailers, and he refused. You're in the wrong spot. This is not right." Elaine set her mouth, and the stare from her deep blue eyes bore into the taller woman.

"We pulled the trailers where your guy in the vest pointed to this morning. I paid for four vendor spaces, and you put us in the worst location. My team is doing our best to maximize the potential. And you're being draconian with all these rules," Tabbi whined and glared at Elaine.

Elaine glared back and pursed her lips. When she wagged her finger, her whole body, including her tall hair, wiggled like a Jello mold. "Those rules are important. We must have order. Besides, I told you twice that you all were in the wrong spots. You're on Candy Cane Alley with the food vendors. Your trailers should be on the other side, on Elf Lane. You have four spots by the stop sign, two on each side of the street. It's marked off in green chalk. Spots one through four."

"What? You want me to move? My team has already done most of the prep work. And both of my Christmas-themed trailers, the *As Seen on TV* one, and the Big Cat Souvenirs took forever to get situated."

"No, you can't be on the food vendors' side. It will ruin everything." Elaine huffed and put her hands on her hips. She puffed out her cheeks, and her fuzzy white coat made her look like a giant snowball. "I would think you would want the better spots." Elaine's eyebrows disappeared in her well-shellacked bangs.

Trying not to show her impatience and hoping to keep the peace, Jules stepped in. "Maybe we could get some volunteers to help you break down and move. I think you'll probably have better sales on the vendor side. You'll be front and center at the entrance. That's a coveted spot."

Tabbi rolled her eyes but considered the idea. "I guess we can move if you think the location is better. We've got a bunch of top-tier merchandise. I drove all the way from Berryville for this, so I hope your festival lives up to the hype. If it doesn't, you'll hear about it. And so will everyone else." The woman turned and stomped down the sidewalk.

Elaine made a face. "I told her twice that she was in the wrong place. Some people." She threw her hands in the air and bustled off in the opposite direction.

Jules was glad to have Elaine's help organizing the festival, but sometimes, the owner of the Birds and Bees nature store was a little prickly. Elaine brought organization to anything that needed planning, but it always came with a side of drama.

Returning to her notes for the upcoming weekend's events, which included two concerts, a tree lighting, a parade of lights, and a big cat demonstration by Cal's Cats at the high school, Jules flipped through the pages on the clipboard. The business council team had planned holiday events for the next three weekends to draw visitors to town to celebrate the season and help the local businesses end the year with a bang.

Jules ran her finger down the schedule. The festival kicked off tonight with concerts at the Baptist and Methodist churches and a performance by the high school drama club of *A Charlie Brown Christmas*. Friday's plans included a parade of lights. On Saturday, the team planned a big celebration with the grand illumination of the town Christmas tree. Jules was excited the festival was extending the tourist season, and as an extra bonus at her resort, all of her vintage trailers and tiny houses were booked for the next three weeks.

She set her clipboard on the notebook and drained the last few drops of coffee. Jules packed her backpack and did a lap around the courthouse to ensure there were no other flare-ups or issues. The spots that Tabbi's team had vacated were already filled with new vendors. Food trucks and trailers lined both sides of the streets. Soon, the town square would be filled with smells rivaling those of any county fair. Jules's mouth watered at the thought of funnel cake and holiday goodies.

3

She crossed the town green in front of the courthouse and administrative buildings. Trailers lined both sides of the street on the other side of the square, too. Brightly colored signs advertised everything from T-shirts to glow-in-the-dark souvenirs.

On the corner, Tabbi supervised the move of two of her trailers. A mountain of a man who looked like a bodybuilder guided the last of her four trailers in place.

Pushing her tortoiseshell sunglasses in her hair, Tabbi said, "Perfect. Thanks, Tony." She blew him a series of kisses. "We'll do just fine here."

He ran a hand through his dark curls and ambled off toward the food trucks.

"That didn't take long," Jules said as she approached. "I hope you like this location better. The people entering on Friday and Saturday will start here. That should be a primo location for your team."

"I certainly hope so." Tabbi turned and adjusted laminated signs of tiger and lion cubs on the counter of her jungle-themed trailer.

A twiggy-looking woman in a blue Tabbi's Tees shirt under her unzipped ski jacket sauntered over. "All done, Tabs. My trailer's ready to go. Do you want me to go ahead and open up?"

"Of course. Let's not waste a minute or a customer." Tabbi waved her bejeweled fingers as she talked. "Jules, have you met Dana Taylor? She helps me on weekends with my booths. And she's been my bestie for more years than either of us wants to count. I can't live without her."

Dana beamed at her friend.

"It's nice to meet you." Jules smiled. "You have quite the variety of wares here."

Dana flashed a toothy grin. "I help Tabbi find the most interesting merchandise. You have to constantly be on top of what's hot at the moment. Otherwise, you end up with a storage unit full of stuff no one wants."

Tabbi nodded. "You have to dance on the razor's edge and be willing to take chances. And you definitely have to be ready to strike when something is hot. Fads are fleeting."

"That's why she's so successful," Dana gushed. "By the way, that tubby

4

woman told me I couldn't open until five. She said that's when the cops will block off the streets to cars." Dana took off her coat and pulled on an oversized Christmas sweater. Jules did a double take. She hadn't seen heavy-duty shoulder pads like that since the Big 80s.

Before Jules could speak, Tabbi said, "Who cares what she said? I said you could open. Send her to me if she gives you any lip. We're here to make money."

Dana's nasally laugh grated on Jules's nerves. "We can take her and that other witchy woman whose name we will not mention." She winked, turned, and strutted back to the trailer across the street.

Shrugging off the mean-girl antics, Jules continued her stroll around the square. *I hope this weekend isn't full of drama and snark.*

Everything looked in order. Done with the business council work, it was time to check on the new arrivals and her team at the resort and then pick up Jake for this evening's date. Nearing the center of the grassy area, she thought about Jake Evans, her resort's maintenance and security guy, whom she had known since they were teens. He'd worked on and off for her dad for the years before two tours in the army in the Middle East. His homecoming coincided with Jules's return to Fern Valley after her divorce from the Idiot. It was the perfect time for a change, a chance to start over. She'd helped her dad restore vintage trailers and revitalize the campground. She had quit her interior design job to make Fern Valley home again after her father passed away, and the resort became her full-time job.

As Jules headed toward her silver Jeep Wrangler, a series of loud shrieks and screams interrupted her memories that had turned melancholic. She spun around without hesitation, jogging toward the noise. Tabbi and a blond, buxom woman in a zebra-print mini-dress with no coat shouted at each other.

"You, again. You just won't leave my husband alone. Why are you everywhere we go? You're a leech. You're trying to make money off the good work we do." The blond stamped her foot and glared at Tabbi.

"It's a free country," Tabbi hissed. "I can go to any festival I want to. I'm an entrepreneur. My products are diversified. I don't do *just* animal things.

And I've always been about animal rescue. Way before you ever entered the picture. And in case you haven't noticed, people prefer my T-shirts. Not those knockoffs you all are peddling." Tabbi looked down her long, pointed nose at the blond, who stood about a head shorter than she. "And when I say I give proceeds to animal charities, I really do." Tabbi's nostrils flared, and her cheeks flashed from a rosy pink to red.

"A lot of our sales go to support animal welfare projects. You better watch your mouth." The blond spat out the words like they were day-old sushi.

"Gimme a break. How much do you really give to charity?" Tabbi sneered. "I think fraud is the correct term. You scam people." She curled her lips into a snarl.

The blond ran her arms across the counter, knocking all the posters in plastic stands to the ground. "This is the sham. You don't support these rescue sites. You're a phony. And if you think you're going to get Cal back, you're dead wrong. I'll make sure of that."

Tabbi took two steps forward, grabbed the woman by the shoulders, and shook her. The blond shrieked like a banshee and grabbed Tabbi's hair, shoving her backward toward the sidewalk. Tabbi teetered in her tall boots and lost her balance. The blond leapt on her with feline precision, and the two women rolled around the sidewalk and into the grass in a jumble of arms, legs, and wild hair.

Before Jules could get closer, several sharp whistle blasts echoed across the green. Elaine James jogged over to the two women and attempted to pull them apart. Within seconds, she was pulled into the punching, kicking, and hair-pulling tumbleweed that rolled across the grass in front of the courthouse.

Tabbi bit Elaine on the leg. The usually prim and starchy owner of the nature shop punched Tabbi in the face. The taller woman scratched at Elaine and rolled off the pile of arms and legs. Tabbi covered her face with her hands and screeched. "I think you broke my nose!"

A burly man dressed like a mashup of Crocodile Dundee and Jack Hannah picked up the blond woman and returned her to her feet. She pushed her hair backward and tried to pat it back in place. Grass and dirt-stained her mini-dress. She tugged on the hem to cover the important parts that probably shouldn't be on display at a Christmas festival.

"What is going on here?" The man's voice boomed as a small crowd gathered. Several people recorded the tussle with their phones.

"She's. . .she's here. Why is she always where we are? I can't stand it. She won't leave us alone." She continued to smooth her zebra dress and pointed at Tabbi.

"Ignore her. She's trying to get your goat. And it looks like she succeeded," he said.

The curvy woman turned and hugged the guy in the jungle-guide get-up. He patted her back, took her hand, and led her across the street to a tiger-striped, tricked-out Humvee with "Cal's Cats" plastered on it. The giant red letters looked like they had been clawed, and bright yellow eyes peeked out of jungle foliage.

Elaine stood and dusted herself off. "I need to go check on some things. Jules, I'll call you later." She glared at Tabbi, who covered her face with her hands.

Jules hoped her mouth wasn't hanging open.

The bodybuilder who worked for Tabbi hurried across the street. "Babe, are you all right?"

"I'm fine," she shrieked, wiggling her nose with her hand. "I need to clean up and find some ice before this turns into a massive shiner. Tabbi, who looked more like a cavewoman than a chic entrepreneur, waggled her finger inches from Jules's nose. "After I calm down, I'll decide whether or not to press charges. I'll let you know."

The large man draped an arm around Tabbi's shoulders, but she shrugged him off like a worn-out sweater. She clomped off between the trailers. The man looked around, ran a hand through his longish, jet-black hair, and followed behind the hot mess.

The crowd of onlookers drifted back to whatever they were doing. With Elaine nowhere in sight, Jules made a quick exit. She could only hope that tonight's events would be more subdued. This was not how she envisioned the start of the business council's first Christmas celebration.

Chapter Two

Thursday

"Come on, puppy. Let's go see what's going on at the office." Jules's brown and white Jack Russell terrier, Bijou, danced for joy when she heard the magic "go" word. Jules pulled on her coat and grabbed the dog's leash. She and Bijou walked briskly from her cabin at the back of the property around the vintage trailers to the large log cabin that served as both store and administrative office for the resort. Even Bijou didn't dillydally this morning.

Jules stamped her boots to knock off the frost on the cement pad under the carport, and Bijou trotted up the stairs, waiting for the back door to open. Hearing voices in the front of the building, the dog tore through the office to the store.

"Hey, Sweetie," Jules's aunt Roxanne said, picking up Bijou for cuddles and dog kisses. "Good morning. How are y'all?"

"Good. Everything's set up in town. How're things here?" Jules asked.

"We're booked solid for the weekend. We checked in all the vendors today, and I expect the other guests to check in tonight and tomorrow. Emily's working afternoons and the weekend to cover the desk." Roxanne, in her stylish baby pink cashmere sweater, black leggings, and signature pearls, straightened the pens on the counter.

Jules's eyes landed on the tall Christmas tree in the corner. White lights twinkled. Burlap and plaid red ribbon intertwined among the branches created a warm, rustic look. Peach baskets full of ornaments representing the Blue Ridge Mountains surrounded the base. Jules tried to showcase area artisans and their creations whenever she could. "The tree looks great," she said, inspecting a hand-painted design of the mountains painted on reclaimed wood.

"Emily helped me with it yesterday. We've already sold some of the decorations. And Lester put up the two trees on each side of the fireplace in the lodge. Mel and Crystal had fun decorating those. We're ready for the holidays." Roxanne smiled as she rummaged through the drawer under the front counter.

"You guys took care of everything."

"You've been a tad busy with all the festival planning. We wanted to surprise you, and we thought you could use the help," her aunt said.

"I love it. Yep. I've been a little distracted lately." Before Jules could comment further, they heard a noise in the back. Bijou yipped and ran through the store like the devil was chasing her.

"Hey, there," echoed from the back room. Jules's handsome security and maintenance guy, Jake, stepped into the store carrying Bijou. The wiggly terrier melted in his arms.

"Hey, back. What are you up to?" Jules asked.

"We finished Kurt Marino's tiny house. Everything's hooked up, and he plans to move in soon. Working on his project gave me some ideas for the next one for our village. I'll show you some pictures when you get a minute."

"Send me the pictures of Kurt's house, too, and I'll update your webpage for you," Jules said.

She and Jake had expanded their partnership the previous summer when they'd decided to add tiny houses to the resort's offerings. It gave Jake an opportunity to showcase them as his model homes, and it offered Jules's guests another unique and upscale vacation opportunity. The tiny house craze had many fans and curious guests who wanted to experience it firsthand.

Jake set Bijou on the floor and pulled out his phone. After some tapping, he said, "Done. And thanks. The new designs have a British look to them. You'll have to come up with a theme for them." Jake stepped behind the counter and looked at the reservation application on the computer. "Anything going on here that I should know about?"

"Nope. It's all good," Roxanne said, straightening fliers for area attractions. "Got a full house this weekend. Mel and Crystal whipped through all the cleaning for our arrivals, and they started breakfast service at the Lodge this morning. It's nice to have a hot breakfast before work."

"I just want coffee today," Jake said, making a beeline for the coffee maker on the counter in the back. Bijou followed him with the hope of scoring more treats.

The bells on the front door tinkled, and Jules pulled the bottom half of the dividing door shut to keep Bijou from being the resort's welcome wagon.

The tall man, who had interrupted yesterday's melee, stepped through the door, followed closely by the blond who'd wrestled Tabbi in the town square. Today, the man sported olive-colored garb. He looked like a guide on Disneyworld's Jungle Safari ride.

Jules had a flash of panic when she remembered Tabbi and her crew had reservations at the resort, too. She made a mental note to see where the two groups were staying. *Hopefully, far away from each other.*

"Good morning. How can we help you?" Roxanne asked from behind the counter.

"Hi, y'all." The man took off his safari hat and bowed slightly. "I'm Cal Collins, and this is my blushing bride, Misti. We're in the Baum house, and we could use some towels."

"We'll get those right to you," Jules said.

Before she could continue, Misti interrupted. "I need at least six towels, and Cal will need a set or two. Is there a grocery store in this town?"

"We have some supplies here," Roxanne interjected. "If you're looking for groceries, there's the Circle K Market on the edge of town about four miles from here."

"Thank you," Cal said as Misti browsed the shelves.

Dropping Twinkies, a bag of Hershey Kisses, and a large container of cheese puffs on the counter, Misti said, "This should hold me until I get to the store."

Cal laid a twenty on the counter, and Roxanne gave him his change. "We've parked our trucks and trailers in the field behind the tiny houses. Your groundskeeper said we could leave them back there on the grass," he said.

"That's fine." Jules moved behind the counter next to Roxanne.

"I have a pair of lions, tigers, and cheetahs. Just like Noah." He chuckled at his own joke. "And chimpanzees, tiger cubs, cheetah cubs, alligator, and an albino python. My son and his assistants are staying in the cat carrier parked by the cages. I put up some hurricane fencing around the area, so people don't wander too close. Especially if they hear animal noises. We have to make sure we don't lose any fingers that might get stuck through the bars. However beautiful, the animals are still wild."

Jules felt a concerned look creep across her face.

"Now, don't you worry about it, little lady. Like I told you when we chatted on the phone, we do everything we can to promote safety. The cages are locked, and we follow every safety mandate. It wouldn't do if our animals ate the audience members. Not good for business."

She attempted a smile. "Please let me or my team know if you need anything."

"You have a lovely resort. You'll have to come up and visit our place sometime. Cal's Cats is in Verona off I-81. Come by, and I'll give you the grand tour of our wildlife preserve."

"I'd love to see it." Jules couldn't wait to see the cubs. "We'll drop the towels off in a little while. Anything else you all need?"

"Nope," Misti said, opening the candy and popping one in her mouth.

Cal patted his wife's shoulder and followed her out the front door.

"What'd I miss?" Jake asked, striding into the room as the screen door slammed behind Cal.

"Cal and Misti. The big cat people," Roxanne said, pulling out an emery board and filing her pearly pink nails.

Jules tapped on the computer behind the counter. She let out a long, slow breath. Tabbi and her team had two vintage trailers on the other side of the resort. One was a 1940 New Moon, decorated in honor of the final frontier and the Apollo flights. The other was a 1936 Masterbuilt Trailer with a rounded roof that she had decorated with all kinds of British royal family memorabilia to mark the year that Edward VIII abdicated the throne and married Wallis Simpson.

Jules shook off thoughts of her themed trailers and the possibility of another Misti and Tabbi dust-up. "I'm going to take towels over to their tiny house and check out the cubs. Anybody wanna come?" Jules pulled out a stack of linens and rummaged through the key box for the master key to the L. Frank Baum house.

"I'll drive you over," Jake said.

"Roxanne, we'll be back in a few. Bijou's back here with you." Jules pulled on her coat and picked up the towels.

"Not a problem. We'll have girl time while you're gone."

Jake took the stack from Jules and held the door. She slid into the front seat of the golf cart, and he jumped in the driver's seat for a quick ride to the edge of the resort.

They bumped over the grass and around the vintage trailers to the tiny houses, where Jake came to a quick stop. Balancing the stack of towels, Jules jogged up the steps and knocked on the yellow door. When there was no answer, she yelled, "Housekeeping."

She counted to ten and fished the key out of her pocket. Leaning the towels on one hip, she opened the door to the home's sitting room, complete with a widescreen TV for movie viewing and a reading nook in the corner. It took five steps to cross the room and leave the towels on the bathroom counter. Cal and Misti had managed to cover the ruby red couch and side chairs in clothes and hats that looked more like costumes than everyday wear.

Jules backed out the door and jiggled the handle to check to see it locked."

"All good?" Jake asked.

"Yup. It didn't take them long to unpack multiple outfits for a weekend gig."

"Sorta like the Hollywood folks. Those movie people last fall brought a ton of stuff with them. Wanna go see the cats?"

"I thought you'd never ask. I am such a sucker for baby animals." Jules

12

climbed into the seat next to him. Jake put the cart in gear and drove behind the tiny house village. As they approached the animal trailers parked in a rectangle behind orange plastic fencing, they heard roars and monkey chatter.

Cal, another youngish guy, and two women stood in front of a cage with two grown tigers. One big cat yawned, and the other rolled over on its back.

"Hey, didn't expect to see you so soon," Cal said, turning to face the golf cart. Jules and Jake walked closer to the fencing where the big cats lazed.

"We dropped off your towels and decided to swing by to see how things were going. This is Jake. He's in charge of security for the resort."

"Nice to meet ya." Cal tapped his safari hat. "We're good to go. These guys will be ready for tomorrow's parade and the wildlife demo this weekend. Glad to be here. This is my son Cody. And this is Angel and Ingrid." Cal pointed to the other three in khaki outfits and boots.

"We're excited that you're part of our first Christmas festival." Jules smiled at Cal's staff, who led the tigers toward the cages.

"You want to see the cubs, huh?" Cal asked with a grin.

Jules nodded.

"Hop over and come this way." Cal held the orange fencing down so Jules could step over it. She and Jake followed Cal past the trailers with cages to a mobile home. Cal and the two women caught up and disappeared inside the vehicle.

When they returned, each climbed down the stairs with a pair of cubs, four tigers, and two baby cheetah fluff balls.

Jules's heart melted.

They set the cubs in the grass, and they hopped around after each other. Two played with whatever they found while the others wrestled in the dirt.

"Do you mind if I take pictures?" she asked. "I'd like to put them in my newsletter."

"Come over here, and Cody can get photos of you all, too," Cal said. "We love to share our animals. Make sure to tag Cal's Cats if you post them." He winked as Jules stepped closer.

Jules handed her phone to the guy who looked like a younger version of

Cal. He snapped several shots and handed the phone back.

She rubbed the fuzzy head of one of the cheetahs. "They're adorable. And they'll be the hit of the weekend. Thanks for letting us see them."

Jake stood and brushed the grass from his jeans. "A once-in-a-lifetime opportunity."

Jules grabbed Jake's hand, and they walked past tigers, chimpanzees, lions, and a cheetah. The wild animal noises echoed through the trees and drowned out the normal woodland sounds of the Blue Ridge Mountains. It sounded like a zoo, but at least the animals seemed content. *I just hope I can keep Misti, Tabbi, and Elaine far enough away from each other to avoid a second round of scratching and clawing.*

Chapter Three

Friday

"I'm going to take Bijou home and head into town. Will you and Emily be okay for the rest of the afternoon?" Jules picked up her laptop and slid it inside her messenger bag.

"Not a problem," Roxanne said, looking up from the computer on the counter. "Emily'll be here soon. It looks like we have six more check-ins this evening. I've got her scheduled first thing in the morning, too. We're expecting about twenty folks tomorrow."

"I'll be at the big green tent in town if you need me. Are you coming to see the parade?"

"Matt's meeting me for dinner, and then he's on duty for the rest of the evening. It's all hands on deck this weekend," her aunt said with a sigh. "His guys are all on overtime this weekend. Just like last fall when they filmed that TV series here. Hopefully, it will be peace on earth instead of all the craziness the Hollywood folks brought. I may see you later after dinner."

A slight smile crept across Jules's face. Her aunt and Sheriff Hobbs had been friends for years, but they'd started seeing each other in the summer when he'd investigated the murder of one of her guests, who was found dead in the woods. Her aunt and the sheriff were good for each other. "Okay, then. Text me if you need me. Jake plans to meet me for the lighted parade. According to the planning team, it will be an amazing experience. We'd love to have you join us."

"Will do. I'll pop in to see how things are going. I heard some good scuttlebutt down at the beauty parlor. The gals were talking about how you're doing as council prez. You and your team keep coming up with ideas to bring people to town to spend money. And Christmas in the mountains is the ideal time to come here for a visit."

"That's our goal. It's just a lot more work than I thought it would be. Come on, Bijou." The terrier made a mad dash for the back door.

In her cabin's kitchen, Jules poured kibble into the dog's bowl and refilled the water. She checked her coat pockets for her hat and gloves. The temperature dropped quickly after dark in the mountains. Zipping her wallet and phone in her coat pocket, she headed for the Jeep. "Bye, Bijou. It might be a late night." There was no comment from her fuzzy sidekick. The dog continued to wolf down her dinner as Jules backtracked to the hall closet and rummaged around for a scarf.

The quick ride to town ended in a traffic jam near Main Street. Deputy Dempsy, who would always be Bubba from high school to Jules, directed traffic to nearby parking lots. When she finally made it to the front of the line, he moved the wooden barrier and waved her through. Jules found parking on one of the side streets and hoofed it over to the town square, where the festivities were set to begin in a few hours. All of the businesses and storefronts sported fresh greenery, bows, and festive lights. Jugglers, clowns, and musicians claimed their places on every block. Fern Valley looked ready for a party.

Mouth-watering scents of fried foods, barbecue, and cotton candy greeted Jules as she approached the business council tent. Her stomach rumbled, reminding her that she had missed lunch. Elaine James flitted around like a hummingbird, straightening all the flier stacks on the information table to ensure they were perfectly aligned horizontally and vertically.

Darlene Denunzio breezed in and set her water bottle on a stack of fliers. She ignored the over-the-glasses stare that Elaine gave her. "All vendors are accounted for and ready to sell, sell, sell. Everybody here ready for the excitement?"

"Excellent," Jules replied, looking at the clipboard Elaine left on the table.

"Yep. We're ready for business. Mitch and Marco will start lining up the parade participants at five. And Elizabeth's taking lots of publicity photos," Elaine added.

"And I saw our intrepid reporter, Jane Jenkins, out and about, too. It looks like she's sniffing around for a story." Darlene's gaze landed on Elaine.

Elaine brushed at her coat sleeve. "Everything is running smoothly," she commented without looking up. "Just like clockwork. No hiccups today. Jane's here to do puff pieces on all the fun and not to stir up controversy where there is none."

"Good to hear. It looks like everything's under control. If you need me, I plan to walk around a bit," Jules said.

"Here, Jules," Elaine interjected. "Take one of the walkie-talkies. Make sure it's on channel three. And here's your red staff lanyard. There. Now you're official." Elaine handed her an "Ask me about Fern Valley" lanyard.

Jules pulled her scarf and collar up and put on her lanyard. A sudden gust caused her to shiver. She hugged her coat closer and jammed her hands in her pockets.

Spectators congregated in the square and on the sidewalks. Jules started her walk on the side with the food vendors and rounded the corner for a quick check on the souvenir trailers. Not seeing anything out of place, Jules wandered to the beginning of the parade route.

"Hey, Jules," Mitch Hill yelled as she approached the starting line. The owner of Lula Belle's gourmet sandwich shop waved with one hand. He held a stake that Marco Hooper hammered into the ground with the other. "How goes it? Great turnout already. We're almost done roping off the viewing area."

Marco, the owner of Lug Nuts, a vintage auto parts store, nodded.

"Looks like you're ready to go." Jules scanned the square. Cindy Johnson, owner of Johnson Motors, Kim Lacy, owner of Knit Wits, and Darlene Denunzio, owner of On Pins and Needles, mingled with parade participants and checked in groups on the side streets.

"Almost done here. We moved the judges' reviewing stand over to that corner. We've already roped that part off. The parade starts here, loops

17

through town, and ends on the other side of the courthouse like we planned."
Marco pointed like a flight attendant to highlight the parade's key milestones.

"Call me if you need me. Elaine gave me a walkie-talkie." Jules waved it in
the air as she spoke.

"Check." Mitch saluted. "We have a couple of things to wrap up here, and
then we'll head over to our food truck. Donna's got sandwiches and drinks
ready to go. We're hoping for a big evening." Lula Belle's had been a fixture
in the valley for years, and Jules was glad that Mitch and Donna saved it
from closure when the original owner decided to retire and move to Florida.
The Hills updated the shop's menu while preserving the classics like pimento
cheese, ham biscuits, and strawberry lemonade.

Jules strolled down a side street to where Kim, Cindy, and Darlene stood
with clipboards.

"Hi, Jules," Cindy said as she approached. "Over half of the participants
are here and checked in already. Everyone is rarin' to go."

"So far, so good," Kim added. "We've got ourselves a parade." She gazed
down the street at the high school marching band that sat in neat rows on
the street. Behind them, the British car club had lined up a series of classic
sports cars two to a row.

As the sun sank slowly behind the ridgeline, casting the last few rays of the
day, Jules spotted the top of Cal's Humvee and several flatbeds with cages
behind the tiny cars.

"The clowns, kazoo crew, and four floats are in line down Elm Avenue.
And then there are some horses and riders ushering in our special guest and
his sleigh," Darlene said.

"Y'all have done an amazing job," Jules said. "This is going to be fun."

"Everything is supposed to light up and glow. Maybe folks will be able to
see Fern Valley from space." Darlene adjusted her green volunteer ballcap.

Cindy turned to talk to two clowns who approached with large red,
squeaky shoes and oversized props.

Jules smiled. "I'm headed back to the tent."

Jane "the Pain" Jenkins toddled down the middle of the street. Jules pasted
on a half-smile as the reporter for the local weekly approached. "Hi, Jane."

Before Jules could continue, the rotund reporter with the gray bowl cut lumbered forward, huffing like she had been running. She edged past. "Can't talk. Gotta interview the big cat people before the animal rights protesters get here. Saw it on the internet. Need to get this posted before I get scooped." The woman, who was as wide as she was tall, bustled down the street toward Cal's trucks.

Jules was about to reply but decided to let it go. Her stomach did a flipflop when she thought of protesters on the first weekend of the festival. Darlene shrugged, and Cindy continued her chat with the clowns.

Pushing anxious thoughts of problems to the back of her head, Jules made one more lap around the square. She spotted Sheriff Hobbs next to a brick building across the street. His expressionless eyes scanned the crowd. Jules wended her way around people on the street and sidewalks until she was within chatting distance.

"Quite the turnout already," he said as she approached. "Looks like people have come from miles around."

Jules nodded. "Just ran into Jane Jenkins on her way to interview Cal and his cat people. She said she was in a hurry to get there before the animal rights people showed up. Anything on your radar?"

"No warnings, but they usually materialize where there are cages or circuses. I've got all my deputies on duty tonight, and there are some extra state troopers if we need them. I don't anticipate any problems." The sheriff eyed the growing crowd.

"Thanks. I'll be at the tent for a while. Elaine and her crew have everything under control on our end."

"I wouldn't expect anything less." His radio squelched and spurted out a series of numbered codes. He tapped the volume control on his radio and stared off at the food vendors.

As Jules turned to leave, a "You hoo" from across the street caught her attention. Her aunt, in a bright red and black paisley coat with a faux black fur collar, waved and trotted across the street with a shopping bag from Lula Belle's. "Hey, y'all. I'm glad I found you in this crowd. Hey, Sheriff, think we can steal away for a couple of minutes? You can take a little break, right?"

CHRISTMAS LIGHTS AND CAT FIGHTS

She winked at her beau.

He nodded and took the bag from her. "Thanks, Rox, for bringing dinner. My car's down that street if you want to get away from the crowd and get out of the cold for a bit."

The pair ducked down the side street where the police cruisers sat next to a fire truck and an ambulance. Jules wandered through the crowd toward the vendors and paused in front of a trailer with hundreds of coats of arms and ancestry knickknacks. Before she could see if there was a Keene one, someone tapped her on the shoulder, and she jumped. Jake materialized next to her.

"Hey, you," she said. "Been here long? You missed Roxanne and Sheriff Hobbs."

"Just got here. Checking out the sights. You hungry?" He pulled her toward him and enveloped her in a hug that sent a charge of excitement down her spine.

"Starving. What looks good?" she asked.

"I've seen everything from chili to turkey legs." Jake pulled her closer and planted a kiss on her lips that curled her toes. Jake took her hand and led her toward a brightly colored truck.

"Everything smells good, but I think I want a hot dog."

"I know. Only mustard." She and Jake stood in a line that snaked around the side of a food truck and into the street. When they made it to the counter, he ordered a burger and fries and a hot dog for Jules.

The woman at the window handed them two white containers and two canned drinks.

The crowds continued to grow, and it took the pair several minutes to find a spot to eat. Leaning against a brick wall of the bank across the street, Jake unwrapped his burger.

Between bites, Jules said, "I saw Jane a few minutes ago. She said something about animal rights protesters. I mentioned it to the sheriff."

Jake wiped ketchup off of his stubbled chin and raised his eyebrows. "Should we be concerned?"

"Sheriff Hobbs didn't seem too worried about it. I hope tonight goes off without a hitch." She popped a bite of hot dog in her mouth. "So far, no fights." She tried to suppress a jolt of anxiety that rocketed through her.

Jake shrugged. "I guess that's good. How did the big cats end up in the Christmas parade anyway?"

"I'm still fuzzy on some of the details. When the call went out for parade participants, somehow Cal Collins got wind of it and contacted Elaine's team," Jules said.

"He owns that cat wildlife rescue place up past I-81. I went there as a kid. It used to be a roadside zoo in the eighties. Somehow it morphed with the times into a cat sanctuary." Jake polished off his burger in two bites and gathered up the trash. "Wanna take a walk?"

"Yep. But let's swing by the business council tent first to see if they need anything. We're getting close to go-time."

A mechanical squeal echoed across the square, and the crowds groaned and looked around.

"Test, test, test….Test, test, test…Testing one, two, three. I said, Testing one, two, three. Don't cry for me, Argentinnnnnnnah!" The male voice boomed from several speakers and made Jules groan.

Jake followed her to the judges' reviewing stand, where J. P. Gross, local business owner and Jules's archrival on the council, thunked the microphone with his beefy finger. Marco Hooper stood behind him, adjusting dials and making a face like he smelled like two-day-old Brussels sprouts.

"Okay," J. P. said. "That sounded good. I'll be back in a second or two to kick off the parade and introduce the dignitaries." He wiped his mouth with the back of his hand and brushed past Jules and Jake with a quick nod.

Jules gave an exaggerated fake smile that made Marco snicker. "Our emcee is satisfied with the acoustics. Soon, his melodious ramblings will greet visitors from one end of town to the other for hours."

"Can't wait." Jules looked around at the throngs of people.

Loud chirps caused the crowds to pause and look around. Two police cruisers moved slowly up Main Street. Lights flashed, and the sirens whoop whooped. A deputy guided guests back to the sidewalk with directions from the speaker in the car's grill. The wave of people parted like the Red Sea, and the cruisers inched down the parade route. People lined all the sidewalks in anticipation and craned their necks for a view of the festivities.

J. P. pushed his way through the throngs without even an excuse me, and crammed his tall frame behind the table. After taking several swigs from his water bottle, he grabbed the microphone and blew into it several times. "Ladies and gentlemen. Children of all ages. This is your emcee and host for the evening, business councilman and entrepreneur J. P. Gross. I am a real estate developer, owner of a landscaping firm, and investor here in beautiful Fern Valley, and I will be giving you updates and fun facts tonight as we're about ready to kick off our lighted parade. Welcome, everyone, to Fern Valley and our first holiday festival. Our town, founded in 1830, was originally an outpost for travelers to points west. We were part of America's great westward expansion, and our little gem in the gorgeous Blue Ridge Mountains of Virginia quickly became a central stopping point on their journeys. Later, it became famous for its timber and other natural resources, such as coal, minerals, and even gold...."

Loud sirens from two fire trucks blotted out the rest of J. P.'s speech. The red trucks rolled slowly down Main Street, followed by the tri-county high school marching band, playing a variety of Christmas classics. J. P. gave up on his prepared statements and turned the microphone off.

When the British car club passed, Jake leaned over. "Be right back."

Jules shifted her feet and stretched. Cal's trailers drove slowly past, and the crowd ooohed and ahhhhed at the animals. Cal and Misti, on the back of a flatbed with the cubs, got the biggest cheers. Illuminated floats drifted by, followed by the Kazoo Crew and the Geezer Squad, puttering through town on their decorated riding lawnmowers. The local horse club with flashing lights on the harnesses and saddles marched by next with the cleanup clowns behind them. Jules felt something touch her hair.

Jake put a flashing tiara on her head. "Oh, thanks," she said. "Where's yours?"

"I got a tiger shirt from Cal's." Jake held up a zebra-print bag and winked.

An hour later, when the final float with the guest of honor and all his elves paraded past, Jules and Jake hiked over to the business council tent and helped the team pack away the fliers and stack the chairs as the crowds dissipated.

"Thanks, everybody. Great turnout." Jules picked up the clipboards and folders on the table and put them in a plastic bin.

"Where are you parked?" Jake asked, pulling her closer with a one-armed hug.

Jules pointed across the square. "What about you?"

"In the church lot."

"Come on, I'll give you a ride," she said.

After dropping Jake off beside his red Mustang, the only remaining car in the lot, Jules headed back to the resort. White lights twinkled on the trunks of all the crape myrtles lining the entrance, and she smiled at all of Jake and Lester's holiday handiwork. Everything looked festive and welcoming for their guests. *No thanks to me. After the next few weeks, things should calm down, and I can focus on my stuff.*

She could barely get the door to her cabin open before Bijou barreled out. "Okay, okay. I know I owe you a walk." The dog danced in and out of her legs until Jules clicked the leash in place. They trotted past the field with Cal's trailers and looped around the tiny houses. A smattering of lights dotted the windows of the houses and the vintage trailers. Bijou had to smell what seemed like every blade of grass.

The icy wind reminded Jules that winter and Christmas were fast approaching. She hoped the specialty woodcarving tools she ordered Jake would arrive in time. She made a mental note to check on the package tracking. She needed to get more wrapping paper, too.

Jules and Bijou skirted the woods. Animal noises caught the terrier's attention. Jules shushed her growls and led her toward home.

As they neared the edge of the woods, Bijou froze and let out an extended guttural growl. Something moved in the underbrush. Bijou started a barking frenzy. Trying to keep the noise down for her guests, she scooped up the dog and walked home. She heard more noises behind her. When she turned, she caught a glimpse of something moving in the woods. *Did she see yellow eyes?*

Jules quickened her pace to a jog and didn't relax until the cabin door slammed behind her. She leaned against the door, her breath exiting in heavy puffs. Bijou jumped from her arms. Something was over there watching them.

Chapter Four

Saturday

J ules jumped out of bed and double-timed her morning routine. Today, the big cats were making an appearance at the high school, and she needed to check on things at the office before the show. Bijou had other ideas. Today was her day to catalog every scent between the cabin and the tiny houses. And then review what she had already sniffed.

As they approached Cal's trailers, Bijou froze, and the fur on her neck stood up. No amount of coaxing could get her to move. The small dog barred her teeth. Every muscle in the little dog tensed. Jules picked her up and walked on, keeping the cages within her line of sight. Cal's people milled around near the animals with buckets, engrossed in their morning routine.

A trailer near the woods caught Jules's eye, and she stopped and stared. The oversized cage stood empty. She cast a wary glance toward the woods where she'd heard strange noises in the brush. Where was the cat that had arrived in that trailer?

Shrugging off the weird feeling that nagged at her brain, she carried Bijou back to her cabin. After feeding her little dog, she made a quick stop by the office before heading to get a good seat for the show.

Jules sailed along through town but came to a dead stop near the tri-county high school, where deputies directed the slow traffic to the overflow parking across the street. She found a spot next to a minivan in the field and followed the crowds to the school's stadium. The bright sunshine warmed her face as she walked toward the school, even though winter temps were in full swing.

Elaine James and Sheriff Hobbs stood by the aluminum fencing between the football field and the track. "Good morning, Jules," Elaine yelled, fanning both arms. "What a glorious day. It's chilly, but thank goodness for the sun. Just a few more minutes, and we'll be ready for the show."

Before Jules could answer, the crowd whooped, and all eyes turned to see Cal, Misti, and Cody leading tigers and lions to the center of the field. Two other women on ATVs pulled three trailers connected to each other like little trains. The crowd cheered as chimpanzees, lions, tigers, a cheetah, a huge snake, and the cubs made an appearance.

Cal talked about each species and showed off their talents. The crowd kept moving closer toward the fence to snap photos, and the deputies had to shoo people back to the stands.

While Cody talked about the cheetah and its land speed records, Misti, in a sparkly jungle costume, rushed over to where Jules, Elaine, and Sheriff Hobbs stood. "Are you the police?" she asked.

Sheriff Hobbs, in full uniform, nodded, and Misti continued, "Then I need you to do something about her." She pointed her manicured red talon toward the street and a blue trailer covered in a jungle motif and "Tabbi's Tees" in bright orange lettering. "She is ruining our lives and our business. I thought vendors paid for spots in town. She's squatting right there on the street. I don't think she even pays taxes on her sales." Misti's hair-sprayed blond curls bounced with each word. She wore enough makeup to make a Vegas showgirl jealous.

"I'll look into it," Sheriff Hobbs said. "And you are?"

"Misti, Misti Miles-Collins. I'm Cal's wife. And that woman is his ex-wife. Cal divorced her last May, but she won't let it go. She's stalking us. Please do something about this." She spun around on her stiletto heels and marched toward the gym.

A puzzled look crossed the sheriff's face.

"Tabbi is, well was, wife number two. Misti is the current Mrs. Collins," Elaine said quietly. "Wife number three. I got their whole family history yesterday when I asked Misti how she was doing. Too much sharing." Elaine waggled her index finger.

The sheriff nodded and disappeared into the crowd. Jules smiled when she spotted him later in front of the blue trailer talking to Tabbi and Dana. *I'm sure he's getting an earful.*

As Cal's team took a series of bows with the animals, Elaine leaned closer to Jules. "Time to wrap up here. I'll be in town about three to ensure everything's ready for the walking tour and the tree lighting. We'll have carolers and street musicians. It'll be a more traditional event, although this was fun. The kids loved the animals."

"Do you need me to do anything?"

"Nope. Elizabeth's flooding the web world with all the event postings. And Darlene has a handle on all the tasks. I'm hoping we'll have a good turnout. And not a lot of drama." Elaine winked.

Jules winked back. "I'll meet you in town this afternoon." She jogged toward the field to retrieve her Jeep.

Back at the resort, Jules took Bijou for a walk. She tried to guide the dog away from Cal's trailers, but the Jack Russell terrier pulled toward the woods, determined to see what was going on with the animals. Picking up Bijou, Jules edged closer to the temporary fencing. Cal fed one of the two cheetah cubs while his son Cody tended to the two tiger cubs.

Bijou stifled a yip as Jules stroked her neck to calm her.

When Cal and Cody glanced their way, Jules yelled, "I enjoyed your show."

"Glad to hear it." Cal flashed his pearly white smile and his showman charm. "We like it here. Maybe we can schedule something to come back in the summer. We take every opportunity we can to teach people about our animals, especially the big cats. These guys are great ambassadors for their species. And they love being around people." Right on cue, the male lion yawned and rolled over on his back.

"We'll keep you in mind as we plan our event calendars. The cubs were a hit." Jules smiled, admiring the wiggly cats. "Where are the others?" she asked.

A scowl crossed Cal's face for a brief second before his handsome smile returned. "What others? Two cheetahs and two tigers."

Jules paused for one long moment but shrugged. "Oh, okay," she said, trying not to roll her eyes. It's hard to keep up. I'll see y'all later." She strode past the line of trailers and the empty cage on a mission to find coffee and check her photos. *I didn't miscount.*

"What's up?" Roxanne asked as Jules popped a pod in the coffee maker.

"Something's off. I want to see if my hunch is right."

Her aunt waited. When Jules didn't reply, Roxanne said, "Folks seem to like our breakfast and all the events. This will be a good model for the spring fling you guys want to host next year. Great job on extending the season."

"The vendors are busy, and the guests are having a good time. There was a big turnout for the cat show today, even though it was a cold morning." Jules flipped through the photos on her phone.

"We've got it down to a science here. Emily will be here to help tomorrow with the check-outs from the weekend. She's excited to get a peek at the tigers before they leave."

"Speaking of that. I was right." Jules said, holding her phone. "There were four tiger cubs."

"Huh?" Roxanne stepped closer to peer over her niece's shoulder.

"I saw Cal and his folks with two tiger cubs. He corrected me when I asked about the other two. And something else is odd. They have an empty trailer."

Her aunt leaned closer to Jules's phone screen. "Those cubs are adorable. You should post those pictures. Animals always attract attention."

"They are cute, but something's not right about this." Jules settled in at her desk and pulled up the resort's camera feeds.

"I'm sure you'll figure it out." Roxanne returned to the store when she heard the bells on the front door.

Jules poured over hours of feeds from the different cameras. None captured the cubs, but she had her photos with Jake to confirm her recollection. She found a segment on Thursday when Cal's trucks arrived and caravanned down her maintenance road. She looked at it frame by frame and counted the trailers. Enlarging the images, she looked for an empty trailer with no success. It looked like everything had an animal when it arrived. She copied her photos and the footage of the trailers to a folder on her laptop.

Jules drained the last few drops of her coffee, turned off her computer, and stepped through the Dutch door. "Hey, Roxanne. Oh, hi, Emily. How are you doing?"

"The cats are so fabulous. I got some pictures. Can't wait to get them posted." The teen held up her phone for Jules to see. "Just adorbs. And almost exciting as having the *Fatal Impressions* filming here with Chavis Ratner." The teen strung the star's name out to about twelve syllables. "I love working here. This is the best job ever."

Jules did a quick tiger cub check from Emily's photo. Two cubs. "I'm headed back to town in a bit to check on the setup for tonight. You all okay here?"

"Sure, where's Bijou?" Emily asked.

"Napping at home on the couch."

Emily pulled up a stool behind the front counter. "I'm going into town tonight, too, with friends. We're excited about all the different food trucks."

"What about you?" Jules asked Roxanne.

"Matt and I are planning to have dinner after the tree lighting," her aunt replied. "I'm opting for a sit-down meal. Last night, dinner was in his squad car. Hopefully, his schedule won't change suddenly tonight."

Jules smiled and gathered her things. After a quick ride to town, she found parking behind one of the sheriff's cruisers. It was standing room only under the business council tent. Marco, Kim, and Darlene chatted with visitors while Elaine held court and explained the rest of the weekend's activities to a couple and their three children. A steady stream of visitors popped in with questions.

When Kim moved closer to her, Jules whispered, "Did I miss anything?"

"Hmmm. J. P. Gross stormed over. He was disappointed that he didn't get to use all his prepared index cards during the parade. He had his whole Regis Philbin act rehearsed with tons of Fern Valley facts and his usual dad jokes. He wanted to be the emcee tonight to make up for it."

Jules made a face. She hoped no one noticed.

"I know," Kim whispered. "Luckily, Elaine was here. She thanked him," and in her steel magnolia way, she convinced him that he has done so much for the council and that we needed to let the sheriff have his time in the spotlight." Kim giggled and patted Jules's arm. "We dodged a bullet. And no one, except for J. P. and his buddies, will complain."

The sun slipped behind the mountains, and the town's streetlights illuminated the sidewalks. White lights outlined the courthouse and nearby businesses. As darkness descended, visitors lined up to purchase glow-in-the-dark items. The line for Tabbi and Dana's trailers snaked down the sidewalk and onto the courthouse greens.

Trumpets blared, and the throngs on the street parted as the James Madison University pep band danced through town with a medley of holiday songs. The students, decked out in festive garb, marched down the street and surrounded the town Christmas tree next to the flagpoles in front of the courthouse. It looked like a sea of red and green.

Elaine frantically flapped her arms like a giant bird and waved to Jules, who picked up her pace and made her way through the crowd to where Elaine and Sheriff Hobbs stood by a forest of tall black speakers and amplifiers.

As Jules approached, Elaine threw her arms in the air. "Where have you been? You didn't answer your phone. And I couldn't reach you on the walkie-talkie."

"Sorry. I didn't hear it. What's up?" Jules felt the heat rise in her cheeks.

"You're business council president. You have to be the one to introduce the sheriff." Elaine planted both hands on her hips.

"Oh," Jules said. She had a moment of panic for not having a prepared speech. She collected her thoughts, and after a mini-concert that turned into a sing-along, the square suddenly fell silent. Elaine thrust the microphone into Jules's hand.

She paused and stepped closer to Sheriff Hobbs. "Good evening, Fern Valley. How are you?" When the applause died down, Jules continued, "How did you like the JMU Pep Band? Let's show them our appreciation!"

Hoots and cheers echoed across the square, and the band played an abbreviated version of "Jingle Bell Rock." When the music and clapping stopped, Jules continued, "Thanks again. I'm Jules Keene, president of the

Fern Valley Business Council, and I'd like to thank everyone for all the time and effort they put into planning this festival. Many thanks to co-chairs Elaine James and Kim Lacy. And without further ado, I'd like to introduce a man who needs no introduction in these parts, our own, Sheriff Matt Hobbs."

The sheriff stepped forward and took the microphone. "Welcome, everyone. I'd like to thank Jules, the business council, and all the emergency responders in Fern Valley. You've all worked really hard to make this event possible. And as much as I love to talk, I think everyone really wants to see the true man of the hour. A spotlight swished around the square and landed next to the tree. Santa and Mrs. Claus stepped out, and the crowd went wild.

When the noise faded, Sheriff Hobbs continued, "Okay, drum corps, let's help Santa count this down from ten. Ready?"

The drummers riffed, and then the snares started the drum roll. When the count got to one, Jules could barely hear anything. Santa flipped the switch, and the tree glowed in gold and silver.

The band played again, and it turned into an impromptu dance party. Even Elaine bopped and swayed.

Sheriff Hobbs patted Jules on the back. "Good job."

"Thank you," Jules said. "One more day, and we've had a successful first weekend of our holiday festival. I don't know about you, but I think I'm headed home after I get one of those incredible-smelling Philly cheese steaks."

Chapter Five

Sunday

Jules flung open the curtains and did a double take at the window. She shivered in her bare feet. Snow covered everything outside. The white stuff, several inches deep, made the trees and mountains look magical. Memories of snowball fights, snowmen, and hot cocoa zipped around her head. A flash of excitement surged through her. Snow days always brought back good memories. She and her dad would always go sledding after the first good snowfall. Jules hurried through breakfast and gathered her things. No sledding today. She needed to check on her guests.

"Come on, Bijou. Let's have an adventure before we get busy."

The dog darted out the door and did zoomies in the snow. She ran and jumped like a wild rabbit. The snow, not quite deep enough for sledding, was perfect for an energetic Jack Russell Terrier to plow through.

Jules finally corralled the little dog when she paused to take a breath. The chilly breeze nipped at their noses on their way to the tiny house village. At the edge of the woods, the fur on the back of the dog's neck stood up, and she let loose with a sinister growl. The same spot that caused the barking jag before.

"What's wrong, Bijou?"

Jules looked down and spotted large paw prints heading into the woods. Pulling out her phone, she snapped several pictures. "Hmmm. A wolf or a coyote? Maybe Jake will know what made these. I love nature, but not this close to the property."

Bijou sniffed the air and bolted toward Cal's trailers. Not wanting another barkfest to disturb guests who were trying to sleep in on a Sunday morning, Jules picked up the dog and walked briskly to the office.

Laptop on and coffee brewing, Jules started her workday by unlocking the front door in case there were any early folks for checkout. She settled in at her desk to peruse emails for the resort and business council. Sixty-seven thank you emails had been delivered from attendees and vendors. She let out a deep breath. Good. *No complaints yet.*

Her thoughts kept bouncing back to the tracks in the snow. She pulled out her phone and looked at the pawprints again. They had had coyotes in the area, but usually, they didn't venture far out of the woods. Bears were usually rare this close to people. Finding a site on the internet with animal tracks, she compared her photos. Hers didn't look like the coyote or bear ones online. Most of them had toenail imprints. After further poking around, she found a match on a wild cat site. Why was one of Cal's cats walking around in the snow? Or did his big cats attract something else? A shiver slid down her spine.

Jules pulled up the feeds to her resort cameras, hoping to catch something near the woods.

After an hour or so of scanning the video feed, Jules jumped when the back door opened.

"What are you so engrossed in?" Roxanne dropped her green Michael Kors Saffiano tote on her desk.

"Bijou found some animal tracks in the snow this morning. I was trying to identify them."

"I wouldn't worry too much. Most of the wildlife gets scared off when people are around. And we don't have trash cans that are easily accessible. The snow was lovely this morning, wasn't it? A perfect ending to the first holiday festival weekend. We couldn't have planned it better." Her aunt dropped a pod in the coffee maker and leaned down to pet Bijou.

"This is interesting." Jules stared at her screen. "I didn't see any wild animals last night on any of the cameras, so I was going back in time for

CHRISTMAS LIGHTS AND CAT FIGHTS

giggles. A truck with a cage in the back came through the gates in the wee hours of Saturday morning. Let's see where you went." Jules scrolled forward through the feeds. "There you are." Jules moved closer to her screen and slowed down the motion.

"What did you find?" Roxanne asked from the store.

"A truck pulled in near Cal's cages, and a tall guy in a cowboy hat opened the tailgate. Someone led a cheetah over on a leash to the cage in the bed of the truck. Then, two guys carried an oversized dog crate and put it in the truck's backseat. There was some handshaking, and the truck drove down the maintenance road to the exit. Something is rotten." Jules made a copy of the truck footage. *Why are they sneaking around with wild animals in the wee hours? Was something prowling around?* She shuddered at the thought and fired off the picture and a text to Jake.

The bells on the front door interrupted Jules's musings about the secret midnight visitors. She stopped to help Roxanne check out a steady stream of guests, several of whom registered for a second weekend of the festival.

It was several hours later before Jules returned to Saturday night's footage. She zoomed in frame by frame on the truck and jotted down a partial rear license plate. Maybe Pixel could help. She pressed the contact on her phone for her former college roommate and computer whiz.

"Hey, girl. What's up?" Pixel answered after a couple of rings. "I wrapped up my class at UVA this week. I'm done teaching this semester, and it may be my final one."

"Is that good or bad?"

"It's bittersweet. I love teaching, but my interviews and background checks with the FBI are progressing."

Jules let out a squeal. Last summer, Pixel helped Jules crack an encrypted file that belonged to a murder victim involved in an extortion scheme. Pixel provided information that Jules used to solve the case, and the FBI was impressed with her abilities. "So, you did go talk to Special Agent Stafford. What are you interviewing for?"

"I was curious at first. And flattered that he called me. But now, I really want the job. It's in forensic data analytics. I'd get to play with all their cool toys and travel to a bunch of different places. But enough about that. What's up with you?"

"Pixel, that's so neat. I am so excited for you. We're knee-deep in the holiday festival over here. Two more weekends to go, and that's why I called. We had Cal's Cats here for the parade. He brought four tiger cubs and two cheetah cubs. Then, later at the demonstration, there were only two tiger cubs. Okay, this may sound way out there, but he did some gaslighting. Then, I spotted an empty trailer. That made my antenna go up, and now I'm curious."

"And you can't help yourself, Nancy Drew, and you do have a knack for tracking down clues. That is odd, but if there's something there, I know you'll find it. And I'll help in any way I can."

"Why lie about something like that? Especially when I knew there were four tiger cubs."

"People don't lie unless they're doing something wrong or hiding something," Pixel said.

"Then, this morning, Bijou spotted animal tracks in the snow. They weren't coyote prints. I'm sure they're from a big cat."

"Hmmm."

"That's not all. I looked through some of my camera feeds, and Saturday morning, when it was still dark, a truck came on the property and left about thirty minutes later. It's not completely clear, but I can see a bit of the license plate. I was hoping you could help." Pixel, a computer programmer by day, poked around the dark corners of the web with her gaming friends. She and her white-hat hacker friends had been able to dig up some interesting information in the past for Jules.

"Send it over. I'll see what I can do."

"You're the best. How can I repay you?" Jules asked.

"How about seats to the local watch party for *Fatal Impressions* when the new season debuts? Y'all are going to do something when the show finally airs, right? It'll make Fern Valley famous."

"Definitely, and I'll make sure you're invited. I got an email from the producer. They're getting ready to start the editing process now. He said he'd let me know when they have a release date. It will be next fall at the earliest." The TV show, with a cult following of binge-watchers, had filmed at the resort, and Pixel's information from the Dark Web had helped Jules uncover a murderer. Jules ended the call and sent the footage to Pixel.

A high-pitched "Good morning" echoed through the store and sent Bijou on a tear through the doorway. Jules shooed the Jack Russell back to her bed and slipped into the store.

Misti, in black patent leather stiletto boots, leggings, and a shiny teal ski parka, sidled up to the counter. She rummaged through an oversized purse and pulled out two keys that she let clatter on the surface in front of Roxanne.

"Was everything okay, Mrs. Collins?" Roxanne asked.

"Yes. We loved the tiny house. We need one at the sanctuary."

Roxanne printed Misti's receipt and handed her one of Jake's cards. "Jake would love to talk to you about building a tiny house on your property."

"Maybe several," Misti said with a wink. "Especially if Cal keeps adding staff. They'd be perfect for housing our trainers and workers."

"I had so much fun at your demo yesterday, and I want to thank y'all for letting us see the four tiger cubs and the baby cheetahs up close. They were adorable."

"It's our pleasure. We love to share our knowledge of wildlife wherever we can." The blond turned on her heels and strode out of the office after a quick look at the snack aisle. *Interesting. She didn't correct me on the number of cubs like her husband did.*

Seconds after the screen door closed, a shriek echoed outside. Roxanne flung open the door, and Jules was close on her heels. The two ran out on the front porch that spanned the length of the building.

In the grassy area, Tabbi flailed her arms around and ranted at Cal. "You can't sue me. It's a free country. I can sell whatever I want wherever I want. And I loved cats way before you, and I ever got together. You can't control me anymore. I'm done with you."

"I don't have a problem with what you sell. I have an issue with your logo, and your website looks like a cheap knockoff of mine. Copycatting is not becoming, Tabbi."

"It wasn't cheap," she hissed. "I paid a boatload for my rebranding. I had to when we divorced. I hired a real artist for my makeover. New life. New look. You took everything, but you have no say over my business now. You'll see. I'm taking Tabbi's Tees to places Cal's Cats will never go."

"We'll see. My lawyers will be in touch." Cal turned. Misti smirked and looped her arm through her husband's.

"Well, I have lawyers, too. And I know how to use them," Tabbi yelled at the back of her ex-husband and his new wife. She plodded up the wooden stairs to the porch. "They're impossible. Here're the keys."

"Let me get your receipts," Roxanne said and disappeared inside.

When Roxanne breezed back through the door, Tabbi jerked the papers out of her hand. "They are too much. Let him try to stop me. I'll see him in court. And I'll see you both on Friday. We'll be back next weekend."

"Can't wait," Roxanne said under her breath.

Chapter Six

Monday

J ules dabbed on some blush and fluffed her long red curls. After a quick glance in the mirror, she returned her makeup and brushes to the drawer in her vanity. "Bijou, I'm having lunch with Pixel to see what she can find on the Dark Web. I'll be back soon."

Not interested in secret internet places, the dog glanced over her shoulder and headed for the fuzzy blanket on the couch as Jules checked to make sure she unplugged her curling iron.

Her phone buzzed as she turned onto the road at the resort's entrance. "Hi, Elaine. What's up?"

"Oh. I'm a little stressed about an email I received a little bit ago. Can you talk for a quick minute?" Without waiting for Jules to respond, Elaine continued. "It's that Tabbi woman. She copied the sheriff, the town manager, and the newspaper. And now Jane's calling me for my side of the story. Tabbi said we would be hearing from her lawyer this week. Oh, Jules. I was trying to break up a fight. I didn't start it. I was trying to keep the peace. Should I talk to my lawyer? I am beside myself. What if she sues? This could damage the town's reputation—not to mention mine. I don't have time to deal with this right now. It's too much with the festival, my store, and the holidays. I don't need another thing to worry about."

"Calm down, Elaine. We'll get this sorted out. Forward me the email, and I'll make some calls."

"Okay. I knew you'd know what to do. To make it worse, that woman is on the schedule as a vendor for next weekend. So we're not done with her, and I'll have to talk to her again. I hope I can maintain my civility and my standards. It's going to be a challenge with this one."

"I know you will. You're the consummate professional. Hey, what about her ex-husband? They're returning, too?" Jules asked, signaling to turn into the lot for Pop's Diner, the place everyone went for burgers and shakes after high school football games. The diner had been part of the Fern Valley landscape for three generations.

Elaine let out a long sigh. "Yes. He's coming back as a vendor next weekend, too. This is not turning out to be the holly jolly festival I dreamed about."

"Don't stress. I'll see what I can find out. We'll get it figured out."

"Thanks, Jules. See you at the planning meeting on Wednesday. We've got a packed agenda. We'll have a lot to debrief from this weekend, especially if that Tabbi woman continues with this nonsense." Elaine disconnected the call.

Jules found a spot to park and fired off a text to the town manager, Tom Berryman.

He responded before she exited the car. **Sit tight. Wait for something official. She might be blowing off steam.**

Jules pocketed her phone and headed for the art deco doors with the portal windows. The center building, originally a traditional diner dating back to the nineteen fifties, had seen several expansions over the years. Jules sat on the red vinyl bench in the lobby and exchanged a flurry of texts with Elaine before her friend Pixel stepped through the doors.

"Hey, how are you? Snow's starting to melt," Pixel said. "My kind of snow. It's pretty for a day or two, but I don't like when the roads get icy."

"Table for two?" the lanky greeter, who looked like an anemic Elvis, asked.

Jules nodded, and the pair followed him to a booth in a corner decked out in doo-wop memorabilia that highlighted the careers of the Drifters, the Coasters, and Dion and the Belmonts.

Before they could continue their conversation, Marsha, a fifty-something waitress with a pink bouffant and sensible shoes, walked up to the table and plunked down menus. "Hey, gals. What can I get for you today? We have plenty of soup and hot sandwich offerings."

"Hi, Marsha. I think I'll have the cobb salad and an unsweetened tea," Jules said.

"Me too, but I'll have my salad with water and a lime."

"Be back in a jiff." Marsha turned and breezed through the swinging doors to the kitchen.

"How are you? What's the deal with the FBI?" Jules asked.

"Nothing new since last week. They subject you to a battery of tests and background checks. And then keep you waiting. And waiting. It must be part of their psych evaluation to see how patient candidates are. It takes a long time, and it's making me antsy."

"You'll do great. I can't wait to hear what happens. Just think of all the cases you'll get to be involved with."

Pixel smiled. "I am excited. By the way, I was able to get a plate off of that truck video you sent me. It belongs to a William 'Mac' McAllister." She pulled a folder out of her bag and handed it to Jules. "He owns a farm near Waynesboro, and his family runs a zoo up there. I found some citations that they've had over the years. Everything from food service violations to animal rights complaints. I also saw some chatter about how they were hacked. Some of their data was for sale out on the dark sites. You know names, credit cards, things like that. Their data security isn't that good." She paused and glanced around the restaurant. "The zoo hasn't been doing well. They've let some of the employees go. I found some nasty comments on Glass Door and other sites. It looks like the tigers, and a couple of new attractions are a last-ditch effort to get people through the door."

"Interesting." Jules thumbed through the sheets in the folder. "How do you get some of this stuff?"

Pixel raised one eyebrow. "I have friends who can find just about anything if it's out there. Check this out. The zoo is bragging about its latest acquisitions on social media. They're even going to have kid birthday parties with the tiger cubs. You can book your next party online."

Jules caught her breath when she spotted a photo of a man and a woman with two tiger cubs.

Before Jules could comment, Marsha returned with their salads and drinks. "Y'all let me know if you need anything else. I'll check back in two shakes of a lamb's tail."

Pixel leaned forward. "The Facebook page says that the cubs were born locally to his pair of tigers. But I guess they'd have to say that if they weren't purchased legally. I glanced at the Game and Inland Fisheries website. There are all kinds of requirements for selling and possessing wild and exotic animals. Something fishy is going on."

"Hmmm. I need to talk to the sheriff about this. Cal and his group will be back next weekend. I wouldn't have even noticed that he was doing a side hustle except that he made such a big deal of correcting me about the baby tigers. And he knew I had pictures." Jules speared a stray cherry tomato and popped it in her mouth.

"So, on to other topics. How's the handsome Jake?" Pixel grinned.

"He's fine. He's been working on tiny houses for some customers, so I haven't seen a lot of him lately. Now that they're finished, he's planning a fourth house for our village. I enjoy coming up with themes and decorating them."

"You do a good job with that. I love all the little touches that tie in with your themes. If I had land, I'd want one. Not sure where I'll end up if I take this job, so I'm trying not to have deep roots anywhere. Renting is fine for now. And I don't think I could live in that tight of a space. My computer gear and bike would take up most of the room. It would be an abrupt lifestyle change for me."

"I like them for a getaway. Not sure I could pare down all my stuff for it to be my permanent residence either. But I love the concept, and we have guests who want to try it out for a few days. Some are as tiny as four hundred square feet, and he has others with second stories. His new modular ones are fairly roomy. We've received rave reviews from the guests who've stayed in them." Memories of the woman who was found dead under one during the filming flashed in Jules's mind. She pushed away thoughts of the murder that had nothing to do with the resort and dug into her salad.

The two women ate in silence for a while until Jules said, "Hey, you had a new boyfriend the last time we talked. How are things?"

Pixel smiled slightly. "He's a game programmer in Seattle. He's working on a zombie killer one right now. Not sure if it's ever going to be more than a long-distance thing, but he's fun to hang out with online. He's really creative and full of ideas for new game concepts. We've never met except on Zoom. We'll see where it goes. If I get this job, I'll be too busy for a social life for a while."

Jules pushed her salad away. "He sounds interesting. Remember all work and no play…"

"From the woman who works and lives at her job," Pixel said with a smile.

Before Jules could respond, Marsha swooped in and grabbed the plate. "Any dessert for you ladies? We have hot fudge sundaes or Coca-Cola cake. Y'all had salads. You could split one."

"Sounds good, but I have to be heading back," Pixel said.

"Me too. Just the check, please," Jules said.

Marsha winked and pulled out her order book. "Come back and see us."

Jules grabbed the check before Marsha set it on the table. "My treat. Thanks for all the info."

Pixel scrunched her mouth. "I think it's my turn to get the tab."

"Nah. It's definitely mine." Jules smiled.

The pair parted in the parking lot, and Jules headed home, but did a U-turn on a whim. At the government center, she found a parking spot near the Sheriff's Office. She flipped through Pixel's folder again about the guy in the mysterious truck. Jules debated about what to do next. Her tale of the tiger cubs and shady dealings seemed a little flimsy to pass on to the sheriff. She needed more information, but something didn't feel right about the whole situation.

A rat-a-tat-tat on the glass caused Jules to jump. She looked up to see Ashley Sharpe. The petite receptionist from the sheriff's office bounced on her toes.

"Hey, there. How are you?" Jules rolled down the window. Her words came out with puffs of white clouds.

42

"Whatcha doing out here? I haven't seen you in a month of Sundays. How's Jake? I haven't seen much of him lately either." Ashley rubbed her mittened hands together.

"We're doing well, and I'm staying busy with the festival. How about you?"

"Good. But busy. We're all doing overtime for the festival. Lookin' forward to next weekend. You coming in? Not sure if the sheriff's in or not if that's who you're here to see. I can check for you."

"Oh, thanks. Not today. I had to look up something and send a couple of texts. I'll tell Jake I ran into you," Jules said.

Ashley raised her hand and gave her a little wave as she headed toward the glass doors.

Deciding to do some research before talking to the sheriff, Jules put the Jeep in reverse. Something wasn't right with Cal Collins and the mysterious guy from Waynesboro. But proving what it actually is might be harder than she imagined.

Chapter Seven

Tuesday

After a double espresso at her office desk, Jules had two folders filled with printouts on Cal's big cat rescue, but Mac McAllister was almost invisible on the social media grid. There was one mention of him on the zoo's website and a couple of pictures on its Facebook and Instagram accounts. She made copies and added them to what Pixel had found.

Footsteps echoed from the carport, and Bijou zoomed into full security mode that turned into wiggly puppy when Jake's head popped in the door.

"Good morning. Do you want coffee?" Jules stood.

"I can get it. What's shaking so early in Fern Valley?" Jake headed for the counter in the back of the workroom.

"Cal and his tiger cubs are bothering me. He left with fewer than he came with. And one of his big cages was empty on Sunday. Too many coincidences going on. Then Tabbi threatens to sue Elaine and the town for the altercation they had during last weekend's festival. It's always something. Tomorrow's planning meeting should be a hoot." Jules pushed a stray curl off her forehead.

"I hope y'all have snacks. It could be quite entertaining. Or it might turn into a smackdown. You may want to bring popcorn. On a calmer note, Kurt's all moved into his new tiny house. Another happy customer. It's close enough for him to check in on his parents but far enough away, so he's not living with them. And he's already talking about adding another one as a guest house for when family visits."

"Great for business! Oh, I forgot to tell you and Lester that Cal asked to leave two of his trailers here. He said they'd get them this weekend," Jules said.

"They'll be fine out there. Nobody will mess with them. I'll let Lester know, but he's not doing regular mowing, just garbage pickup."

"Anything else going on around here?" she asked. She smiled when she thought of the sexagenarian groundskeeper who had worked here as long as she could remember. Lester Branch lived in the smaller cabin next to Jake and did the landscaping and some maintenance.

"Nope. All normal stuff. I moved what felt like a ton of lumber in the barn yesterday for house number four. I'll be starting the framing soon. Here, look at these. The loft part on this one makes it look like a castle."

Jules leaned over to get a better look at Jake's phone. She got a citrusy whiff of soap and aftershave that made her heart flutter. "That will look great in our little village. I need to come up with an author castle theme."

Jake massaged her shoulders. "You'll think of something. Dinner tonight?"

"Movie night?" Thoughts flashed to what was in her freezer that she could throw together for dinner.

"I'll bring a pizza."

Jules smiled, relieved she didn't have to stress about dinner or make an emergency grocery run. Bijou yipped. "She approves. Sounds like fun. What time?"

"Sixish."

"Hey, do you know anyone from Game and Inland Fisheries?" Jules returned to her laptop.

"Sam Azevedo. Why? You suddenly interested in hunting and fishing?" Jake had a twinkle in his deep green eyes. "Sounds like my kind of fun."

Her handsome boyfriend enjoyed camping, fishing, and kayaking. Basically anything outside. A flutter of panic caused her heartbeat to increase. She worried that she didn't like to do all the rugged outdoorsy things that he liked. A slight frown crossed her face. She pushed thoughts about whether they were a good match out of her mind. With a slight blush, she thought about all the activities they did enjoy together. "I wanted to talk to someone about the big cats. Cal acted weird when he was here. I know there were four tiger cubs, and he kept insisting that there were only two. Oh, look at this." Jules thumbed through the pictures on her phone until she found the one of the tracks in the snow. "The one I sent you."

"Looks like a coyote or bobcat." Jake leaned over for a closer look. "I haven't seen big tracks around here in a while."

"Maybe. With all the stuff that's going on with Cal, it feels weird. We haven't had wild animal issues in a while, but it made me wonder if something was running around loose on the property. I didn't catch anything on any of the cameras."

"I'll text you Sam's number. He's a good guy. He'll know what to do. But it may be because all those big cats were here. The other animals were probably curious about the new smells and sounds. I'll be in the barn if you need me." Jake headed for the back door.

"The check-ins start on Thursday. Lester said he'd make his rounds this afternoon to do any last-minute touch-ups," Jules yelled after him.

"I'll tell him to let me know if he needs any help. See you later." Jake saluted and sauntered out.

Jules googled Game and Inland Fisheries and checked their banned species page. Then she texted Sam to see if he had some time this week to talk. Jules flipped through her files on Cal and Mac again. Bored by all the paperwork, Bijou curled up in her puffy bed for a morning nap.

Unable to sit still or focus on spring planning, Jules slipped into her coat. "You guard the place, Bijou. I'll be back in a sec. I want to check on something."

She jumped in the golf cart and sped over the frozen ground to Cal's trailers. Not sure what she was looking for, Jules parked and wandered around the perimeter. The snow crunched under her boots.

Not finding anything out of the ordinary, Jules climbed up on the wheel well of the trailer closest to her. On top sat a double metal cage bolted to the floor of the flatbed. The bars were staggered, preventing anyone or anything from squeezing in or out of either cage. A thin layer of hay bedding covered the floor. No animals, but the area smelled like it had been inhabited lately. Jules hopped down and circled the trailer. She climbed on the wheel of the second one. Same view and same smells.

Disappointed that nothing jumped out as weird or out of place, Jules continued her circuit around both vehicles. She'd go back to the office and make hot chocolate and leave the tiger cub thing to Game and Inland Fisheries.

Jules fell when she tripped on a root poking through the remnants of the snow near the back of one of the flatbeds. She stood and wiped the heels of her hands, checking for cuts. Two big wet spots spread on her jeans where she landed in the melting snow. Grumbling over the tumble, Jules dusted off her hands on her jeans. Something glittered. Jules leaned over and picked up a gold-colored charm with a broken connector. She fingered the heart that was about the size of a quarter. On one side, someone had engraved "Jira" in a fancy font.

Jules turned it over in her hand. It didn't look valuable, but she'd take it back to lost and found. With nothing to show except the charm and two wet knees, Jules hopped back in the cart.

As she posted a picture of the charm on the resort's Instagram site, her phone rang, and Bijou jumped. She dropped the charm in her purse when she fished out her phone.

"This is Sam Azevedo. How are you? I got your text. I'm on the road, but I have a minute or two if you can talk now."

"Thanks so much for calling. Fern Valley is having a Christmas festival, and Cal Collins from Cal's Cats was an exhibitor this past weekend. To make a long story short, he arrived with four tiger cubs, two cheetah cubs, and a lot of other grown animals. And when they got ready to leave, there were only two tiger cubs. When I asked him about it, he acted like I couldn't count. So that made me suspicious."

"Interesting," he said. "Anything else?"

"Uh, when I was walking my dog, I thought I heard something in the bushes. And I saw a large paw print in the snow. It could have been from one of Cal's animals, but it was closer to the woods and not really in the area where they were." Jules paused to catch her breath.

"We have bobcats, coyotes, and bears in the valley, and every once in a while, there are mountain lion sightings. Not sure if those are all legit. I mean, we get a few Bigfoot sightings reported each year, too," he said. Jules heard the squawk of a radio in the background. "So, you're certain about the cubs."

"I have pictures. When I went back and looked at the security footage, I saw a strange truck near Cal's trailers. Oh, and then I caught the same truck on one of my camera feeds, leaving with one of the cheetahs and another cage in the middle of the night."

After a long pause, he said, "Interesting. Can you send me copies?" He rattled off his email address.

"He made such a big deal about the number of cubs when I know good and well how many animals there were. The whole thing was weird."

"I'll look into it. I've got to head to the far side of my district today, so it may be a couple of days before you hear back from me. We'll get to the bottom of this. Tell Jake I said hello."

"Will do. Thanks for your help." Jules ended the call and texted him copies of her pictures and the video. Maybe he could shed some light on the missing cats. Cal, Misti, and Tabbi would all be back for the weekend's events. More opportunities for Jules to poke around and uncover whatever they were trying to hide.

Chapter Eight

Wednesday

J ules balanced her briefcase and coffee and hip-checked the Jeep's door. She wished she had worn boots instead of pumps, but the look wasn't right with her navy business suit. She followed a family with four small children through the library's front door and waved to Gail Matthews, who coordinated all activities at the circulation desk like a drum major at homecoming.

"Hey, Jules. They moved the meeting to the big conference room." Gail pointed to the back and managed a book check-out at the same time.

"Thanks." Jules dodged children, toys, and bookshelves on her way to the meeting room already packed with business council members. Usually, there was not much interest in the committee's work. Butterflies awakened inside of her. *This should be interesting.*

Kim and Marco slid three tables to the front of the room and placed them end to end while Elaine supervised Mitch's placement of the lectern. Turning toward Jules, Elaine said, "Oh, hi. We had some interest from our members, so we'll meet for updates first and have our working session afterward. We'll see if we need to schedule a follow-up. Hopefully, it won't be too distracting with such a big audience."

Council members huddled around the sputtering coffee machine and the two boxes of doughnuts from member Jocelyn Mercer's The Grateful Bread. The fancy doughnuts called to Jules, but she resisted the urge in favor of several moments of mental prep time before things got rolling.

"Okay, everyone. It's time to get started. Please take your seats. It looks like we have enough chairs. If we don't, you can grab some from the closet in the back. Kim, Marco, Jules, you ready?" Elaine moved up the aisle, shooing members to their spots.

Jules stood behind the lectern and checked the red light on the microphone. She scanned the room and got a nod from Elaine. Not an empty chair in sight. The ones who trickled in stood against the back wall next to the glass doors.

"Good morning, Fern Valley Business Council. Thank you for coming today for our Christmas festival committee meeting. We'll start with an update on this past weekend from the event and committee chairs."

Elizabeth Rhoney, owner of Between the Covers, slid into her seat. "Sorry, I'm late."

Jules did a quick finger wave at the bookseller on the front row. "We'll start with Elaine James, the event co-chair. The expenditures and monies collected will be detailed in the December treasurer's report for our January meeting."

Elaine approached the front and lowered the microphone. "Thank you. Welcome. We had a full slate of food and merchandise vendors this past weekend. Sheriff Hobbs's team estimated that we had over three thousand people at the parade and about that many at the tree lighting. The big cat demonstration was also a success, with over fifteen hundred attendees at the school. I'll let my co-chair Kim Lacy provide an update about what to expect this weekend."

"Thanks, Elaine. Hey, Fern Valley, aren't you excited? It's been nothing but Christmas central around here, and that should get you in the holiday spirit. And I don't know about you, but I'm ready for round two. On Friday night, we have a walking historical tour that starts here at the library. There will be carolers, musicians, and lots of food vendors. Saturday is the big craft fair at the high school and the classic car holiday cruise-in and lights tour. And Sunday, we have our first Christmas music festival. Think of it as Fern Valley Idol. We have about thirty individuals and groups from the tri-county area competing for the five-hundred-dollar prize for adults and a two-hundred-dollar savings bond in the kids' category. Come out and see some awesome talent."

When she paused, Jules rose and said, "Thank you, Kim. Darlene, could you give us an update on the vendors?"

"Gladly." Darlene made her way to the lectern. "We had a waiting list of folks who wanted to be vendors this year, so I say that's fabulous. We received fees for the first weekend from forty-two vendors. We have thirty-seven signed up for next week, too, and we sold one hundred and twenty-five spaces for the craft show. And Kim already said we have thirty-some contestants for the singing competition. We decided to make the cruise-in a free event, but we'll have volunteers out with a bucket brigade. They'll collect donations for our animal shelter." She paused. "Marco or Mitch, do you have any updates?" Darlene scanned the room for a response.

Marco approached the front of the room and adjusted the microphone. "Good morning. The parade and tree lighting went off without a hitch, and it looked like everyone had a festive time. I checked in with the sheriff's office. They wrote two citations during the weekend. Both were for speeding. The sheriff's team spearheaded our traffic control efforts. And we'd like to thank all our police, fire, and rescue workers who put in some long hours to support us. Any questions?"

J. P. Gross cleared his throat and stood. "I heard that there were some rabble-rousers and animal rights protesters. We should vet our participants so that we know that they are high caliber and worthy. And don't attract controversy."

Sheriff Hobbs piped up from the doorway. "There were no protests this weekend. There may have been online chatter, but nothing materialized. No issues."

"That's not what I heard," J. P. muttered, scrutinizing the room. "Jane, do you have any comments? It was your hot story. Tell us your thoughts."

All eyes landed on reporter Jane Jenkins, who scrunched down in her seat in the corner. "I have no comment, but I stand by my research," she said in almost a whisper.

After an extended pause, the sheriff repeated, "There were no protests or issues."

"Any other questions or points of discussion?" Elaine took the microphone from Marco. "Well, then, we'll get down to the planning for this weekend. Let's move those tables closer together so all the teams can sit up here." As the committee members pulled out folders and moved to the front of the room, some of the crowd started to thin as lookie-loos slipped out the door, nabbing the last of the doughnuts.

"Okay," Elaine said to a smaller audience. "Let's go over the agenda for this weekend." She rattled off the events and the team contacts. Jules's mind wandered when she reviewed start times and locations. Without pausing, Elaine launched into a review of emergency numbers and contingency plans.

Jules snapped back to reality when Elaine looked at the faces around the table. "Does anyone need any resources?" The committee members shook their heads. "What about you, Sheriff? Your team is locked and loaded?"

A slight grimace crossed Sheriff Hobbs's face. "We're fully staffed, and we've secured additional resources for traffic and crowd control from the state police. We don't anticipate any problems."

"Any other business?" Before waiting for any responses, Elaine continued, "If not, then before we adjourn, I want to bring up an issue. Some bad behavior. As you may know, I tried to break up an altercation between two of the sellers, and I got dragged into the tussle. Both vendors are slated to be a part of this weekend's events. I will monitor the situation closely and work with the sheriff's team in case there are further issues. They will be asked to leave if they are not professional. Any other business? Jules, do you have anything to add?"

Jules rose. "I'd like to thank everyone for all the hard work they've put into this festival. And if the rest of the weekends are like the last one, we should have really good numbers."

"Well, if there's nothing else..." Elaine said.

J. P. Gross stood and cleared his throat. "Jules, Elaine. I do have one question," he bellowed.

The rest of the room froze in anticipation of what was coming.

"I heard that that vendor was very unhappy with the altercation and how it was handled. She plans to sue. Are you all prepared for a lawsuit and bad press? What does the council plan to do to mitigate risks to our members?"

Elaine blanched. She opened her mouth, but nothing came out but a squeak.

Jules stood and reached for the mic. "We have notified Tom Berryman and Sheriff Hobbs about the complaint. We will handle it like we do all complaints. We hope that it doesn't materialize into a lawsuit, but we have a process in place if it does."

"Well, I hope you're ready for all the bad publicity. And I hope you know what you're doing and that you don't ruin us all. You know how quickly bad publicity spreads." J. P. turned and stalked out of the room.

Elaine took a sip of water and seemed to recover. "Any other comments or questions?" She looked frantically around the room. When there was no response, she quickly added, "Meeting adjourned."

The butterflies danced and flitted around Jules's stomach. *Deep breaths, girl. You don't even know if this is a thing yet.* She smiled pleasantly and scanned the room, hoping that the nerves weren't showing.

The noise level grew as people chatted in small clusters.

Sheriff Hobbs approached Jules. "Good job. That's why you got this job."

Jules offered a weak smile. "Thanks." She gathered her things and said her goodbyes.

On her way to her Jeep, Jules cataloged all the tasks she needed to get done before the guests started to arrive tomorrow. Distracted, she reached for the Jeep's door. Jane "the Pain," rushed toward her before she could climb inside.

"Any comment, Jules, on the pending litigation? I talked to Tabbi Morris, and her plan is to sue everyone and his brother. She said she was even planning to hold a press conference about it. What is your plan? Are you going to get ahead of this? What effect will this have on the weekend events?"

Jules paused. "Jane, it would be inappropriate for me to comment on pending litigation. The town authorities have been notified, and we are following all established protocols."

"So. Are you prepared to be sued? What if you're called as a witness?"

Jules frowned. "I've said all that I can say. If you will excuse me, I need to get back to work." She jerked open the Jeep's door, causing Jane to take several steps back.

"You haven't seen the last of me," Jane sneered. "I hope you know what you've gotten yourself into."

Jules tried not to let the Tabbi issue dampen her enthusiasm for the Christmas festival. This season had always been her favorite, but she hadn't celebrated as much since her divorce and her father's passing. She hadn't been in a festive mood in a while. This year will be different, and Tabbi, Jane, and J. P. weren't going to diminish her spirits.

Trying to think of Christmases past to push melancholic memories out of her thoughts, she jammed the Jeep in reverse. When she backed out faster than she anticipated, her purse flew off the seat and onto the floor. Sighing at her impatience and the inconvenience, Jules put the Jeep into park and hopped out.

Scooping up the myriad of lipstick, pens, and sunglasses, she noticed something that glinted in the light. She had meant to put the Jira charm in the lost and found. Jules pocketed it and drove back to the office. Maybe she could find the owner in her registration files.

Settling in at her desk, Jules pulled up the registration database. No Jiras as guests. Nobody responded to her Instagram post either. For a lark, she googled Cal's Cats and spent an hour combing through his site. *Maybe it was someone on his team.*

There you are. Jira, the cheetah, appeared front and center in several photos with a smiling Cal and Cody. *Cal and I will have to talk. I don't believe in coincidences.*

Chapter Nine

Thursday Afternoon

Jules opened the back door, and Bijou zoomed after the voices in the store. Relieved that the Dutch door blocked the four-legged tornado, Jules decided on coffee first. Roxanne had things out front under control. She rummaged through the coffee pods for a mocha, but a high-pitched squeal echoed through the store and interrupted her plans. Jules abandoned the coffee machine and shooed Bijou away from the door.

"I was here first. Why does she get to push to the front of the line and get preferential treatment?" Misti Miles-Collins banged her fist on the counter and shook her other hand in the air. "This is so unfair. She is always trying to weasel her way in where she's not wanted."

"You were over there rooting through the snacks," Tabbi Morris sneered at the younger, Rubenesque blond. "I have things to do. I can't wait all day for you to pick out unhealthy things to stuff your face with."

Jules stepped behind the counter. "How can I help you?"

"I'm here to check in. We're back this weekend." Misti looked around the store and then stared at her ruby-red fingernails. "We're not performing this time. We're vendors. But we'll spread our rescue message from our souvenir trailers." She cut her eyes toward Tabbi.

"Very good. I have the Collins party for two in the Baum house again. I hope you enjoy your stay." Jules printed the check-in information and handed it to Misti, who turned toward the snack shelves.

Jules waited until she returned.

"Put these on my tab." Misti stacked gum, red licorice, and a pack of snack cakes on the counter.

"Better be careful. You keep eating like that, and you won't fit into those trashy costumes." Tabbi picked up her keys and welcome packet and walked toward the door like she was on a red carpet.

Misti hesitated. "Mind ya business," she yelled to Tabbi's back. She grabbed the bag of snacks and stomped toward the front door.

"Have a nice day," Roxanne yelled after the two women.

Jules shook her head. "Where did you put Tabbi?"

"She and her team are back in the same two vintage trailers. Far, far away from the Collinses."

"Good. Maybe they won't bump into each other while they're here. They always seem to find each other." She pasted on a fake smile that made Roxanne giggle. "Oh, the drama."

"I've got a date with the sheriff for dinner. We've got two more check-ins tonight," Roxanne said, scrolling through the reservation app.

"I can handle those. Have fun on your date." Jules scooted her stool closer to the laptop on the front counter.

"Everything for today's guests is right there. You have big plans?" Roxanne gathered her lunch container and purse.

"Jake wants to start framing the new tiny house. I told him I'd bring dinner and help."

"You kids have fun. Bye, Bijou." Roxanne leaned down and kissed the terrier.

By the time five o'clock rolled around, Jules had checked in the two families, provided overviews of the town's eateries, and sold enough snacks to tide folks over.

"Come on, puppy. Let's go whip up our dinner. We could do that cheesy chicken pasta bake and then go help Jake."

About an hour later, Jules carried a picnic basket with garlic bread, iced tea, salad, and the still-warm chicken pasta to the barn.

They walked toward the hammering. A flash of neon pink near the barn caught Jules's eye. She led Bijou to the back, and the dog barked when they turned the corner. Tabbi's boyfriend, Tony, and a young brunette in a pink ski jacket were in the middle of a make-out session.

Bijou yipped, and Tony turned.

Jules's eyes widened. "Sorry. We didn't mean to interrupt. We were out for a stroll."

"What, you havin' a picnic in the middle of winter?" he asked. "Whattya think, Sheena? Should we go on a picnic?"

The rail-thin woman shrugged.

"Not an outdoor picnic," Jules said. "In the barn. We're working on the latest addition to our tiny houses. Y'all have a nice evening." *Why did she feel the need to explain? He was the one kissing someone other than Tabbi behind the barn.*

"And in case you're wondering, ya didn't see nuthin' here." The bodybuilder turned to face his companion.

The petite brunette giggled as he returned to her embrace.

Jules pulled on the leash, and the dog ambled around the barn. Her ears perked up when she heard whistling. Jules balanced the basket and managed to slide open one of the massive doors. Bijou yipped and tore inside to find Jake.

"Hey, guys. What's up?" Jake put down his hammer and dusted his hands on his jeans.

Jules laid out the plates and plastic utensils on a piece of plywood on two sawhorses. "Dinner is served."

"I'm starving. Smells good."

"It's a cheesy casserole that tastes like chicken enchiladas. I found the recipe on Pinterest," she said.

"Perfect timing. I missed lunch."

The pair ate while Bijou stood on high alert for anything that happened to hit the floor.

Jake reached for another bread stick. "This house will be wider and taller than the others. It's modular, so it'll have more living space. The early ones were built to be transported, so they had to fit within one car lane. This one has a taller loft."

"Can you do the roof on it like this?" Jules pulled out her phone and searched for images of Jay Gatsby's mansion.

"Sure, but it's not a castle or the Biltmore Estate."

"I was thinking of a roaring twenties Fitzgerald theme. But maybe it could be a Bram Stoker house with a castle vibe. We could have fun with that."

"I kinda like the Dracula idea. Lots of possibilities. I'll figure out something for the 1920s for the next one."

"What kind of surprise are you going to put in this one? I love the under-the-stairs reading nook in the Rowling house. But my favorite is the revolving bookcase in the Baum one."

Jake grinned. "It was a cool touch to put gray, white, and black books on one side of the revolving bookcase and books with bright-colored spines on the other. Just like the movie's switch to color."

"Maybe for this one, you could have a secret passage." All kinds of decorating ideas bounced around in her head.

"I'll work on it. We need something new to surprise the guests," he said.

"The tiny houses village has been a popular addition to the resort." Images of the sweet tiny houses merged into darker memories of one of the murders during the filming of *Fatal Impressions*. She brushed thoughts of horrific crime out of her head as she repacked her basket with the leftovers from their meal.

"Babe, that was good. Thanks for making dinner."

"No problem. Bijou and I like hanging out with you in the barn. Speaking of that, you'll never guess what we saw on the way over."

"Another wild animal?"

"Sort of, I guess," Jules said. "Tabbi's boyfriend Tony was making out with the brunette who works their souvenir trailer. They proceeded with what they were doing, and Bijou and I moseyed on along." Jules shrugged.

He wiggled his eyebrows. "Interesting, I guess."

"Tabbi's kind of a terror. She's already had one fight on the courthouse lawn, and she had an altercation with her ex's new wife in the store earlier.

58

I'd hate to see what she'd do if she found out about Tony's shenanigans with the younger gal." Jules dusted her hands off and stood. "What can I help you with?"

"I'd like to finish the framing and get the subflooring in place. It might be ambitious for one night, but we'll see how far we get. Here, hold this board in place, and I'll secure it at the top and bottom. When I'm done, we'll come back and add two-by-fours in between the boards for stability. There's a pair of gloves over there on top of my toolbox." Jake pointed to the storage area on the other side of the frame.

After hours of stretching and bending to hold boards, Jules's muscles ached. She knew it would be worse tomorrow. She did several yoga stretches, but they didn't help. Tonight called for a hot bath and a couple of aspirin. "What's next?" she asked. "You made a lot of progress on all the framing."

"I'm ready to call it a night. Tomorrow, I'll work on the subflooring. Then it's the tiny attic and roof. Thanks for all of your help and dinner."

Jules rubbed her arms and the back of her thighs. "This is fun, but it makes me appreciate my day job. Time for us to head home."

"I'm right behind you. I want to do a quick walk-through and lock up here. See ya tomorrow."

He kissed her, and that turned into a long embrace that Jules didn't want to end. When it did, she said, "Good night. See you in the morning."

Bijou, recharged from her latest nap, zipped around the barn and danced at the door. When Jules slid the giant door open, a blast of arctic air whipped through the barn. "Brrr. Come on, Bijou. No dilly-dallying tonight."

Bijou walked as fast as her short legs would carry her, stopping to sniff the fence near the parking lot. Jules jiggled the leash, but Bijou froze, focused on a clump of grass near the sidewalk. She dug in the grass and picked up something she didn't want to share. Nervous about what the little dog had found, Jules straddled her and wrestled what looked like a doll out of her mouth. "Let go of that. It belongs to someone. That's not something you should chew on."

Large hat pins stuck out at all angles. Jules dropped the doll and checked

Bijou to make sure she didn't get any pins in her mouth or paws.

Reassured that there were no pins stuck or hiding in the little dog's mouth, Jules picked up the doll. She turned the homemade doll with curly brown hair, jutting out in all directions. Someone had drawn big eyes and a large red mouth. A leopard-print dress hung off one shoulder.

"Come on, Bijou."

Jules hurried home and snapped a picture of Bijou's find. She texted the sheriff. If it wasn't important, at least he'd get a laugh out of it. She put the voodoo doll in a bag and set it near the front door.

Was this supposed to be Tabbi?

Chapter Ten

Friday

Despite the chill in the air and the frozen ground, Bijou bounded around the field on her morning walk. Near the vintage trailers, Tony and Sheena packed his truck. Sheena waved and continued her work. *Did Tabbi know about Tony's extracurricular activities? And was the voodoo doll some kind of message or a weird practical joke?*

Glad to be inside, Jules shed her coat and popped a hot chocolate pod into the machine. She rummaged around the snack drawer for marshmallows. Not finding any, she settled for a squirt of whipped cream in her mug.

She needed to work on the resort's next newsletter before the rush of check-ins started.

"Good morning, peeps." Roxanne breezed in and dropped a black Coach purse and a shopping bag from Between the Covers on her desk.

"Catching up on your reading?" Jules cropped a photo of the leopard cubs.

"Something like that. I cleaned my den. These are books that I thought you might want to add to the reading corners in the tiny houses. Or maybe Jake could build me one of those little free libraries," Roxanne said.

"Both are good ideas. How are you this morning?"

"I'll be better after coffee. I need to get fortified for today's onslaught." Roxanne winked at her niece.

"I'm showing twenty-three check-ins today. Busy. Busy." Jules grinned at her aunt.

"We can handle it, and Emily will be in after school. And she's on the schedule tomorrow, too. We've got this. We've done it hundreds of times." Roxanne puttered around her desk while her coffee brewed.

Jules returned to her marketing tasks. Moving on to her email, she answered all but J. P. Gross's passive-aggressive follow-up about how the committee should better vet the vendors it selects to represent the town. Jules could feel the heat rising to her cheeks when she thought about J. P. and his snide comments. She'd marinate on her reply for a couple of days. Determined not to let him get to her, she focused on creating a to-do list for this week, but the bells on the front door interrupted her internal grumbling and signaled the arrival of new guests.

After a steady stream of new arrivals and phone calls that went on for several hours, Roxanne rested on the stool behind the counter. "Whew. From my count, that's everyone for Friday. We'll have some questions or drop-ins this afternoon, but it should calm down."

Before Jules could comment, Lester, the groundskeeper, rushed in the front door. He waved his arms in the air like a windmill in March. "It happened again. Call the Sheriff!"

"What happened?" Roxanne asked.

"I was weed whacking over by the fence line, and I checked on those trailers with the cages that fella left here after they took the animals. Something caught my eye when I walked by. Something in the trailer."

"What?" Jules asked, and Roxanne stared at Lester.

"It looked like a pile of clothes," he said. Roxanne squinted at Lester. When she didn't say anything, he continued, "I moved in for a better look. And it was a leg, sticking out between the bars." He wiped his brow with a folded bandana that he pulled from his back pocket. "It was missing a shoe, but it was definitely a leg," he added.

Jules dialed 9-1-1. "Do we need an ambulance?"

"Nah. She was kinda stiff. No pulse. The body's cold. No breathing, of course. I'm guessing it's been there a while."

Jules connected and explained to the dispatcher what Lester had found. When she ended the call, she said, "Lester, come with me. Roxanne, can you call Jake?"

"Call Jake what?" he asked, stepping into the office.

"Lester found something bad near Cal's trailer. Can you wait for the sheriff here and send him over when he arrives? Roxanne'll fill you in. Thank you," Jules said, scooting out the door as she blew him a kiss.

Jules jumped in the golf cart, and Lester slid in the passenger seat. Jules floored it and zoomed into the area behind the vintage trailers. The groundskeeper clutched the dash with both hands, but he didn't say anything about her driving.

"Over there, Jules." Lester pointed to the trailer with the cage. "You can kinda see it from here."

Jules stopped abruptly. They could see a leg in black stretch pants jutting out at an angle between the bars. Jules jumped out and inched closer.

A gasp slipped from Jules's mouth. "No!" she said, a little too loudly.

Tabbi, in her leopard skin top, lay in a crumpled heap at the bottom on a bed of hay. She wore one black stiletto. Jules covered her mouth with her hand.

Jules's stomach sank. Then her pulse raced. This would be the fifth murder in Fern Valley in a year. Another murder would give J. P. and his cronies more ammunition to argue that her resort was attracting unsavory elements to the area. What was supposed to be a happy holiday celebration had turned into something sinister. Dread and panic weighed heavily on her thoughts. All she wanted to do was continue her parents' campground legacy. It felt right to offer glamping opportunities to a whole new generation, but now her place was ground zero for murder. She closed her eyes for a couple of beats.

Trying not to disturb the scene any further, she and Lester waited in silence for the sheriff by the golf cart. Thoughts about Tabbi's murder ping-ponged around in Jules's head.

After what felt like an eternity, the sheriff's truck, followed by a police cruiser, flew down the maintenance road. Sheriff Hobbs stepped out and slammed the door. "Mornin', Jules. Lester." He approached the cart and peered over the edge into the trailer. Deputy Mario Caswell ambled across the grass.

"Mario, get a hold of someone in forensics and see when they can get out here, and then please get Lester and Jules's statements."

Mario nodded, pulled out his phone, and started tapping on the screen.

Jules spent the next hour alternating between answering Mario's myriad of questions and watching the forensic team photograph and catalog everything around the trailers.

Jake jogged over and stood next to the golf cart. "Doin' okay?"

Jules nodded. "Just watching them work. How are things over there?"

"Roxanne's got it all under control. We got a bunch of calls from folks in town, but nothing from the guests. Roxanne said to tell you she talked Elaine down from calling an emergency meeting."

"I'm gonna head back home," Lester said. "As exciting as this is, these bones can't take the cold for too long. Call me if you need me."

"Will do." Jake nodded his head as the older man climbed out of the golf cart and moseyed toward his cabin.

The sheriff took off his latex gloves and approached the couple. He leaned over and rested his forearms on the golf cart's roof.

"The medical examiner will have to weigh in, but it looks like she was killed sometime overnight. Gunshot wound to the chest. When did you last see her?"

"She checked in yesterday and had an altercation at the desk with her ex-husband's new wife," Jules said.

The sheriff jotted something in his notebook. "We're going to be here a while. Tell Roxanne I'll call her later." He rubbed both eyes.

"You need us for anything else?" Jules asked.

"Nah. I'll swing by before we leave unless it's really late."

"Thanks, Sheriff. Tabbi Morris and her team were staying in two vintage trailers across from each other."

"I'll talk to them soon. Do me a favor; text me the names of the people in her party when you get back to your desk."

"Will do.

Jules's phone continued to buzz with texts and emails as they headed back to the office. Fern Valley's gossip mill worked at warp speed. The rapid-fire ones were from Elaine James. Before she could answer about the need for an emergency business council meeting, her phone rang. Obviously, whatever Roxanne said didn't convince her.

"Elaine."

"Oh, my stars, Jules. They found a body during our holiday festival. What are we going to do? This is not a holly jolly Christmas." Jules imagined Elaine wringing her hands as she fretted.

"I know. The sheriff's team is here now."

"Where are you?"

"At the resort," Jules said in a low tone.

"We have to figure out what to do with today's planned events. The vendors have already set up. I think it'll cause more problems if we have to shut down." Elaine sighed heavily. "Everything will be ruined. That woman caused problems alive and dead."

"Hang on a sec." Jules cleared her throat and yelled, "Hey, sheriff. Do you see any reason why we need to postpone the events in town today?"

"Nope. You should be fine to continue as planned."

"Good to hear. Elaine…"

"I heard. Good news about the festival," she said, disconnecting. *Elaine's on a tear.* Jules looked up at Jake. "Wanna ride back?"

He nodded, and she put the cart in reverse and bumped over the frozen ground. Jules burned a little rubber on the carport when she slammed on the brakes.

"Okay, Mario Andretti, leave some tread on the tires." Jake grinned.

"Got stuff to do. Just like Elaine." She hopped out and trudged up the steps.

Roxanne and Bijou raced to greet them. Roxanne had a barrage of questions before Jake had time to close the door.

"Well," her aunt said. "I need details of what happened out there."

"It's Tabbi. Lester found her in that empty cage," Jules said as her aunt's hand flew to her mouth.

"I'm terribly sorry," Roxanne said gravely.

Jules turned on her laptop and researched Tabbi's party. She texted the list of names and where they were staying to Sheriff Hobbs.

"I'm going to see if the sheriff needs anything." Jake kissed her on the head and nodded at Roxanne.

"Maybe the cameras caught something that will be helpful. I'll be here," Jules mused. She settled in her chair and flipped through camera feeds. Skimming through hours of recordings from several camera angles, Jules looked at the previous day, frame by frame.

Not finding anything that looked related to Tabbi, Jules yawned and stretched. "Oh, crud. I'm going to be late. Can you lock up here? I need to get to town. And can Bijou stay here with you?"

"We'll be fine. Have fun, if you can, under the circumstances," her aunt said with a crazy grin on her face.

Elaine will surely have something to say if I'm late.

Jules hurried to her Jeep and made it to town in record time with a little help from her lead foot. After finding parking, she walked briskly to the courthouse and the green business council tent, where Mitch Hill had set up coffee, brownies, and gingerbread cookies from Lula Belle's. Kim, Darlene, and Elaine chatted while Deputy Dempsey helped himself to snacks and coffee.

"Oh, Jules. I'm glad you're here." Elaine stepped closer, wringing her hands. "Any updates?"

Jules shook her head. "The sheriff and his team are still working at the resort." Jules poured coffee in a to-go cup and watched Elaine's expression darken.

Elaine shook her head and made a tsking sound. "Bubba, I mean Charles. Sorry. Any news from the sheriff's department?"

The deputy finished chewing. "Just like Jules said, forensics is still working the crime scene." He took a huge bite, and brownie crumbs tumbled down the front of his uniform inside his partially unzipped jacket. "I'm sure the sheriff's planning to notify the next of kin and her coworkers."

Jules nodded. "Anybody else have any updates?"

Mitch and the women shook their heads. A somber mood descended on the tent, even though they were surrounded by so many festive decorations and twinkling lights.

"Not to be callous, of course, but it would have been a huge hassle to cancel and do refunds. I hate disappointing people, especially during the holiday season." Elaine let out a heavy sigh that sounded like air escaping from a punctured balloon. "We're ready to go." She refilled her to-go mug. "All the vendors are set. The historic walking tour begins at six-thirty and ends with cocoa around the bonfire. Tomorrow's the craft show at the high school, and the classic car cruise-in is tomorrow evening. Let's make the best of it."

"And don't forget the Christmas sing-off on Sunday. Then we can rest," Kim added, stirring her coffee.

"We're fully staffed here in case there are questions. So, we roll along. Keep calm and carry on," Elaine said. "Mitch, you wanna come with me? We need to check that those portable fire pits are set up on the courthouse lawn properly. Nick and the rest of his fabulous firefighters will have to give them the FVFD seal of approval before we light them."

"Sure." Mitch followed Elaine toward the courthouse.

Charles nabbed another brownie. "Have to get back to my post, too. One for the road." He took a huge bite and topped off his coffee.

"I'm going to do a quick walk around, and then I'll head home to check on things there. Call me if you need me." Jules waved to Kim and Darlene.

Jules made a quick circuit around the courthouse grounds. The vendors looked ready to go, and scents of hamburgers and French fries wafted through the air. Making a detour, she ordered two cheeseburger sliders and a Dr. Pepper. She took a bite of the juicy burger and wiped her chin as she walked down the row of souvenir vendors.

Tony's latest squeeze, in a leopard-print ski vest, hung over the counter at Tabbi's Tees and waved at passersby.

"Hi. You all are back. I hope you had good sales last weekend," Jules said, inching closer to the trailer's counter.

"Oh, hey. You're from the resort. I'm Sheena. Yes, we had a blast. And I love your vintage trailers. I saw the one you decorated for the British royalty and the one that's moon-themed. Or is it for space exploration? Anyway, they are great. I'm going to come back sometime for a vacation."

"Thank you. Each one has its own theme, usually based on the year or model." Sheena turned her attention to a prospective customer. *No mention of Tabbi or a reaction to the murder. Does she even know?*

Across the street, Tabbi's friend Dana staffed the Christmas trailer. She had a steady line of customers buying holiday garb and decorations.

When Dana handed a woman at the counter her items in a plastic bag, Jules jogged across the street and said, "Hi there. It's good to see you again."

"Uh, hi. It's been busy around here today." The woman played with multiple rubber bracelets on her arm. The bracelets and the oversized lace bow attached to her headband gave Jules flashbacks to Madonna wanna-bees from the Big Eighties, her mom's favorite era. Pushing sad thoughts away, she said, "Those are interesting." She pointed to Dana's getup that almost looked like a costume.

"Oh, I collect vintage clothing." Dana smiled and wiggled her arm with the stack of black rubber bracelets. "Today, I'm wearing clothes from the era of MTV and big hair. Tomorrow, I have a vintage fifties outfit."

"Then you'll love Pop's Diner in town. He's got a ton of memorabilia on the walls. Hey, do you need anything?" Jules asked.

"Nope. I have my energy drink. I can go all night," said the tall brunette with her nasally accent. "I'll be glad when Tabbi gets here. It's not like her to be late."

Something behind Jules caught Dana's eye, and she leaned forward over the counter. "Hey, Tony. Where's Tabbi?"

"Who knows? Something musta come up. She's not answering her phone. It's not like her to leave us hanging. Can you handle both trailers, or do you want me to close up the cat one?" The guy in the shiny workout suit pointed to the nearby trailer. He fidgeted on the sidewalk and then ran his hands through his wavy hair several times.

"No, Tabbi'll have a stroke. I'll manage somehow." She pulled out her phone and tapped furiously.

Jules quashed guilty feelings about not telling the team about Tabbi, but it didn't feel right, especially before the sheriff talked to them. She continued her stroll to the Jeep. Her phone binged several times, announcing a series of texts. Taking the last bite of burger and wiping her hands, Jules fished her phone out of her purse. Three rapid-fire texts.

The Sheriff wants to talk to me.

What should I do?

This is too crazy. What is he thinking? I had nothing to do with this.

Jules's stomach lurched. She dialed Elaine's number, and before she could get a greeting out, Elaine blurted, "Did you get my texts? I can't believe it. Why does he want to talk to me, especially now? I'm kinda busy. He's got to know I had nothing to do with this. Why me? I didn't know her or like her. I bet a lot of people didn't like her. Do you think I need a lawyer? This is too much."

"Elaine, take a breath. If the sheriff didn't say he was going to arrest you, then he just wants to ask you some questions. It's up to you whether or not you want a lawyer. Do you need me to come back and cover for you?"

"No, no, I need to stay busy. I can't keep thinking about that awful woman and what happened to her. I'm fine. I'll let you know if I need to leave. I have a job to do here. I'll take some cleansing breaths and center myself. Keep calm and all that."

"Okay. Call me if anything changes." Jules backed out of her spot and pointed the Jeep toward the resort.

She wondered if she should check on Elaine anyway, despite her protests. Kim and Darlene were with her, and they'd call if anything went awry. Jules resisted the urge to swing by Tabbi's booths again. She'd leave the notification to Sheriff Hobbs.

Jules floored it through town and down a back road to the resort. She slowed down ever so slightly as she made the turn beside Cal's animal trailer. A Fern Valley cruiser, the sheriff's truck, a forensic van, and a state trooper's cruiser surrounded the trailer. No spectators in sight. Jules mashed the brake and skidded to a stop outside her garage. Slamming the Jeep's door, she jogged to Lester's small cabin on the other side of the barn.

She knocked, and a moment later, her groundskeeper pulled the door open.

"Oh, hey, Jules. I didn't expect to see you this afternoon. What's up?"

"I'm sorry to bother you, but I came from town and wanted to see if you had heard anything on your scanner?"

"Come on in. It's colder than a brass toilet seat in the Yukon out here."

"Any news? It looks like the sheriff and his folks are still at the scene." Jules stood in the entryway between the living area and the kitchen of the groundskeeper's cabin. The well-worn furniture looked like it was from the seventies when the campground originally opened. Lester's police scanner and headphones sat on his cluttered desk in the corner.

"They took the body to Richmond. It's been pretty hush-hush. That's about all I know. They didn't say anything about how or who? I think the sheriff got on his team about chatter on the radio. They've been pretty tight-lipped about this whole thing," Lester said.

Good for the sheriff, but bad for those who are trying to find out information.

"I did hear one little snippet that might be a clue. I didn't recognize the voice, but someone said they found a voodoo doll under her when they moved the body. Can you believe it? My momma and grandmomma grew up in Louisiana, and that stuff is nothing to mess with."

Jules's eyes widened.

"Bad stuff. Anyway, that's all that was said about it. The chatter died down when the medical examiner arrived."

"Thanks, Lester. I'll let you get back to what you were doing." Jules hightailed it to the office. She barely made it through the back door before Roxanne and Bijou pounced on her. Roxanne wanted information. Bijou, just hugs.

"So, what's going on?" Roxanne stared at her niece.

"Somehow, Elaine found out that the victim was Tabbi," Jules whispered.

Roxanne sunk into her desk chair. "Wow. But why are you whispering?"

Jules raised her eyebrows. "I'm not sure. It felt like it was a secret. I talked to Tabbi's team in town. I don't think they know about her murder yet. They acted bothered that she was late. Lester said they haven't identified her on the police scanner either."

Roxanne pursed her lips. "Hey, the Fern Valley rumor mill is right more often than not."

"Sheriff's got his hands full with this one. She rubbed a lot of people the wrong way. I know his suspect list is going to be long." Jules fired up her laptop and settled into her desk chair to take another look at the camera feeds. She started with this weekend to see if anything looked out of place. Then, she moved backward in time to the previous weekend.

Jules scrolled through the feeds from all her cameras. Something flashed on her screen, and she paused and replayed it. Cal Collins strode across the field to the lodge. Even in slow motion, his swagger exuded confidence. She glanced at the timestamp, seven-thirty on Thursday night. She jotted down the camera information and switched cameras. Jules zoomed to about the time of the last Cal sighting. "There you are," she whispered to herself.

She slowed the feed and watched Cal walk toward the barn. He stopped near the door and looked around as Tabbi approached. She waved her arms around, and they argued for several minutes. Tabbi took several steps forward and embraced Cal. The couple kissed for several minutes and then separated. Cal walked toward the lodge, and Tabbi headed to the vintage trailers. Jules's jaw dropped.

"Well, I'll be," Jules said loud enough for Bijou's head to turn.

"What did you find?" Roxanne asked.

"A clip of Cal and Tabbi in a liplock. Some interesting dynamics with this group." Jules copied the footage and sent it to the sheriff.

Roxanne whistled and rummaged around her desk. "I'm old enough that people shouldn't surprise me, but they do. I'm heading out soon. Matt and I were supposed to have dinner in, but that's probably not going to happen now. You going into town?"

Jules stood and stretched. "I was, but I got lost in the camera feeds. I think I'll stay here. I'll head over to the craft show and the cruise-in tomorrow."

"I'll be in at my usual time. Ciao." Her aunt blew kisses as she sauntered toward the front door.

Jules made an espresso and did some yoga poses while she waited for it to brew. "Bijou, it's harder when I don't know what I'm looking for. Tabbi had dust-ups with almost everyone. And now she and Cal are sneaking around

71

the resort like love-sick teenagers. And what about Misti? Tony? And Tony and Sheena, for that matter?"

Bijou opened one eye. When she didn't see any snacks, she rolled over. She didn't care about love triangles.

"Let's see. I'm looking for Tony, Dana, Sheena, and Cal. Any one of them could have been involved in Tabbi's murder. And Elaine thinks the sheriff is interested in questioning her. There's no way anyone could think Elaine was involved. When she dies, her headstone will read, 'I always followed the rules and made sure others did, too.'"

Jules stirred creamer into her coffee and settled in her chair. She clicked through hours of footage frame by frame. She copied the files and sent the cloud link to Sheriff Hobbs in case his guys found something she missed.

Around nine o'clock, Jules shut down her laptop and yawned. "That's enough for tonight. All that effort for hours of clips of people walking to and from their trailers or tiny houses. I got one shot of Tony and Sheena walking toward the parking lot, but it didn't look as scandalous as Cal and Tabbi's dalliance. Some Nancy Drew I am."

Chapter Eleven

Saturday

The bells on the front door announced the resort's latest arrival of the morning. Jules saved the draft of the newsletter she was working on and headed for the front counter.

"Good morning, Sheriff. How are you?"

He closed the door behind him and took off his Smokey Bear hat. "Mornin', Jules. Gotta few minutes?"

"Sure, come on back. Coffee?" her aunt's beau nodded, and Bijou yipped her greeting.

"It's good to see you, but I'm guessing this isn't a social visit." Jules handed him the mug after the machine stopped sputtering and let out a blast of steam.

"Nope. All business today. I got the videos you sent. Thanks. Just wanted to get your take on Tabbi Morris and get you to describe what you witnessed. We'll know more when the autopsy results come back."

Jules sighed. "I'm sorry about her fate. It was horrific, but she was a little prickly. She and the current Mrs. Collins had words in town and here. Tabbi also had a run-in with Elaine and some of the Fern Valley folks, but I think that was minor in comparison to the battle of Cal's wives, past and present. Their altercations were more like smackdowns. And you saw the clip of the make-out session with her ex-husband that I sent you. This seems like a soap opera. Especially after Cal and Tabbi had a loud argument in front of a

73

small crowd. He claimed she copied his marketing designs."

The sheriff raised an eyebrow and pulled his black notebook from his front pocket. "Anything else?"

"I also ran into Tabbi's boyfriend, Tony, out behind the barn with one of their workers, Sheena, who's a lot younger than Tabbi."

He raised both eyebrows this time. "What about her interactions with the Fern Valley folks?"

Jules nodded. "Tabbi was snippy in the office a couple of times. Roxanne put her in her place once." A smile crept across the sheriff's face. "After Elaine tried to break up that fight in the town square, Tabbi sent that email full of threats and complaints and lawsuits." Jules took a breath. When he didn't comment, she continued, "Uh, Misti and Tabbi seemed to have a dustup every time they encountered each other."

"I'll look into it. Lots of folks with reasons to dislike the victim." He took a swig of his coffee and set the mug on the edge of Jules's desk. "Let me know what you hear. Anything else?"

"I told you about Cal and the tiger cubs. Not sure that that has anything to do with this, but it was odd. Anyway, I called Game and Inland Fisheries about the tiger cub thing, but I haven't heard back from him."

The bells tinkled again, and Roxanne breezed in. A smile crossed Sheriff Hobbs's face. He stood, pocketing his notebook.

"Hey, Rox. Lookin' good as usual."

"You're not so bad yourself. Didn't think we'd see much of you until you wrapped up this investigation. Did you get any sleep?" She dropped her royal blue Gucci bag on her desk.

"A coupla hours. Always something going on around here. Gonna try to get away from work this evening after the cruise-in."

"Dinner at my place?" Roxanne batted her eyelashes.

"Sounds great. See you then." He leaned over and kissed Roxanne. "Bye, Jules."

When the sheriff left, her aunt asked, "So, what's new around here?"

Jules's eyes widened.

"Sorry. I was trying to lighten the mood a little. It's sad, but Matt has plenty of suspects. Tabbi wasn't going to win any popularity contests. He's going to be busy for days unless he catches a break."

"Elaine is in a tizzy about all this."

"She and half the town. Elaine didn't do anything except be her usual self. I don't think she has anything to worry about." Her aunt rummaged through her purse and pulled out a gold tube of lipstick.

"Tabbi threatened to sue her and others in an email. She and Misti and Cal have a pretty good hate triangle going. And then I saw her boyfriend Tony with someone else behind the barn." Jules's voice trailed off.

Roxanne's eyebrows shot up, and her mouth formed a small "o."

The bell rang again, and Bijou sprung into security mode. She calmed down when Emily Owens hung over the Dutch door.

"Good morning, everybody. And happy Saturday. Jules, got anything special you want me to work on today?"

"It's good to see you. All the guests are checked in for the weekend. We had a situation today, and the sheriff and his team were here. If you get questions about it, let Roxanne know."

Roxanne interrupted with, "I'll fill you in later."

Emily nodded, and Jules continued, "We may get more calls or questions than normal, so if you could staff the front, that would be great. And if it gets too quiet, I'd love for you to do some posts on the resort's social media sites. There should be some newish pictures on the computer out there."

"Awesome," the teen said, making a dash for the counter. "And my dad said that I'd never get paid for spending so much time on Instagram."

"I'm going to run over to the high school and check on the craft show. I'll be back to get Bijou before you leave for your date," Jules said.

"We'll be fine here. It's payroll day, and I'll take care of the sales tax and quarterly reporting. I want to knock that out before the holidays. We'll all need a good rest after this festival," Roxanne said.

Jules waved and slipped out the back door. Spotting the empty sheriff's car in the parking lot, she scanned the area to see what he was up to.

She walked briskly to her driveway and threw her purse on the Jeep's passenger seat. As the engine roared to life, the sheriff exited the 1940 New

Moon vintage trailer. It didn't look like he had anything in his hands.

Deciding that he probably wouldn't share if he found anything in the trailer, Jules decided to prime the Fern Valley rumor mill. She turned up a song on the oldies station and cruised to the high school.

Jules entered the building through a large green, red, and white balloon arch. High school students in elf costumes chattered and greeted visitors with red maps and candy canes.

She wished she had left her coat in the car. The building felt tropical, so she wiggled out of it and made a beeline for the information table. Kim and Darlene answered questions from a gaggle of vendors while Elaine buzzed around the hallway, straightening everything.

When the line died down at the table, Jules said, "Good morning, ladies."

"Whew! It's been a blur. I think all the vendors are squared away. And now the shoppers are coming in droves," Darlene said.

"Everything looks nice. Your committee did a great job." Groups of people filed into the gym at a steady pace.

"The food trucks out in the bus loop. The school's bake sale is down that hallway." Kim pointed past the trophy case.

"Need anything?" Jules stared at the throngs of people filling the hallway.

"Nope. We're good. Reinforcements will be here to give us a break at lunchtime. I'm really pleased with all the foot traffic. The vendors should be happy with the sales." Darlene took a swig from her water bottle.

As more visitors approached the table, Jules blended in with the crowd and followed the candy-cane-striped arrows that guided her through the maze of tables in the gym.

After hours of browsing, Jules found a cute collar for Bijou, a carved wooden box for Jake, and a handcrafted pendant for Roxanne. She carried her purchases out and waved to neighbors and friends. Unfortunately, she didn't overhear any gossip about Tabbi's murder.

The blast of cold air on the other side of the main doors was a welcome relief from the heat inside the school. Her phone buzzed several times in rapid succession. Shuffling her packages, she reached for her phone as she spotted Tony at the Tabbi Tee's trailer across the street. She glanced at her phone. Emily had tagged her in several posts.

Dropping the phone back in her purse, she walked across the grass as Tony hung T-shirts on hooks around the opening above the counter. Jules walked past the food trucks with their myriad of delicious smells that made her stomach rumble. Her phone dinged again, but she ignored it.

As Jules approached the robin's egg blue trailer, Tony bellowed, "Hey, I hope you're not coming over here to hassle me. We've got a right to be here. Tabbi paid for a vendor space, and there's not as much traffic in town this weekend. We need to make a living."

"Excuse me?"

"Huh? I thought you were coming over here like that other mean lady to make us move. We're not blocking traffic." He looked over at Sheena in the "As Seen on TV" trailer.

"No. I was going to ask you how you all were doing," Jules said.

"Oh, uh. Fine, I guess. Sales are better here than they were in town. We left the other trailers there with Dana."

"She was in such a mood that Sheena and I didn't want to be around her." Tony added several T-shirts to the rack.

Jules hoped she didn't roll her eyes. *This guy's girlfriend was found dead, and he was more interested in selling T-shirts.* "I'm so sorry for your loss. The sheriff came by my office this morning."

His mouth formed a straight line, and he chewed on his bottom lip. "Thanks. She'll be missed. But she would have wanted us to finish the job, right, Sheena? Especially since we're paid up through the weekend. Never waste an opportunity, Tabbi always said."

Sheena nodded and arranged cans of magic sealer and microwave egg containers in front of her.

"If I can help with anything, please let me know," Jules added.

"I'll call you in the spring," Sheena yelled. "I want to come back and stay in your trailers in the summer. Right, Tony? It's beautiful here." Tony nodded so vigorously that Jules feared he might shake something loose.

Jules waved and made her way to her silver Wrangler. Remembering the text, she pulled out her phone.

77

Wanna go to the cruise-in with the 'Stang?

Dinner at Pop's? She texted back and added several heart emojis in a follow-up text.

Jules had enough time to get Bijou and find an outfit for her date tonight.

On her ride back to the resort, she replayed her conversation with Tony and Sheena. They cared more about selling their wares than they did about Tabbi. The whole discussion was awkward. Jules made a mental note to talk to Dana. *That may give me a whole other side to the story.*

Around three-thirty, Jules heard Jake's red Mustang pull up in her driveway. Pushing thoughts of Tabbi's death and guilty feelings about enjoying her date out of her head, Jules locked the door and trotted down the sidewalk.

"Let's go see what kind of trouble we can get into," he said.

She laughed and kissed his lightly stubbled cheek. "Hope we won't need bail money. I've never been to a cruise in. Can't wait to see what this is all about."

"I've been on a couple of poker runs, but not a cruise-in. When I was in the army in South Carolina, people would cruise around Myrtle Beach. It's probably like that." Jake found an upbeat channel on the car's satellite radio. "Too chilly to put the top down."

"We'll save that for summer."

"Anything new in your investigation?" he asked as they turned onto the resort's driveway.

"I'm trying to help Elaine. She's worried about this whole ordeal with Tabbi. First the threats and now the murder. I've never seen her this nervous before. I'm not really investigating. Just asking some questions."

"The sheriff couldn't possibly think Elaine did it." Jake pursed his lips.

"It seems impossible. She's the one who always plays by the rules, the organizer and list maker. She's really wound up about all of this."

Their conversation ended abruptly when traffic came to a standstill on the outskirts of town. Jules hadn't seen so many classic, specialty, and muscle cars in one place before. Two guys in fluorescent vests made their way down the line of cars.

"Hey, Marco," Jake said as he rolled down the window when the man appeared at the side of the car.

"You're here for the cruise-in?" Jake nodded, and Marco Hooper continued, "Follow the car in front of you. We're going to get everyone lined up in the church lot. When we start, you'll follow the car in front of you. Obey all traffic laws and cruise around the town. We'll all eventually end up at Pop's. Have fun."

"Good turnout," Jules said. "These look like a lot of your clients."

"Yep, word got out, and all the gearheads and vintage car lovers are here. I let everyone on my shop's mailing list know." Marco, owner of Lug Nuts vintage auto parts, saluted and moved to the next vehicle.

They found a spot and waited for what seemed like hours. Then Mitch Hill waved a checkered flag, and the drivers started their engines. The roar and whine of a variety of vehicles filled the evening air and merged into a large rumble. The line of cars snaked through the lot and slowly paraded through Fern Valley. The drivers and their passengers waved at the folks lining the sidewalks.

When they rounded the corner near the government center, Jules spotted Tony and Sheena chatting at the T-shirt trailer. What would happen to the business now that Tabbi was no longer around? She seemed to be the driving force of the operation.

After a slow cruise around the square, Jake followed the line of cars to Pop's and found a place to park in the back. He and Jules strolled by the rows and rows of cars. Many of the owners sported costumes that matched their car's era or color, and they had decked out their rides for the holidays. Jules's favorites were the classics and rat rods that looked like something out of *American Graffiti*. Jules snapped photos for her next newsletter.

Volunteers wandered through the crowd with bright green Fern Valley buckets, collecting change for the animal shelter. After dropping in a donation, Jake wrapped his arm around Jules, and she snuggled in. It was nice to hang out and relax for a change. Lately, her thoughts fixated on the murder, work, and business council. She spent most of her waking hours trying to drum up business for the resort and couldn't remember the last time she took a full day off. "This is fun," she said as he gently squeezed her shoulder.

A high pitched "Joooooooooooles" echoed across the parking lot. Elaine James bustled toward the pair. "Hey, y'all. Sorry to interrupt, but Jules, I need to talk to you." Before Jake could excuse himself, Elaine launched into her story, "Jules. I got a letter today from an attorney in Staunton. Tabbi filed a lawsuit over the skirmish at the courthouse. It said that she's involving the town manager and the sheriff, too. Oh, Jules. I'm not sure what to do. How could something so dumb mushroom into a big deal?"

Elaine, in her white snowball coat, tapped her black boot on the asphalt.

"Can there be a lawsuit if the plaintiff is dead? I'll get in contact with Sheriff Hobbs and Tom. They can advise us. Don't panic," Jules murmured.

"I don't need this right now with all the festivities and the holiday season fast approaching. That woman! I wish she'd never shown up in Fern Valley." Elaine stuffed her hands in her coat pockets and stalked off.

Jake shook his head and guided Jules to the restaurant. While they waited in the packed lobby for a table, Jules sent a flurry of texts to the sheriff and town manager.

Almost an hour later, a girl in a poodle skirt seated them in a cozy booth in the Beatles' section of the restaurant. Jules's phone dinged with a text from Tom Berryman. **I'll check. The heirs may want to pursue it. Stay tuned.**

Jules let out a sigh as Marsha approached in her trademark pink bouffant and pale pink waitress uniform with the white Peter Pan collar. "I hope that wasn't a sign of exasperation. Sorry about the wait. What can I get for you all tonight?"

"No, it's not that. It's been a long day. Let's see. I'll have the grilled cheese and a cup of tomato soup with an iced tea," Jules said.

"I'll have the Coney dog with everything and onion rings. And a chocolate malt." Jake handed her the menus.

"Be back in a flash." Marsha winked and moved on to the next table.

"What's up?" Jake asked, leaning forward, taking both of her hands in his.

"Tom Berryman said he'd contact Tabbi's lawyer. Her lawsuit could still be a thing. Elaine is going to freak out even more."

"Who knew a case could live on after a person died?"

Jules shrugged and slumped back in the booth. She watched people, many in fifties costumes, drift in and out of the restaurant. They sported leather jackets, poodle skirts, and saddle oxfords. More than one Elvis-look-alike sauntered past the table.

Her thoughts bounced around from topic to topic with no clear connection. The altercation wasn't that big of a deal, but it and whether the heirs would continue the lawsuit would worry Elaine for days. Then, images of Tabbi's lifeless body kept flashing across Jules's thoughts. *How in the world did Tabbi end up in one of Cal's cages at my resort?*

Chapter Twelve

Sunday

J ules took a bite of her pecan pie muffin and put the Jeep in gear. She wanted to pop in at the high school to check on the singing competition before she did any research on Tabbi. Elaine had looked frazzled the day before. Maybe she could help with the setup.

She finished her muffin during the ride and dusted her hands on her jeans. Draining the last bit of coffee from her travel mug, she pulled into the lot in front of the school and scored a spot near the main entrance. Jules wiggled out of her coat and dropped her keys and phone in her purse. Jules ducked under the balloon arch at the entrance, and her boot heels clicked on the industrial composite floor as she trekked down the front hall to the registration table.

"Welcome," Kim Lacy boomed. "You going to sing today, Jules?"

Jules laughed. "I'm better at lip-synching." She stepped up to the table where Kim and Darlene sat behind stacks of red envelopes. "How goes it?"

"We're ready," Darlene chirped. "Elaine and Marco are inside with the AV club doing a sound check. We've got lights and an incredible sound system, everything except the revolving chairs on *The Voice*."

"Or Simon Cowell from the early days of *American Idol* or that other show," Kim added.

"If you get hungry, the food trucks and vendors should be outside by eleven. We open the doors around noon for a one o'clock show. Y'all ready to rock 'n roll?" Darlene did a fist pump in the air like she was a cheerleader.

Jules laughed. The gals' enthusiasm was contagious.

"We've sold a bunch of tickets, and I'm sure we'll get some walk-in traffic. Can't wait to see who wins. We've got a great lineup of solo acts, choirs, and bands. Let's see who the new voice of Fern Valley's going to be." Kim fished through her purse and pulled out her lip gloss. "Elizabeth sent out a ton of press releases. We're expecting reporters from two of the local channels."

"Sounds like fun. Y'all need any help?" Jules asked.

"Nope, we're good. Just waiting for the contestants to arrive." Kim pulled out some registration packets from under the table and added them to the stack.

"I'll be back in a sec. I want to see the auditorium." Jules's footsteps echoed as she walked down the long hallway lined with trophy cases and lockers. She stopped at a water fountain that offered the option for water bottle refills. Things had changed since she was in school, but the distinct smells, a mix of some kind of cleaning solution and stinky gym socks, flashed her back to her days of scrunchies and backpacks.

Smaller lockers and modern classrooms with more technology than an overhead projector caught her eye. The tri-counties built this school about ten years ago, and it was a boon for the nearby towns that needed an updated facility.

Jules slipped into the auditorium and walked down the sloping floor to the first row. Elaine, standing under a spotlight on the stage, tapped the microphone and waved to Marco and a pair of students in the sound booth. "Okay, we've tested all the equipment. Do you have everyone's music?" Marco gave her two thumbs up, and she continued, "You've got everything queued up in the right order?"

Another thumbs up from Marco. Jules thought she caught an eye roll from the sound booth.

"Run through the first couple of songs so I can check out the volume from the seats." Elaine gingerly climbed down the wooden steps and stood in front of the first row.

Snippets of several songs blared from all sides of the auditorium.

Elaine flapped her arms up and down. "Good. Now, let's try the lights one more time."

Lights flashed slowly and then rapidly. Then, the spotlight morphed from pink to blue to bright white.

"I think we're ready." Elaine waved her arm in the air. "I need to go check on the green room. The performers should be arriving soon. Very good. Things are in order here. Good job, y'all."

As Marco clicked switches, the auditorium went dark except for the running lights on the aisles and other emergency red ones around the doors.

"Lookin' good, Elaine. Do y'all need anything?" Jules asked.

Elaine shook her head as she hustled out the side door.

Jules waved to Marco and slipped out the side door, too. Scads of people, some carrying garment bags, gathered in the main hallway. Not seeing any opportunities to help, Jules walked outside to see what the food trucks had to offer. Her stomach rumbled at the first few whiffs of hamburgers and barbecue. She perused all the brightly painted trucks and settled on a lilac one that offered tacos.

After two street tacos and a bottle of water, she checked the time on her phone and hustled back inside to find a seat for the competition before it was standing room only.

Retracing her steps to the auditorium. She found a spot in the middle of the fourth row and tried to settling in on the hard seat.

The lights dimmed while she checked her email and the resort's Instagram feed. Jules looked around. A steady stream of bodies still filed in from the doors at the back. The lights flashed again, and the noise died down.

Darlene Denunzio stepped on the stage, and applause erupted. "Good afternoon, Fern Valley. I hope you're as excited as I am for our first-holiday sing-off. We have so much talent here today. But before we get started, I'd like to introduce you to our judges. Marco swung the spotlight to the edge of the stage. "First, we have our town manager, the honorable Tom Berryman." When the applause faded, she continued. "Next to him, we have local businessman J. P. Gross, along with Marti Baskerville, principal of this beautiful facility. Thank you, judges, for giving up your afternoon to help us find the best voice in the valley. Let's give them another round of applause."

The judges waved, and Darlene continued, "Without further ado, our first act is Claire and Lilly Davis, the Darling Dumplins."

Fifteen kid acts later, Jules was ready for a break. She excused herself and moved up the aisle as Darlene returned to the stage. "Weren't they awesome? Let's give them all one more round of applause. Now we'll have a ten-minute intermission. Don't be late. You don't want to miss any of the adults."

Jules bought a bottle of water at the 4H Club bake sale booth and greeted friends as she made her way back to the auditorium.

The music blared, and lights flashed again as Jules settled in her seat for the second part of the show.

About the time that she started to fidget and wonder if she should sneak out, Darlene introduced the Skyline Singers. Jake, Ashley Sharpe, and Carlene "Red" Tucker ambled out on stage. Her boyfriend, the sheriff's receptionist, and the owner of Red's Honky-tonk sang a medley of seventies country songs and tunes by Kenny Rogers, Barbara Mandrell, and Eddie Rabbitt.

Her mouth fell open. She didn't know if she was more shocked at how good Jake sounded or that he entered the contest without mentioning it to her. *You'd think it would have at least merited a casual comment.*

She snapped some pictures of the handsome Jake on stage and smiled to herself.

After three other acts, Darlene announced a fifteen-minute break for the judges to confer. Hardly anyone left their seats. Jules had enough time to post her pictures of Jake before the judges handed Darlene two envelopes. She tapped on the microphone with her ring. "I am pleased to announce that the youth winner of the first Fern Valley sing-along is Tyler McKensie." Applause echoed through the auditorium as the young man with the blue guitar who sang an Elvis medley took the stage to claim his prize.

Then, Darlene tapped on the mic again. "And now, the moment you've all been waiting for. Could I have the Campbell Sisters, the Ridgerunners, and the Skyline Singers on stage, please?" When the groups reassembled around her, Darlene said, "Let's give a big round of applause for all our contestants. Don't forget our judges. They deserve a big thank you. This was such a hard decision for them. Okay, now, without any more hubbub, I'd like to congratulate the Ridgerunners, our third-place winners. And first place in the adult category and the grand prize winner is…the Skyline Singers—Jake Evans, Ashley Sharpe, and Red Tucker. And congratulations to the Campbell Sisters for their second-place win."

The Skyline Singers hugged each other, and Ashley jumped up and down and squealed. Jules stepped into the aisle to meet Jake when he came off stage. The three singers were still celebrating on stage when Red Tucker grabbed Jake around the waist and planted a long kiss on his lips. The crowd made an ooooing sound. Jules felt her cheeks flush. Jake seemed to be in no hurry to pull away.

Memories of her cheating ex-husband, the Idiot, flashed across her thoughts. *I can't go through that again.* She didn't know if it was the shock of the moment or the sting from the betrayal or both. Jules felt the blood pulsating in her head. Her first instinct was to march on stage, and then her second thought was to flee. She had the urge to get as far away from him and memories of the Idiot as she could. Not waiting to find out if there was more to the Red and Jake story, she turned and rushed to her Jeep.

Chapter Thirteen

Monday

Jules charged toward the office coffee maker for her second espresso, hoping it would improve her mood. She knew she should have congratulated Jake on his big win, but she couldn't after Red Carlson had kissed him like that in front of everyone. And he looked like he liked it. Stunned, she wasn't sure quite what she felt, so she'd hurried home and sulked, and that had turned into a night of tossing and turning and a foul mood this morning. *Girl, you have to confront him. This can't be like life with the Idiot. And he didn't even call or text me last night.*

Trying to put it out of her mind, she looked at the bookings for the last quarter. Work would distract her until a stray thought reminded her of Jake. Pushing him out of her thoughts again, she glanced at her spreadsheet. The fall and winter were on track for record numbers. Potential bookings for January were low, though. Maybe she should use that time to take a vacation to somewhere warm.

Beach thoughts turned into Jake thoughts, and she gritted her teeth. She opened her calendar to check for dates and fired off an email to Elizabeth Rhoney at Between the Covers, hoping that she would want to partner with some kind of book event in January.

Then she started sketching out Valentine's Day romantic getaways. She sent emails to area businesses to see if they wanted to offer any specials that she could offer her guests as package deals. Thoughts of Jake kept popping into her mind, and that made her think of her ex-husband, the Idiot, and all his philandering. She let out a heavy sigh and bit her lip to keep from crying. Down deep, she knew Jake wasn't like the Idiot, but her disappointment in him cut deeper than she wanted to admit.

Before Jules could gather her thoughts and clear her head, Jake and Roxanne came in through the front door. The pair shared a joke with lots of laughter.

"Hey, Jules. How are you?" Roxanne dropped her pink Michael Kors purse and her insulated lunch bag on the desk.

"Fine," she said without looking up.

She could feel Jake's stare. Ignoring it, she pretended to look for something in her desk drawer.

Her aunt paused and looked at Jake and then at Jules. "We were talking about Jake's exciting weekend. Who knew he could sing like that?"

"Yes, he's a man of many talents." Jules stared at her fingernails.

When she didn't say anything else, Jake retreated to the coffee maker. The machine sputtered and released a blast of steam. Jake filled a to-go cup with the brew. "I'll be in the barn if anyone needs me." He strode through the office and out the door before Roxanne or Jules could reply.

After a pause, Roxanne said, "Okay, what's going on?" She glared at her niece.

"Nothing. I've been staring at this computer too long. I need to come up with some ideas for January and February to make it worthwhile to stay open year-round. Finding another dead body on my property hasn't helped." Jules leaned her elbows on the desk and put her head on her arms. "I'm tired."

"I wouldn't worry too much about the murder. You didn't do it, and the past has proven that it probably causes people's morbid sense of curiosity to kick in. We've not lost any bookings in the past, even after the other unfortunate events. And so far, none of our guests have even said anything about it."

"I know." Jules sighed. "But I'm trying for a wholesome family environment, and lately, it's been a magnet for trouble."

"Time for breakfast. You want anything?"

"No, I'm good. Thanks." Jules stared at her screensaver.

"It's not the numbers." Her aunt cut her eyes at Jules. "Whatever is bothering you, work it out with Jake. Don't let it blow up into something bigger than it truly is." Roxanne put her purse in her desk drawer and sashayed out.

Jules swallowed her retort and sent a text to Pixel instead. **Need a favor. Can you see what you can dig up on Tabbi Morris, Tony Yates, Sheena Dobbins, and Dana Taylor?**

Pixel responded quickly with, **No problem. Saw the news.** Her text ended with a string of unhappy faces and a skull and crossbones.

Not wanting to sit and stew about Jake and the murder, Jules toyed with the idea of paying a visit to the truck guy. *It couldn't hurt to accidentally run into him.* She thumbed through her folder and googled William McAllister. She found a match at the zoo in Waynesboro and jotted down the contact information on a sticky note. *A road trip may be just what I need.*

When Roxanne returned with a yogurt parfait and an omelet, Jules said, "I'll be back later. I've got a couple of errands to run."

"See ya." Her aunt picked out a raspberry from her parfait and popped it in her mouth.

Jules jumped in her Jeep and headed west. As she crested Afton Mountain, the morning sun shown on the valley and gave it a golden hue. She resisted the urge to pull off at the viewing area for some quiet time. Although the mountains and undulating peaks and valleys were breathtaking, her curiosity about the guy in Waynesboro outweighed her desire to look at the spectacular view. She passed the scenic roadside pull-off that always made her look up at the abandoned motel and restaurant on the hillside. It was the opposite of the breathtaking mountaintop view. The building had been left to rot for decades after the interstate came through, cutting off its access as a roadside motel. Her mind wandered to the creepy abandoned place, the perfect setting for a horror film. Jules shook off the thoughts of the spooky motel and followed her GPS's directions through some curvy backroads.

About fifteen miles from Waynesboro, she spotted a small wooden sign that said "Zoo" in red with an arrow. She followed the arrows on a series of these signs until she noticed a long, graveled driveway. Turning in, she drove down the narrow strip, surrounded on both sides by woods, to a white farmhouse and barn. She pushed more thoughts of horror movie settings out of her head and followed the arrows to a field, surrounded by a rope border. Jules parked between a minivan and a daycare bus.

Jules walked over to a small cabin with a sliding window and perused the many colorful, hand-lettered signs that offered a menu of pricing options, including anything from a basic tour to zip-lining over the animals.

"Hi, can I help you?" asked a bleached blond with aqua highlights. The woman smacked her gum as she talked.

"This is my first time here. I guess I want to start with a general admission ticket."

"Oh, you'll want to get a bag of zoo treats for feeding. If not, you'll miss out."

"Okay." Jules pulled out her wallet.

"That'll be eighteen dollars."

While waiting for her change, Jules asked, "So what are the must-sees here?"

"The monkeys and tigers are my favorites. But the nocturnal exhibit and the snakes are pretty freaky."

"Any baby animals?"

"Uh, not sure if the new chimpanzees are out on exhibit or not. Same with the tigers. They might be. Don't know." The clerk continued to smack her gum.

Retrieving her change and the bag of zoo treats, Jules followed the sidewalk past monkey and bird enclosures. She watched a group of daycare kids walk like little ducks in a line between their teachers. Stopping to get her bearings from a signpost, she followed the orange arrow to the big cats.

Bird and ape noises broke the morning stillness. Every once in a while, a roar reverberated over the other sounds. Jules watched the lions laze in the winter sun. A tiger paced the fence line while the other lay on a rock. No sign of any cubs.

Jules peeked at the bear, who was playing with a large ball. As she walked toward the giraffes, a young guy in a fluorescent yellow Zoo T-shirt zoomed by on an ATV. She caught up to him at the giraffe exhibit that featured a viewing area at eye level with the majestic creatures.

The twenty-something refilled bubblegum machines with zoo treats. Jules shook her bag, and three giraffes came running.

"Be careful, or they'll help themselves to the whole bag. They can slime you from several feet away with those purple tongues."

Jules laughed. "Thanks for the warning. They're beautiful. Hey, guys, wait your turn. I have enough for everyone." She put the brown pellets in her hand, and the giraffes retrieved them with their massive tongues. "You're right. I'm a little slobbery now. What a great job. I'd love to hang out with the animals all day. How long have you worked here?"

"All of my life. I kinda have to. It's in my parents' backyard. By the way, I'm Zac Robinson." He pushed his bangs out of his eyes and grinned.

"It's nice to meet you. I'm Jules. I thought the McAllisters owned the zoo."

His brows made a "V," and he shook his head. "That's my uncle. He works here, but my mom and dad own the property. He lives next door." Zac pointed toward the exit.

"How cool is it to live at a zoo." Jules tried to divide the treats among the three hungry giraffes, who were all concerned about having a turn.

"It's more work than you think, but it's fun. I mean who else got to take exotic animals to school for show and tell?"

"Any cute babies to play with?" Jules asked.

"We have some chimps, a bat, and two tiger cubs. We're hoping we'll have some baby leopards in the spring."

"Your tiger had cubs?" Jules balled up the paper bag when the giraffe emptied the last of the crumbs.

He hesitated. "They won't be on exhibit until we start the spring season. They're still acclimating to the environment."

Jules put on her best pouty face. "Then I guess I'll have to come back. I bet they're adorable."

He stepped closer and pulled out his phone. After tapping on the screen, he held it up for her to see. "They're cute and cuddly, but they're still tigers."

"Can't wait to see them." Jules let out an overly dramatic sigh and pulled out hand sanitizer from her purse to get rid of the giraffe slobber.

"I'm almost done here. You wanna peek at them?"

Jules turned on her brightest smile. "That would be awesome. I am such a cat lover."

"Hop in." He bowed and waved his hand toward the passenger seat.

Jules slid in, and Zac started the vehicle. After several engine revs, he put it in gear and sped off to a building behind the barn.

When he skidded to a sudden stop, Jules braced herself by grabbing the dashboard. "Whoa," she said, probably too loudly.

Zac hopped out and grinned. He unlocked the wooden door and held it for her. Inside what looked like a kitchen and storage area, a tall metal cage sat in the corner. Two tiger cubs roughhoused on a pile of baby blankets.

"Oh, they are so cute," Jules cooed, stepping closer for a better look.

"What are their names?"

"We'll do a contest for their spring debut. That always creates a buzz on social media."

"Where's the mom?" Jules stepped closer to the cage.

"She's with the male in the enclosure. We need to keep them separated so he doesn't hurt the cubs."

Jules frowned. "Oh. Can we do a picture?"

The lanky guy hesitated. "Yeah, sure."

Handing him her phone, they took several shots with the cubs in the background. "I didn't mean to keep you from your job. Thanks so much for the behind-the-scenes tour and the free peek at the babies," Jules said.

"No problem." He tapped his contact in her phone before handing it back to her. "In case you want to see them again."

Jules smiled as he held the door for her. Shading her eyes with her hand, she stepped outside in the sudden glare.

She moved along the path, passing zebras, tortoise, and deer. Pausing to take some pictures, Jules glanced around to see if Zac was still watching. No sign of him, so she headed to the parking lot.

For good measure, she drove by the property next door. Maybe she could get a look at Mac McAllister. Turning into an overgrown driveway that ended at a locked animal gate, Jules stared at the giant no trespassing sign and the electrified fencing that made her wish she had a drone or at least binoculars. Squinting, she caught a glimpse of a truck on the property next to a rusty double-wide. Why were they getting cats from Cal and then passing them off as their own?

Unable to see more, she gave up. The drive back to Fern Valley gave her time to think about the players and who could have wanted to kill Tabbi. Too many thoughts about Tabbi and Cal vied for her attention as she drove.

Back in the office and after several good handwashings, Jules settled in her desk and sent emails to Pixel and Sam Azevedo, the conservation officer. At least she knew what had happened to the tiger cubs and the big cat.

The zoo seemed like a nice place, not a roadside attraction with animals penned in tiny cages. Jules didn't see any evidence of it looking run down. Was sneaking around to buy the tigers a sign of financial issues? Why wouldn't they trade or buy them outright? A memory of Tabbi in the animal cage jarred Jules back to the present. The midnight animal swap and Tabbi's death were too coincidental not to be related. Did the cage where she was found have some sort of significance, or was it chosen to point the finger at Cal's team?

Chapter Fourteen

Tuesday

Jules's phone vibrated almost off her desk. She looked up from her spreadsheets and clicked the button. Pixel's face appeared on the screen for a video chat.

"Hey, girl. You gotta minute? I found some stuff for you that you might find interesting."

"Sure. It's good to see you. What's up?" Jules asked.

"All's well. I'm going to put all of this together with the contact information and put it in Dropbox for you, but I wanted to give you the highlights," Pixel said with a lilt in her voice.

"You are the best. What did you find?"

"I looked up Tony Yates. He was a former bodybuilder, and he works as a professional trainer at a gym in Berryville. He did a stint on the power-lifting circuit about five years ago. It looks like he's been dating Tabbi on and off for a couple of years, and he helps her with her T-shirt business." She paused and flipped through her notes. "He and Sheena are about the same age. He got in some trouble with steroids in his early twenties and in a couple of bar fights."

"Hmmmm," Jules said.

Pixel took a swig from a water bottle. "There wasn't much on Dana Taylor. She's a receptionist at a doctor's office and does essential oil parties. She and Tabbi are neighbors in a condo complex. Let's see, what else did I find?

Sheena Dobbins is a waitress at a place called Amigos, and she works a lot of odd jobs, including being a Lyft driver. I'm not sure where she met Tabbi."

"You always find interesting information." Jules brushed a stray curl off of her forehead.

"Oh, I saved the best for last. Let's see. Ms. Morris has been married three times. The first was as a teenager when she dropped out of high school. That lasted a couple of years. She left him for her boss at an auto parts store, and she dumped husband number two when she met Cal Collins online. She lived with him for a couple of years before they married. Cal already had two kids when Tabbi appeared on the scene. Tabbi and Cal were married for eight years until he left her for a newer model. I had more on her. Just a sec." Pixel paused and then clicked staccato style on her keyboard.

"Tabbi seems to have had an interesting life," Jules mused.

"It's been colorful. Lots of jobs. Let's see. She tried out as a cafeteria worker, waitress, shop clerk, and manager of a Dollar General. In her business life, she seems to flit between get-rich-quick schemes. She's done candle, makeup, cookware, and vitamin sales. A couple of these look like pyramid schemes." Pixel paused.

"Anything else?"

More tapping and Pixel continued, "Somewhere along the line, when she was married to Cal, he had her running the concessions for his shows. Now, she does the county fair and show circuits with her wares. It must be lucrative. She's got four trailers and staff now. I don't see any other day job, but she does advertise on her website that people can order custom T-shirts through her company. According to her Facebook page, she met the love of her life, Tony, a few years ago, and he's been such a support for her after her terrible divorce. She posts a lot of angry stuff about how Cal took away her love, life, and livelihood. Her rants seem to be on Friday and Saturday nights. Maybe a little too much wine with her social media?"

Jules laughed. "Interesting. But it's not all hate. I have a video clip of her and Cal at my resort last week caught in a rather lengthy liplock."

Pixel whistled. "Sounds like some of those Hollywood folks you had at your place. Maybe they're not over each other yet."

Jules smiled. "And thanks for checking on that license plate earlier. I drove out to Mac McAllister's place yesterday. He lives next door to a family zoo, and guess what I got to see? Baby tigers! I was right about the four cubs. It seems Cal's got a side hustle selling wild animals."

Pixel winked at her. "That's about all I had. I wanted to check in with you before I sent you the notes. Let me know if you need anything else. Oh, I head to Quantico tomorrow for another round of interviews. Wish me luck."

"You'll do awesome. The next lunch or dinner is on me to celebrate."

"You paid for the last one. It's my turn. See ya." Pixel waved and disconnected the video chat.

Jules created a spreadsheet and listed all the players and what she knew about them. A lot of people had a reason to want Tabbi dead. She downloaded Pixel's files, skimmed through them, and copied key information to her spreadsheet.

Jules had an idea to fish for additional information. She crafted an email about a pair of stilettos left at the campground to send to Sheena, Dana, and Misti separately. She hoped she could use it to start a conversation. She also sent Tony a condolence email and asked about funeral services for Tabbi. Maybe she'd learn something new. Fingers crossed.

Minutes later, Dana Taylor responded with, "Not mine. Don't wear heels that often, but mine are always vintage." Not hopeful that she'd get any additional information, Jules sent a response back, offering her thoughts, prayers, and condolences for the loss of her friend.

Roxanne trudged in with a box. "Hey there. How're things shakin'?"

"Can I help you with that?"

"I got it. We're low on supplies and some of the restaurant fliers. I popped over to storage to pick these up. What are you up to?"

"I sent some condolence emails to Tabbi's team and asked about the funeral arrangements."

"That's sweet of you, but why do I think there's an ulterior motive? Oh wait, sounds like you're on the case. Anything you want to talk about?"

"Nope. Just poking around to see what I can find about Tabbi." Jules looked up at her aunt and furrowed her brow. "What?"

"No reason. But before you go whole-hog on the sleuthing, I think you should talk to Jake. I still don't like whatever is going on between you two."

Jules pursed her lips. "It's nothing. We're both busy, that's all."

Roxanne's eyebrows shot up about an inch. "If you say so, but as a casual observer, both of you look like the Grinch. This is the holiday season. Don't make me kick you in the butt." She lifted her foot to show off her black leather boot with the pointy toe and three-inch heel.

Roxanne took the box to the front, and Jules sulked in her chair. She knew she should talk to Jake about the Red incident, but she was hurt. She wanted him to explain or apologize, and when he didn't, her temper flared. And now she didn't know what to say to him. *This can't be how it ends.*

Pushing thoughts of Jake aside, she skimmed through emails. Elizabeth Rhoney wanted to partner with her for a writers' weekend in January. She was thinking of a romance theme ahead of Valentine's Day that would bring fans and readers to town for a long weekend. Excited about filling the resort with voracious readers, Jules sent an affirmative and a promise to meet for lunch to start the planning.

Tony also replied to her email. "Hey, thanks. Nothing formal for the services. We're going to meet at the lake to spread her ashes and have a wake at a nearby bar, Amigos, on Thursday at seven. Come by if you want."

Jules thanked him for the invitation and added it to her calendar. Berryville was a two-hour drive. It would be a late night with the round trip. *It would be nice if Jake wanted to go with her, but she wasn't in the mood to ask him. He'd been scarce lately, the invisible man. I'd rather go by myself.*

The resort phone rang, interrupting her internal discussion with herself. "Welcome to the Fern Valley Luxury Camping Resort. How may I help you?"

"Uh, hi. This is Sheena Dobbins. I stayed in one of your trailers. May I speak to Jules."

"Hi, Sheena. This is Jules. How can I help you?"

"I got your email. Those aren't my shoes. You may want to try Dana, or I guess they could be Tabbi's. Dana would know either way. They were close buds. Hey, while I've got you, when can I make reservations for the summer at your place?"

"We'll take them anytime by phone or the website. We're booking now for next spring and summer."

"Ooooooh awesome. Ton—Uh, my boyfriend and I have an anniversary in June, so I'm thinking a long, romantic weekend." Sheena cooed.

"We specialize in themed packages. Check out our website for romantic getaways and anniversary celebrations. We have everything from couples' spa packages to chocolate baskets. We can customize it any way you'd like it."

"Perfect. I'll check out your website. We want to come back for a vacay."

"It will be great to see you again. There's lots to do here. Hiking, fishing, biking, antiquing. The list goes on," Jules said.

"Can't wait. And I know we can find something to keep us occupied." Sheena bit down on something crunchy.

"Uh, when the vendors were here, some of them asked to be put on a mailing list for future events. We're planning a spring fling. Do you know if someone is taking over Tabbi's business?"

After a long pause and some chewing, Sheena answered. "Probably Tony. He owns a couple of the trailers, and he paid for some of the inventory."

"Thanks. I'll check with him. He invited me to the wake, so I'll see you there if you're going."

"Yep, I'll be there. See you then." Sheena clicked off, and Jules stared at her phone.

She opened her spreadsheet with all the players and grabbed a notebook to do a drawing of the connections. She started jotting all the names. Then, she drew arrows between the relationships. Misti, Cal, and Tony had the most arrows.

Before she could ponder further, her phone buzzed.

"Hi, Lester. What's up?"

"Good morning, Boss. I was checking to see how tall the grass had gotten near the fence and the amphitheater, and I spotted something. You may want to see this."

"It's not another dead body, is it?"

"Nah. Nothin' like that."

"Good." Jules sighed. "Where are you?"

"By the fence line between the tiny houses and the trailers. You'll see the mower."

"Be right over." Jules pocketed her phone. "Roxanne, I'm going to go see Lester. Be back in a few."

"Okay," drifted up from the front. "Bijou can hang out with me."

The dog lifted her head when she heard her name, but she didn't move from her napping position.

Jules pulled on her coat as she stepped out on the carport behind the office. She double-timed her walk in the December temperatures.

Lester stood near where Cal had parked the big cat haulers and stared at something in the distance. "Hey, there," he said as she approached. "Something red caught my eye over there, and I stopped to check it out. See, it's a lady's fancy purse."

Jules didn't see anything until she took a couple of steps where Lester pointed. The groundskeeper must have had a better vantage point from atop the mower. Then she zeroed in on something red in a clump of grass. Jules slid on her winter gloves before she lifted the flap of the red evening bag. The sparkling rhinestone clasp clicked open. A gold compact, a voodoo doll with curly brown hair, and a small handgun fell out. Jules snapped several pictures. Stuck inside at the bottom was a curled picture of Tabbi and Cal.

"That's interesting," Lester said. "Who's been to a shindig lately?"

"I'm sure Sheriff Hobbs will be interested." She texted him the photo. "Maybe he can send someone over to look at it."

Jules's phone dinged with a response. **Leave it be. I'll have someone there in a little bit.** Jules held up her phone. "He's sending someone out to get it."

Lester returned to his zero-turn lawnmower and climbed on the yellow seat. "I'll hang out here with you until they get here. Not sure if they'll need me to make a statement or not."

Jules smiled and leaned against the split rail fence. What was an evening bag doing out near the woods with a picture of Cal and Tabbi and a gun?

And what's with the voodoo dolls?

About the time Jules needed to stretch her legs, a police cruiser kicked up dirt along the maintenance road. The car came to an abrupt stop, and a small dust cloud took a minute to settle.

Sheriff Hobbs stepped out and greeted the pair. "So, what did y'all find this time?"

"I saw something red in the grass and weeds. It turned out to be a party purse." Lester pointed to the spilled purse near some tree roots. "I called Jules, and she opened it to see who it belonged to."

"And?" the sheriff asked.

"I had my gloves on. No wallet in the purse. But there is a picture inside. There was another dark-haired voodoo doll."

"Okay," he said, pulling his own latex gloves out of his pocket. He took several pictures. "Was it like this?"

"No, the contents spilled out when Jules opened it," Lester added.

"A gun and some makeup." The sheriff took more pictures of the items, put the purse and its contents in a paper bag and sealed it. "The ground's been frozen. I don't see any prints. Just weeds, and some of them look like they've been stomped on. I'm guessing somebody tossed it back here." He took a video of the area.

Lester beamed from ear to ear. Jules knew listening to his police scanner was his favorite pastime, and now he was at ground zero of an investigation. She wasn't the only one of the resort's staff who was a true crime fan.

The sheriff looked around and walked in concentric circles around where the purse had lain. Lester watched in rapt fascination to see what else he would find. The sheriff stopped twice to take pictures and bag whatever he picked up.

Satisfied that he had seen everything there was to see, Sheriff Hobbs adjusted his gun belt and hiked back to where Lester and Jules stood.

"What else did you find?" she asked.

"A quarter and a bright pink button. We'll see. Might be a collection of junk. Call me if you find anything else."

"Will do," she said.

"I'm on it. But I don't like the voodoo dolls," Lester muttered. He started his mower's big engine and roared off toward the barn.

Jules waved to the men and jogged back to the office. Why would there be an evening bag near the woods where Cal's trailers were? Was this the murder weapon? And what is with the dolls? Today's finds spawned more questions than answers.

Chapter Fifteen

Wednesday

J ules opened the back door, and Bijou tore up the stairs and through the backroom toward the voices in the store. Jules dropped her coat and phone on her desk and stuck her head through the opening. "Good morning."

Jake and Roxanne stopped their conversation. "Morning," he said, picking up the wiggly dog who rewarded him with face licks.

"Hey, I heard you and Lester found a gun. You didn't mention it when you got back yesterday. In fact, you weren't all that talkative. I had to find out from Matt." Her aunt closed one eye and glared.

"Lester spotted something red near the woods. It was a purse with a gun in it."

"Not just any gun." Her aunt waved one hand around. "Matt thinks it might be the murder weapon. This could be the break his team has been looking for. I'm sure Lester's over the moon with his find."

When no one else said anything, Jules asked, "Anyone want coffee?"

"No. I'm good. I'll be in the barn if you need me." Jake set Bijou down and strode out the front door.

"I can't believe you didn't say anything about what y'all found," her aunt said, scowling at her. "And you and Jake haven't worked out whatever it is that's in your craw. What are you waiting for? Don't let this fester."

"It's nothing." Jules selected a strong brew and popped the pod into the machine. Hoping the caffeine would help the tension headache behind her eyes, she booted up her laptop and tidied her desk while she waited.

"You'll be sorry," her aunt called out in a sing-song voice from the front room.

Jules bit her tongue. The ding from her phone distracted her from her funk. **You might find this interesting.** Pixel had texted a link to some old newspaper articles. Jules sank down into her chair and skimmed the files.

Jules let out a gasp. Eight years ago, Misti Miles was a suspect in the sudden death of a fellow beauty pageant contestant, Lizzie Edmunds. Both were contestants in the Star City Beauty Pageant. From a follow-up article, it was never clear if Edmunds had been poisoned or whether it was an accidental death. Misti was never charged, but the *Roanoke Times* listed her as a strong suspect that the police questioned on multiple occasions. There was a link to another story where a podcaster interviewed Edmunds's sister, and she blamed Misti for Lizzie's death.

Jules tapped her pen on her desk. Did Misti murder her pageant rival, and could Misti hate her husband's ex-wife enough to want her out of the picture permanently? She forwarded the link to Sheriff Hobbs in case he hadn't seen the articles.

Her phone dinged again. **Come to the barn now. Jake's hurt.** Puzzled, she looked around the office. She never heard Roxanne leave.

Rushing out the back door without her coat, she ran to the barn with her cell phone in her hand. Panic welled up in her throat. Flinging open the heavy wooden door, she got a whiff of sawdust. A tool whined in the background. Puzzled, she trudged through the dimly lit front section toward the lighted area in the back. The sanding sound got louder.

A prone Jake hung over a large beam. His head wasn't visible from where she stood. Jules stifled the feeling of dread and hurried closer. His leg twitched, and his body arced forward. *Was he convulsing?* She squeaked and moved beside him. A cloud of sawdust danced in the air. Where was Roxanne?

As she reached out to touch his back, he stood up and turned off the sander. He pulled off this respirator and stared at Jules.

She let out a heavy sigh and tried to will her heart rate back to normal.

"What's up? You okay?" Jake unplugged the sander. A puzzled look crossed his face.

"I could ask you the same question." Jules felt the heat rising in her cheeks. "Roxanne texted me that you were hurt."

Jake snickered. "She asked me what I was doing, and I said swearing because I hit my thumb with the hammer. It sounds like Roxanne is playing both of us." His grin showed the dimples on either side of his cheeks.

"I didn't mean to interrupt your project." Jules took several steps backward.

Jake stopped and approached her. "I love that you ran all the way over here without your coat."

"Under dubious circumstances and based on some faulty information. Just wait until I see Roxanne." She could feel her face getting hotter.

"There was a little bit of truth to it." Jake held up his swollen thumb. "It shows you care." He dusted off his shirt and pulled her closer to him.

The pair stood there for a while in an embrace. Jules got lost in the warmth, and the mixture of his citrusy aftershave and the wood smells in his flannel shirt. She was having trouble staying angry at him. Part of her wanted to hug him, and the other part wanted to tear off into a rant about how he embarrassed her in front of everyone.

"Still mad at me?" he whispered in her ear.

"Yes. Very."

"It wasn't my fault. The gals got excited over our win. Red and I have been friends a long time. She was good to me when I got out of the army. She let me sleep on her couch when I wasn't sure what I wanted to do in civilian life. I was planning to hike across the country, and she's the one who talked me into getting a job and staying put. She didn't mean anything by the kiss. In fact, she scolded me for not going after you when you tore out of the auditorium."

"Why didn't you?" Jules asked, pulling away and staring into his green eyes.

"I dunno. I was happy about our win and a little ticked that you didn't hang around to celebrate. You missed pizza at Pop's, And you didn't say

104

anything for days," he said, staring at her.

Trying not to look sheepish, she said, "I get a lot of exercise jumping to conclusions after life with the Idiot. Seeing you two like that brought back too many memories from a bad marriage. Old wounds that I don't ever want to deal with again."

"I'm not him. I'm sorry, Jules. Let me make it up to you. Dinner tonight?" he asked.

"We'll celebrate your win," she said.

"And us." Jake pulled her in close for an extended hug.

Jules got lost in the warmth of his embrace. *Maybe this time was different.*

Not wanting to disturb the moment, she broke the silence anyway when she spoke. "This house is starting to take shape."

"The framing should be done by tomorrow for this part. There's a second module that will be connected on-site."

"Looking good. I gotta get back to the office. Be careful, and don't hurt yourself again."

"Should I warn Roxanne?"

"No, she likes surprises," Jules muttered.

Jake grinned. "But will you come running again if I do get hurt?" he yelled behind her as she slid out the front. "Never mind, I'll be over around six."

Where are you? Jules texted her aunt.

Checking on Mel and Crystal. How's Jake?

Headed to the emergency room.

Very funny, her aunt responded.

I could say the same to you.

Don't be crabby. I'm always happy to help. Everybody needs a cupid. Roxanne ended the conversation with a string of heart emojis.

Jules's phone rang and distracted her from Roxanne. "Hi, Sam. How are things in the woods?" Jules pushed her annoyance with Roxanne aside and focused on her conversation with the conservation officer as she walked to her desk.

"Just fine. I'm journeying across the district again." Swooshing sounds like he had the window down, which made it hard to hear.

"You're on the road every time I talk to you," she said.

"That's what I do most days. But I get to be outside and see all kinds of stuff, even in winter. I wanted to loop back with you. I've opened a case on the two tiger cubs. No details yet, but the investigation is ongoing. We're checking into it. You provided enough information to raise a few eyebrows on my team."

"I appreciate the update."

"And I appreciate the tip. Anything else going on?" he asked.

"Nope. No news," she replied.

"Y'all take care and tell Jake I said hey," Sam said.

Jules disconnected, and her phone buzzed again before she could set it down. "Hi, Elaine. What's up?"

"Planning meeting. We need to go over the logistics. Where are you? Please tell me you're on your way."

"I am. Sorry. I got tied up with a phone call. Be there in a second. Y'all start without me." Jules disconnected and chided herself for forgetting the appointment. Jeans, a sweater, and boots would have to do. She patted Bijou, grabbed her coat, and raced out the door.

Making it to the library in record time, she waved at Gail Matthews, who tapped her watch and pointed to the room in the corner.

Jules saluted and whizzed through the stacks, dodging bookcases and a couple of small children. She slid into the nearest chair and tried not to cause a disruption. Darlene nodded at her arrival and continued her update on the weekend's activities. Jules took a moment to catch her breath, then sent Roxanne a text to let her know where she was.

"I hope y'all ate your Wheaties," Darlene said. "This is the final weekend of our holiday festival. We need to end with a bang. Then we can all rest up before our own festivities. Friday night, there is the Taste of Christmas Spectacular. It's an all-you-can-eat samples event for guests and a contest for those showcasing their recipes. For Saturday, there is the Breakfast with Santa Craft Time and the Jingle Bell Run/Walk. All the proceeds from the race will go to the Christmas Mother program. We have supporters, entertainment, and vendors along the route. And to wrap it all up, we've got the holiday music concert at the high school on Saturday night. Whew! Y'all really outdid yourselves with keeping our guests entertained."

"Thank you, Darlene," Elaine said. "Thanks to everyone. We will have a celebratory luncheon in January for all the volunteers who've worked so hard. I think it's been a successful inaugural event. Well, almost everything." She paused and added, "Okay, Marco, Mitch, what about your team?"

"There's not much to tell. Everything's good," Mitch Hill said. "We all have our schedules. I checked in with Sheriff Hobbs, and we have plenty of support from his office. Everybody knows the drill. We are ready."

"Very good," Elaine added. "Any other updates?" She paused for about ten seconds as she scanned the faces around the table. "Good. Then let's bring this festival home with a really big finish."

As the committee members packed their belongings, the chatter died down. Jules gathered her purse and said her goodbyes as she edged toward the door. She missed a good chunk of the updates at the beginning of the meeting.

"Jooooooles, Joooooooooles rang through the room."

She turned to find Elaine barreling her way around the other members. "Do you have a minute before you leave? I'll walk you out."

"Sure. What can I do for you? Sorry that I was late and missed the first part."

"Oh, no worries. You'll get the minutes." *That was an about-face from her excited phone call earlier.*

Elaine let out a heavy sigh and looked around to see who was nearby. "I talked to Tom Berryman yesterday. He said that the lawsuit is still active unless that woman's heirs decide not to pursue it. He even said to be prepared to give testimony if I'm called. Can you believe it? I'll need you to be my witness. I was only trying to break up the fight between those two women. I had nothing to do with their problems or that horrible woman's demise. This is too much."

Jules held the door for the shorter woman, who continued talking as they walked to the parking lot. "And to top it all off. Sheriff Hobbs wants to see me this afternoon to go over some questions he has about my previous statement." She stood in the cold, wringing her hands. "What could he possibly want? I told him everything I knew when it happened. Why does he keep contacting me? Do you think he's trying to see if I'll change my story? Oh, my stars. Maybe I need to call my lawyer again."

Jules shrugged. "Not sure, but the sheriff has some questions or things he wants to run by you. Let me know if you need me to give a statement." Jules patted her on the shoulder. "Don't worry. It'll be okay. I'll see you on Friday."

"Will do. Here's to the last weekend of the festival. Maybe we'll be able to put this nonsense behind us." Elaine shook her head and trotted off toward her minivan.

Jules hurried to her Jeep and turned on the heat full blast. She thought of several reasons the sheriff would want to see Elaine again. Hopefully, none were because he truly suspected her of Tabbi's murder.

A little after six, a knock on her cabin door interrupted Jules's reading. She put her Louise Penny novel on the coffee table and picked up her coat and purse. Bijou yipped as Jules pulled open the door.

Lester stood on her small porch in his brown parka, his hands in his pockets.

"Hi, Lester. What's up?" Jules looked behind him to see if Jake was on his way.

"Going somewhere? Did I catch you at a bad time? I know it's near supper time, but I had something on my mind."

"Come in and sit down." Jules pointed to the living room.

Lester's lanky frame sunk into the guest chair, and Bijou danced around his feet until he patted her on the head. "That fancy purse is still bothering me."

"The gun?" Jules perched on the arm of the couch.

"No. That voodoo thing." He shuddered slightly and leaned forward, resting his elbows on his knees. "The killer's dabbling in something dark. I wanted to let you know I called the sheriff and let him know of my concerns." Lester looked down at his work-worn hands. "My grandma grew up in Louisiana, and this stuff is nothing to mess with. She used to tell stories of voodoo curses that would curl your toenails. I shy away from that mess. You poke the bear. You never know what could happen."

"Thanks, Lester. I'm sure the sheriff appreciates all the information."

He twisted the hem of his coat. "I thought those Hollywood people who were here were too freewheeling. But this is serious. I want you to be careful and not get mixed up in this." A door slammed in the distance, and Lester rose and looked toward the front door. "I'll let you get back to what you were doing. I felt like I needed to tell you my concerns. I have books full of tragic things that happened because of voodoo curses."

"I appreciate it." Jules followed him to the front door.

"Oh, hi, Jake." Lester stepped out on the stoop.

"Hi. We're going to get some dinner in town. Wanna join us?" Jake stomped his boots on the mat.

"I've already eaten. I heat up dinner and watch the local news every night. Y'all have something good. See you tomorrow." The older man gingerly descended the steps and headed for his cabin.

Jules slid on her coat and pulled the door behind her.

"Lester okay?" Jake asked as she climbed into his car.

"I think so. He wanted to share some concerns about the murder." Jake looked at Jules.

"The purse he found with the gun and a picture of Tabbi and Cal. It also had a voodoo doll in it with a bunch of pins."

"Hmmm," Jake said, backing out of her driveway. "When he gets fixated on something, he's like a bulldog. And a tad superstitious."

"He was so worked up about it. I didn't have the heart to tell him that I found a second voodoo doll on the property earlier," Jules said in almost a whisper.

"It's probably better not to." Jake cocked an eyebrow. "Whatcha feel like for dinner? I was thinking the Good Thyme Bistro. You okay with that?"

Jules nodded and sunk back into the Mustang's leather seat. Could there be something more sinister to all this? Jules was more concerned about the gun and photograph than the two dolls. *Did I miss something?*

In what felt like an instant to Jules, Jake cruised through town and found street parking near the restaurant. Foot traffic was steady on the sidewalks. Jules smiled. She was glad to see shoppers out and about. She and Jake hustled around the corner as a cool breeze whipped around the buildings.

After the hostess seated them in a cozy corner near the front by the big oak bar, Jules slid out of her coat and reached for a menu.

"You're awfully quiet." Jake set his menu down and leaned forward.

"Sorry. Lester surprised me. I haven't seen him get that animated about anything except his police scanner."

"And the time those kids took his mower for a joyride." Jake shrugged as the waitress approached.

"Welcome on this chilly evening. What can I get for you?" The waitress with the jet-black pixie cut asked. "Would you like to start out with some drinks and appetizers? We have some really good specials up on our chalkboard." She pointed to the board with the fancy script.

"Hmm. Not quite sure what I want. I may need a few minutes," Jules mused.

"No problem," the waitress said with a bubbly lilt. "Can I get you some drinks?"

"I'll have an iced tea," Jules said.

"Same. And I like lots of lemon," Jake added.

"You know what? I'll take the chicken Caesar salad," Jules said.

Jake set his menu on the table. "I'll have the loaded steak burger with baked beans and onion straws."

"Got it. Be back in a flash," the waitress said.

Jake took both of Jules's hands in his. "Not sure how important that doll is."

"It didn't faze me really. It was another thing in the purse. But it really bothered Lester."

"Might be worth looking into, especially since there were two." Jake paused. "Hey, I had an idea. Since both of our birthdays are coming up after the new year, why don't we find a warm spot and take a vacation? When was the last time you took a holiday?"

Jules paused. "Before I got divorced."

110

"I think my last one was an extended pass when I was on leave in the army. We're overdue. Find a warm place in January or February."

Jules smiled. "Sounds heavenly."

The pair sat quietly, holding hands across the table. Jules enjoyed the warm sensation that coursed through her. It was nice to be still and people-watch the families at the tables around them.

The waitress zipped over with a large tray that she balanced on one shoulder. "Here you go." She passed out the drinks, Jake's steakburger, and Jules's salad. "If you need anything else, let me know."

Jules bit into a crouton. "There are some nice places in Florida. You want to drive or fly?"

"Let's take the scenic route. I hear Key West is nice." Jake wiped his chin with the cloth napkin. His juicy burger, topped with red onions, lettuce, and three kinds of cheese, oozed juice, and mustard when he squeezed it.

"A road trip in the Wrangler sounds like fun. We can stop in Charleston, Savannah, St. Augustine. Or we can do the historic Florida route on A1A." Her voice trailed off.

"Daytona Beach might be fun, too. Whatever you want. We could even stop at that tiny house site in South Carolina since we didn't get a chance to visit in the fall. I'd kinda like to see some of their designs."

Jules smiled. "There's so much I want to see. Key West sounds great. I've always wanted to see the Hemingway house and the six-toed cats."

Jake popped the rest of an onion straw in his mouth. "Six toes?"

"The cats that lived on his property had an extra toe. The genetic trait has been passed down to the descendants."

"Sounds like a new theme for another tiny house," Jake said.

"You better get busy. We can do that one after the Stoker one."

A flutter of excitement jolted Jules. The road trip sounded fun and romantic. Now, she had two projects for the night. Research voodoo dolls and plan a winter vacation with destinations warmer than the Blue Ridge Mountains in January.

Chapter Sixteen

Thursday

J ules revved the Jeep's engine as Jake trotted across the grass. He hopped in and clicked his seat belt in place.

"You look nice." Jules put the Jeep in gear and headed for I-64 and eventually I-81.

"I clean up well. You do, too. Date night at a wake. You really know how to show a guy a good time." Jake's smile lit up his entire face.

"Dinner was nice last night. I have a whole bunch of places to send you to look at for our trip."

"Looking forward to it. I haven't been on a road trip in a while, if you don't count this one."

"Speaking of that, thanks for coming with me tonight. It's a long haul, and it's nice to have company. I want us to mingle and see what we can find out about Tabbi and her team. Also, we should ask about the red purse and the gun. The sheriff has been pretty tight-lipped about them, and I'm curious about the possibility of Tabbi being killed with her own gun."

"So, I'm playing sidekick tonight?"

"Just turn on that southern charm and see what information you can worm out of folks. You're good at getting people to talk." Jules winked and turned up the radio.

After a few miles on I-81, Jules asked, "Wanna stop for dinner before the wake? Not sure if there will be any food at Amigos."

"I missed lunch, so anything sounds good." Jake scanned through the radio channels. He picked a classic rock station and settled in his seat.

"I know the perfect place." Jules exited and took Route 250 to Mrs. Rowe's Restaurant. "The best pies on this side of the mountain. Or anywhere."

The hostess showed them to a table in the corner of the diner, where they perused lots of comfort food options on the menu. Jules settled on turkey and gravy over mashed potatoes with green beans, and Jake ordered the meatloaf special.

"Y'all save room for some pie," the waitress said. "I'll be back with your iced teas in a jiff."

Jules studied the room packed with early evening diners. Her eyes lit on the glass case, filled with at least twenty kinds of pie, some topped with mounds of meringue. Her mouth watered. Tonight, she'd get dessert.

The food tasted like Sunday dinner at grandma's house or what home-cooked used to taste like. Before she could bask further in the delights of the meal, the waitress returned. "Can I get y'all some dessert?"

"I'll have a slice of your coconut pie," Jake said.

"Lemon meringue for me."

When the waitress returned to the counter, Jake leaned forward. "Anything special you want me to ask tonight? What should I be on the lookout for?"

"You almost need a scorecard to keep up with all of the players involved. Misti didn't like Tabbi. Though divorced from Cal, I saw Tabbi having a rendezvous with him. Tony, the boyfriend, seemed attentive to Tabbi, but I also saw a romantic encounter between him and Sheena. Tabbi was rude to everyone she encountered, including Roxanne and Elaine. Let's look at how people react and listen to what they talk about. Maybe we'll find something interesting."

The waitress returned with two oversized slices of pie. "Can I get y'all anything else?" She left the check on the corner of the table, and the pair dug in.

"This is really good," Jules said, taking another bite.

Jake's pie disappeared quickly. Jules took one more bite and pushed her plate to the middle of the table.

"You done?" When she nodded, he finished off what she had left on her plate.

Jules picked up the check and her purse. "I'll be right back."

By the time she returned, Jake had left the tip. She followed him through the front door to the Jeep.

Darkness blanketed the mountains as the pair drove north. She flipped on her headlights and mashed the accelerator to keep up with the truck traffic on I-81. Miles later, Jules exited in Winchester when she spotted the Berryville sign and followed the GPS to Amigos, the end unit of a small strip mall.

Jules pulled into a spot between two oversized pickups sporting all kinds of patriotic stickers. She climbed out and smoothed her black dress pants and gray sweater. Leaving her purse and coat in the car, she took Jake's arm, and the pair walked briskly to the front entrance.

Country music pulsated from the bar's open doors. Jules and Jake wandered in. Oddly, no one worked the front door. People packed the edges of the dance floor, and all the tables looked filled.

"Want something to drink?" he whispered in her ear.

"Ginger ale." Jules looked around to see if she recognized anyone. Dana, Sheena, and Tony stood out in a sea of faces.

When Jake returned and handed her a glass, she stretched and cupped her hand near his ear. "Thanks. Let's split up and see what we can find."

He nodded and moved through the crowd toward the dance floor. Jules dodged people and ended up near the pool tables. Spotting Dana at a table near the DJ, Jules pushed her way through the throngs of standing people.

When she was close enough for the woman to hear her, Jules said, "Dana. Hi, how are you?"

"Hey. Thanks for coming all this way for Tabbi's celebration." The tall woman wiped a tear that slipped out of her eye. "That was nice of you."

"Jake and I wanted to pay our respects. How are things going? It looks like a lot of folks are here."

Dana nodded. "She was a good boss and great friend. I've known her for years. People admired her for being a smart businesswoman." Her voice

114

cracked, and she swallowed hard to choke back the tears. "I miss my bestie. Things aren't going to be the same. I don't know what I'll do without her."

"She would have appreciated the great turnout tonight." *Or would Tabbi have complained about things that didn't meet her standards?* Jules shook off the sassy thought and patted Dana's arm.

"Thanks." Dana dabbed her eyes and turned toward two women who approached.

Grateful for the chance to escape, Jules waved and moved toward the bar. Sheena flipped through her order book.

"Hey," Jules said.

Sheena slammed the order book closed like she was protecting her answers on an algebra test. "Oh, hi," she said, looking around.

"How are you doing?" Jules moved closer.

"Fine. Racking up the tips. So, it's a good night." The waitress looked past Jules. Her glance darted around the room.

"A good send-off for Tabbi," Jules shouted to be heard over the latest Top 40 country hit blasting from the speakers.

Sheena's overly stylized eyebrows shot up past her bangs. "Most are here for the two-for-one drink specials. Some came for the entertainment and to see who else showed up."

Jules tried for a puzzled look. "Oh, I thought these were all her friends celebrating her life."

"Not hardly. Most people in town knew of her get-rich-quick schemes and short temper. Dana and Tabbi's cousin Fiona over there are probably her only true friends." Sheena pointed to a table where Dana sat close to another woman who was hunched over, clutching a glass with both hands.

"And you and Tony," Jules added, hoping to keep Sheena talking.

"Yes. Me and Tony." Sheena continued to glance around the room.

"Did you plan this for Tabbi? That's so nice of you," Jules cooed.

"Yes. It seemed fitting since she spent most of her time here. I suggested it to Fred, the owner, and he agreed. He even threw in the drink specials and some appetizers. I gotta go." Sheena blended with the mass of people before Jules could reply.

Not seeing Tony, Jules weaved through the crowd toward Fiona's table to offer her condolences. She approached the platinum blond, who tapped on her phone with her long blue nails. The woman's thick makeup had settled in her wrinkles and made her look older than she probably was.

"Hi, are you Fiona? I'm Jules Keene. I worked with Tabbi recently at an event I hosted."

"Oh." Fiona looked up from her phone. "I think I remember her saying she had a gig near Charlottesville for a couple of weekends. In hindsight, it wasn't that good of an idea for her. She complained about the sales, some rude woman, and Tony...." The woman's voice trailed off, and it looked like she was lost in thought.

"I am so sorry for your loss. Is there any other family here?" Jules inched closer to the woman, who must have been in her mid-fifties. "I'd like to pay my respects."

"No, she and I are pretty much the last of the line. Who knows? Maybe it's better that way. There's another cousin, but he's in jail somewhere in Florida. I haven't seen him in years. I guess you could sort of count Tony, but he's really the latest in a long string of worthless boyfriends."

"There's a lot of her friends here tonight. She would have liked that," Jules added.

"She would have wanted a much larger venue and the concession contract." Fiona looked down her nose and made a pickle face.

"Tabbi supplied souvenirs at our event. Do you know who I would contact if we wanted to have them back for our spring festival?"

Fiona paused. "I guess that would be me. I'm in charge of her estate, such as it is. I've got to talk to Tony when he sobers up to see if he wants to buy me out. If it's up to me, I'm having a fire sale to get rid of all that junk. Who needs that kind of hassle? I don't think it's worth my time or effort. I'm certainly not going to drive all over creation to be a T-shirt barker."

"By the way, we found some things at the resort after Tabbi's death," Jules said, lowering her voice.

"What kind of things?" The woman straightened up in her chair and stared at Jules.

"My groundskeeper found a purse with a picture of Tabbi and Cal, a voodoo doll, and a gun." Jules's voice dropped off as she looked around the room.

Fiona chuckled. "I don't think voodoo was her thing. She was into self-help books and new-age mumbo jumbo. Maybe it was something new for her. She tended to flit from fad to fad. The picture might have been hers. She never quite got over Cal, but she wouldn't own a gun. That wasn't hers. She hated guns. One of our friends growing up was shot to death. He was a kid. He and his brother were playing with a loaded weapon. Tabbi was very vocal about her opposition."

Jules nodded. "Then I guess it didn't belong to her. Thanks so much for chatting with me. Again, I'm sorry for your loss."

The woman waved her off with a bejeweled hand. She had quite a collection of oversized rings on each finger.

If Tabbi didn't own a gun, then how did it get in her purse? This didn't make sense.

Jules moved through a sea of bodies toward Tony, precariously balanced on a barstool. Nearby, Sheena pulled beer bottles from an ice chest and picked up her tray. She set it back down on the bar hard enough for the bottles to wobble when she saw Jules approach.

"Hi, y'all. I wanted to pop over and offer my condolences before my boyfriend, and I drive back to Fern Valley."

"I'm glad you could come," Tony slurred. "It's nice to see you again, June."

"Jules. It's Jules. We wanted to pay our respects since you graciously invited us."

"I did?" A puzzled look crossed Tony's dark brow. He stared at her for a few seconds and then fingered his beer bottle. He picked at the edge of the red label. "It's been a rough day. I'm still trying to figure out what to do next. It's all giving me a headache."

When he continued to pick at the label, Jules asked, "How long had you and Tabbi been dating?"

Sheena set a beer bottle down on the counter with a little more force than needed. She coughed and glared at Tony.

"What? On and off for a coupla years. Maybe five or six. She used to come into the gym where I worked. She hired me as her personal trainer. Then she wanted to make a deal for us to go into business selling things on the carnival and festival circuits. She said I'd be an asset to her organization," he slurred.

Sheena didn't add anything, but her countenance darkened to a scowl. She stared at Tony like she was trying to send him a telepathic message.

Jules did the math. Tabbi and Toni must have started their relationship while she was still married to Cal. "My groundskeeper found a purse near where Tabbi was found. I'm wondering if it was hers," Jules added.

"Any money in it?" Tony looked up and stared at her.

"No, just personal items."

Sheena coughed and glared at Tony.

"You sure there was no money or credit cards in the purse?" Tony stared at Jules.

"No. Sorry. I need to go find Jake. We've got a two-hour ride back home. This was nice. Thank you for inviting us."

"Anytime," Tony said. "We'll have to get together again soon. I like that Jake guy. He's a cool dude."

"We're hosting a spring festival. Maybe I'll see y'all then." Jules added, hoping to extend the conversation.

Sheena picked up her tray and disappeared into the crowd.

Tony returned to peeling the label off of his long-neck beer bottle.

Jules put on her best fake smile and waved. She glanced around the room for Jake. Spotting her boyfriend chatting with two guys and a girl at the pool tables, she waded through the crowd like a fish swimming against the current.

"Hi," she said, probably too loudly, as she approached Jake.

"Hey, babe. This is T. J., Rita, and Maurice. They live near Tabbi."

"I'm so sorry about what happened to her," Jules said. "It was so sudden."

T. J., leaning on his pool cue, looked at Jules. "Somebody finally did a number on her. I always thought someone would teach her a lesson eventually."

Rita giggled.

"A lot of people showed up tonight for her send-off," Jake added.

Maurice coughed to cover up a laugh and lined up his next shot.

T. J. snickered. "Most of them are here for the drinks. Lots of angry wives and jilted boyfriends. They're here to see the show." T. J. raised his bottle.

"Hopefully, they'll find out who did it. Though if they're looking at people who were mad at her, then it's most of the crowd here," Maurice added.

T. J. laughed loudly and took a swig from his beer bottle.

Maurice nodded. "She ticked off everyone. The list of those she cheated or sued is long."

After an uncomfortable pause, Jules looked at Jake. "'Bout ready to head out. I've got an early morning tomorrow."

"Yep. Nice to meet y'all." Jake saluted and put his hand on Jules's lower back. The warmth from his hand sent a spark through her.

The three-some nodded and returned to their game as Jake followed Jules out into the chilly night air.

Once locked inside her Jeep, she started the engine and blasted the heat. "It'll be warm in here in a minute. So, did we find out anything that made a four-hour round-trip worth it?"

"I talked to two women who worked with Tabbi. They liked her because she always gave them leftover merchandise. But they thought she catted around and gossiped too much. Their words, not mine." Jake adjusted his seat belt.

"I talked to her cousin Fiona. She wasn't a great character reference for the deceased, but she did say that Tabbi was very anti-gun and that there was no way the gun we found was hers." Jules signaled to turn onto the interstate.

Jake turned and looked at her. "So, whose gun was it? Maybe Sheriff Hobbs can get prints off the purse."

"Or maybe off the contents. There are a bunch of pieces missing from this puzzle. But I guess we did find out some new tidbits of info tonight. You'll never know what might be important later. I'll let the sheriff know about the gun comment."

"Sheena wasn't fond of Tabbi, and Tony was totally drunk. This may be the weirdest wake I've ever attended," he said. "It's bad when more people showed up for the discounted drinks and to see who's who rather than celebrate her life."

Jules merged onto the interstate and followed a tractor-trailer who was at a good cruising speed. Jake hunkered down in his seat and was snoring before they had gone thirty miles.

Cal and Misti didn't like Tabbi, but Cal was still having make-out sessions with her up until the time she was murdered. Tony was her boyfriend, but he was stepping out with Sheena. Then T. J. said that half the bar had a bone to pick with her. The list kept getting longer instead of shorter. Tabbi hadn't won any friends in Fern Valley either. There was some weird vibe tonight between Sheena and Tony.

Jules yawned and turned the heat down. She had another hour and a half to think about the murder and the possible motives. The list of suspects seemed endless.

Chapter Seventeen

Friday

Jules dropped Bijou off at the office and hiked to the lodge to see what Mel and Crystal had whipped up for breakfast. Today was the big weekend check-in day, so she needed sustenance before the onslaught of guests.

Filling a to-go cup with coffee, she added enough creamer to turn it a light tan. Today's selections were omelets or French toast with fruit. She chose the latter and garnished it with raspberries and powdered sugar. She added a couple slices of turkey bacon to her carton for good measure. "Crystal, you and your mom outdid yourselves this morning."

The twenty-something with the long blond braid beamed. "Wait until you see what we have up our sleeve for tomorrow and Sunday's brunch. Are you going to the Taste of Christmas Spectacular tonight?"

"Can't wait. I'll skip lunch and dinner, but I'll be ready."

Crystal's eyes sparkled. "Mom and I are entering our holiday candies."

"Jake and I will be sure to stop by and vote. And our guests will love the special breakfasts. You all have come up with some amazing recipes."

Jules hurried back to the office, hoping that her food would stay warm during her trek across the frozen field. Overnight temperatures had dropped, and they would be in for more snow over the weekend. She'd keep an eye on the weather in case Jake and Lester had to pull out the plow or salt the walkways.

Inside the office, Bijou got a whiff of the bacon and followed Jules to her desk. "I'll save you some. I promise."

"Some of what?" Roxanne breezed in and wiggled out of her coat, faux fur hat, and gloves.

"Bacon. She wants to share my breakfast."

"That sounds better than mine. I brought yogurt. Matt and I are going to that tasting thing tonight, and I know I won't be good there. So, a light breakfast it is." Her aunt winked and headed for the coffee maker. "Anything special on the agenda today besides check-ins?"

"Nope. Just watching to see if it'll snow. I texted Jake and Lester to make sure they were ready with the sidewalk salt." Jules hurried to the supply closet and rummaged through the sports equipment. "There, I knew I bought these." She pulled out three clear snowman containers filled with plastic snowman parts. "In case anyone feels like building a snowman or woman." She set the containers on the front counter.

"The check-ins are a mix this weekend. Some are here for the race, and others brought their kids for the Santa events. And a lot of the vendors are back. It should be a fun wrap up to the festival." Roxanne tapped her designer boot on the floor while she waited for the coffee to brew.

"Jake and I went to Tabbi's wake last night." Roxanne raised an eyebrow, and Jules continued, "Definitely interesting. The bar had drink and appetizer specials for the event."

"Classy."

"It seemed like a normal bar night. Nobody spoke in honor of Tabbi while we were there. I talked to Tony, who was clueless, and Sheena, who seemed annoyed at everything. Tabbi didn't have that many people singing her praises, and only one family member was there. That reminds me. I need to text the sheriff. I asked her cousin Fiona about the gun, and she was adamant that it didn't belong to Tabbi." Jules typed a quick message to Sheriff Hobbs.

Roxanne added sugar and cream to her mug and sat down at her desk.

"Is Emily coming in today?" Jules asked.

"No, she went to see her sister for the weekend. It's you and me, kiddo."
The bells jangled on the front door, interrupting their conversation.

Roxanne hopped up, and Jules heard, "Well, hello, Sheriff. What brings you to this neck of the woods." Bijou yipped and ran to greet him.

The conversation was muted, and Jules didn't want to eavesdrop, so she logged in to see what was going on in the social media world.

About twenty minutes later, Jules jumped when Sheriff Hobbs said in his deep baritone voice, "Hey, there."

"Good morning. Did you get my text?"

"He looked all business when he came in, so I knew he was here to see you," Roxanne yelled from the store.

The sheriff smiled and stood in the doorway where he could see both women. "You'll have my full attention tonight at dinner and at the tasting fundraiser thing. But for now, I have some questions for Jules."

"Jake and I attended Tabbi's wake," Jules said.

"To pay your last respects since you were such old friends?" He pursed his lips.

"To be polite, since she died at my resort. And while I was there, I talked to her cousin Fiona. Somehow we got on the subject of guns."

"Somehow—"

"Anyway, she was adamant about Tabbi's disdain for guns. She said she bordered on fanatical about gun control. They had a friend who was killed by gun violence, and I thought you'd be interested."

"I am. Especially since it wasn't Tabbi's purse."

Jules's jaw dropped. "Well, then that confirms what Fiona said." She waited for the sheriff to continue, but he didn't offer any other information.

After what seemed like an eternally long silence, he said, "Anything else I should know about?"

Jules shook her head.

"Rox, I'll pick you up at six," he said, striding toward the front door.

Roxanne asked, "Hey, Sheriff, wanna walk over for breakfast?" Her aunt must have changed her mind about the yogurt.

He nodded, and the wooden door slammed behind the pair. The office fell silent.

Jules pulled out her folder and flipped through her notes. She added what she and Jake had uncovered at Amigos and the sheriff's bombshell about the purse Lester found.

A little after five, Jules plopped down in her desk chair. She and Roxanne had a steady stream of check-ins, including Tony, Sheena, and Dana again. She and Roxanne had answered hundreds of questions about the resort's amenities, local restaurants, and the festival. Sold-out weekends were Jules's favorites. She did a little happy dance from her chair and a quick check of her email. It was time to pack up for the evening. "Come on, Bijou. I owe you a walk before I change and do a quick touchup."

After putting on a bright green sweater and floofing her hair, Jules texted Jake. **Headed over to check on things for tonight. Wanna come or meet me there later?**

Pick you up in a few minutes, he responded.

After one last swipe with the mascara wand, Jules straightened the counter and went to the kitchen to feed Bijou.

When Jake's Mustang roared in her driveway, she pulled on her coat and headed for the door.

Jake jumped out of his car before she got to the passenger side to open the door. "Good evening. Ready to paint the town?" he asked.

"Always, but hopefully, it won't get too wild and raucous at the Taste of Christmas. Elaine will be watching."

"You know Fern Valley. A surprise around every corner," Jake said with a smirk.

Jules laughed and snapped her seat belt in place. "The ticket proceeds are funding the prizes and the scholarship at the high school. Darlene said we sold over three hundred tickets, and they're selling some at the door. She's got chefs and reps from some of the local cideries and wineries, as well as town folks whose favorite show is *The Great British Bake Off*. Mel and Crystal have a booth. We have to cheer them on. It should be a fun event."

Ten minutes later, Jake found a spot, and they walked in the main entrance through a candy cane balloon arch. The hallways looked festive with the balloons, and the volunteers sported Christmas sweaters and Santa hats.

Elaine fluttered around the information table and the silent auction items, arranging things.

"Jules, where is your tacky Christmas sweater?" Darlene asked, showing off hers with a giant Rudolph and his big, light-up nose.

"I need to get one. I was going with festive colors." Jules spread her arms wide.

"We've got to get you some bling." Kim jumped up and grabbed a reindeer antler headband and a light-up Christmas bulb necklace.

Jake snickered as they decorated Jules.

"Oh, you're next, buddy. Everyone needs some festive swag." Darlene plunked a Santa hat on his head and wrapped a red and white scarf around his neck. "There. That looks more jolly. Y'all check out the great items in the silent auction. Your giant basket from the resort is about midway down the table. And it looks faaaaab-u-lous. We're giving adults red wristbands, and anyone under twenty-one gets a green one. There is unlimited tasting. We'll have some games and contests throughout the night. Use the tickets in your bags to vote for your favorites. Enjoy!"

"Anything we can help with?" Jules asked, looking at all the gift baskets on the red and white table.

"Marco, Mitch, and the gals made quick work of the setup. Darlene and I will keep order here. Elaine's making the announcements throughout the evening. Go check out the tables and bid on our items. Here's what you need." Kim handed them each a bag and wristbands and winked.

"You all outdid yourselves. Great job!" Jules rifled through the contents of the event bag.

Jake and Jules wandered around and perused the decorated tables laden with decadent samples. There were more food and fancy desserts than Jules had seen in one place before. It was a good thing they'd skipped dinner. The table decorations were so creative and inviting. Jules snapped photos to save for her idea file. She kept all kinds of boards on Pinterest for decorations, table settings, crafts, and recipes for the resort.

When the crowds started pouring through the doors, she and Jake moved to the far wall and made their way from table to table to sample all kinds of food and drinks.

While checking out a table full of peanut candies, Jules felt a tug on her elbow. "Hi, Elaine," she said, turning around. These fudgy peanut butter things are really good. Want one?"

"No. I'll taste it later. I'm too keyed up to eat. I have to tell you what happened." Elaine yanked on Jules's sleeve and led her to the middle of the floor between the rows of tables where it was less crowded.

"What's up?" Jules popped the last bite in her mouth and licked her fingers.

"The sheriff called me again. He and a state trooper had some questions for me. This is the third time, Jules. It's so unsettling. I keep telling them that all I did was break up a fight between two vendors. That was basically my only contact with that crazy woman. Sheeesh. I mean, I'm sorry that she's dead, but why does he think I'm involved?" Elaine looked crestfallen.

Jules leaned in closer to talk in lower tones. "What exactly did they ask you?"

"The same questions over and over. I gave a statement when it happened. Then, the sheriff had a ton of questions. And now this. It feels like they're trying to see if I mess up and contradict myself. You're good at finding out information, and well, Roxanne is close to him. Could you talk to him to see what his angle is? This is so unnerving, and I'm starting to lose sleep over it. I don't want this to turn into something that airs on *Dateline*."

"Sure. But he's not always forthcoming with information about active investigations. I'll see what I can find out."

"You're a peach. I appreciate it." Elaine patted Jules's shoulder and returned to her normal high-octane level of exuberance in a span of less than thirty seconds. "Enjoy the night. I want to go check on the silent auction. Gotta keep things humming along."

Why would the sheriff's team keep questioning Elaine? There were plenty of witnesses there that day the fight broke out, and lots of other suspects with a bigger motive to do Tabbi in than Elaine. She'd retired here to open her gardening shop after years in risk management for a firm in Northern Virginia. She has high standards and always wants perfection. She's picky and sometimes demanding, but she's no killer.

Jules sampled a cherry cheesecake bite and a swig of peppermint hot chocolate while adding the vendor's business cards to her little bag. Good connections were always important, especially in her business. After she visited all the booths on that row, she sidled up next to Jake.

"Have you tasted everything? I picked up some brochures from some of the newer wineries. We should go on a wine tour when it gets warmer." Jake draped his arm around her.

Jules snuggled in. "Sounds fun. I'm about sugared out. I wanna peek at the silent auction before we leave, but that's about it. I'm so glad about the turnout."

"I'm ready to head out, too," he said as they made their way to the exit under the basketball hoop.

They mingled with the crowd and checked out all the gift baskets and offerings for the silent auction one last time. Jules added a bid for an overnight stay in Virginia Beach and then stopped in front of her basket with the large candy cane bow. The current bid was five hundred and fifty dollars for a weekend stay in one of the tiny houses, two bottles of wine, snacks, a couples' massage, a picnic basket, and a pair of resort wine glasses. Pleased with herself, she moved on down the long table of baskets in all shapes and sizes. Jake grabbed her by the shoulders and spun her around before she could get to the end of the table.

Curious about what he was trying to hide, she decided to poke at him. "Just a sec. I didn't see everything down at that end."

"Uh, okay. Not much down on that end to see that's interesting. I did a quick cruise by. Hey, there's J. P. Gross. Wanna say hi?" he asked.

Jules rolled her eyes and decided to dodge a bullet. She ducked behind Jake and followed him out the main entrance before J. P. tried to corner her with a barrage of complaints and suggestions of things she could do better and how he should be leading the business council.

The icy breeze stung her face and chilled Jules to her spine. She stuffed her hands in her coat pockets and tucked her chin in her collar. "Man, the temperature's dropped."

Jake unlocked her door and shut it after she slid into her seat. He jogged around to his side pulled something off the windshield, and climbed inside. He started the car and blasted the heat.

Jules turned on her heated seat to knock off the chill. "What's that?"

Jake crumpled up the paper. "I thought it was a flier, but it looks like a stupid joke." He handed the scrunched wad to her.

"You're going to get in trouble. Stop it now," was scrawled in big loopy letters in black marker on a piece of copy paper.

"You think this was directed to you?" Bats bounced around in her stomach. Who'd be threatening Jake? Goose bumps popped up on Jules's arms. Was this related to Tabbi's murder?

Jake shrugged as he backed out of the parking spot. "Who knows? I'm not worried about it. I haven't done anything to tick anyone off. Maybe it's just a prank."

Jules folded the paper and slipped it into her pocket.

Chapter Eighteen

Saturday

Jules sat up in bed and tried to shake the drowsy feeling, but Bijou had no issues with the pre-dawn hour. She was ready to roll and insisted that Jules play with the rope bone before any other activities commenced.

After a quick, hot shower, Jules relocated to the kitchen for coffee and peanut butter toast. She checked the news and her social media sites. "I better get a move on. The race is going to start soon."

Finding the warmest outfit she could for the Jingle Bell Run, Jules added her tall boots, polar coat, gloves, and hat. She kissed Bijou on the head and hurried to the garage.

Today's lineup included a series of races for different skill levels. Runners in brightly colored holiday outfits milled around the town square, waiting for their race, while spectators swarmed the food trucks for hot food and beverages. The Breakfast with Santa event would start later that morning in the school's gym. Fern Valley was abuzz with all the early risers.

Jules parked and walked over to the registration tent. Deputy Dempsey stood behind the barricade with a breakfast sandwich in one hand and his phone in the other. He nodded and chewed as she passed. The business council volunteers huddled under the tent and drank coffee.

"Hey, Jules," Kim said as she approached. "Ready for the fun run?"

"I'm a spectator today. I only run if there's a bear chasing me. And I don't quite have the right gear today." Jules flexed her foot to show off her tall boots.

"The 10k is underway. They should be heading to the finish line any minute now. The 5k will be lining up momentarily. Then we wrap up with the 3k, fun run, and costume contest."

"It's been a seamless morning. Everyone picked up the registration packets last night, so there were only a handful of people with questions today," Marco added. "Smooth sailing. Just the way I like it."

They paused to watch the runners, many in shorts, line up. Mitch Hill did the starter's count and fired a blank into the air. Hundreds of runners in brightly colored outfits trotted past.

"Do y'all need any help with anything?" Jules asked when the noise level subsided.

"Nah. After the fun run, we'll pack up here," Marco said.

"We had an amazing turnout." Jules filled a to-go cup with coffee and used it to warm her hands.

"I'm really excited about the participation. We need to do something like this again in the spring. I didn't realize how big the running community was in the valley and how many folks came in from out of state," Kim said.

Thirty minutes later, participants for the next race gathered at the starting line. Mitch repeated the count and the shot to start the race. The runners jogged off, and the noise level subsided again.

"This team has the logistics of this down to a science. I'm impressed at how organized it is since it's the first one we've hosted," Jules said.

"It's all thanks to Kim. It was her idea to color-code the runners' tags. They follow the route signs for their race." Marco took a swig from his water bottle.

Kim blushed. "We have monitors along the course to assist in case anyone gets confused. It's almost time to get the fun run lined up. This is my favorite part." She gathered her things and walked to where Mitch stood, clipboard at the ready.

Kim and Mitch herded the runners, who came in all shapes and sizes, behind the starting line. Mitch used Elaine's bullhorn while Kim shooed them in place. Jules loved all the costumes. Participants sported hats, funny signs, boas, and other props. Jules's favorite was a group that built a cardboard sleigh for their Santa. Eight reindeer lined up in front of him to complete the ensemble. She spotted several grinches in the crowd, as well as ballerinas, toy soldiers, and a bunch of elves in all shapes and sizes.

After hundreds of runners whooshed off, Mitch trotted over to the tent. "Do you want us to take the tent down and move to the finish line?" Mitch asked.

"It's about that time," Kim said. "Let's pack up everything here and head over there."

Kim and Jules picked up the papers and folded the tables and chairs. Marco backed his truck close to the group.

After loading the tent and other equipment, Mitch, Marco, and Kim hopped in the truck bed. Jules followed them in her Jeep.

They found parking on a side street near the finish line, marked with red, green, and white balloon arches. Spectators lined the sidewalks and cheered for the runners from the different races. The four stopped at a green tent where Darlene and Elaine sat in folding chairs.

"I'd say all was quiet here except when the groups ran past. The crowd is having a blast and whooping it up." Darlene said. "It's all been very exciting."

Jules leaned over near Elaine. "You doing okay?"

"Fine and dandy. Have you talked to the sheriff yet?" Elaine whispered.

"No, not yet. Have you talked to him again since the last interview?" Jules asked.

Elaine shook her head and wrung her hands. "It's all very upsetting. Let me know when you talk with him. I want to put this behind me and move on to things that are more important. It has sucked up way too much of my time."

Jules patted her on the back. "Will do. It'll be okay." She made a mental note to call the sheriff when she got back to the office.

Elaine bustled around to the front of the table. "I'm headed over to the school to check on the breakfast with Santa."

"I'll go with you." Kim jumped up and grabbed her purse. "Can't wait to see all the kiddos."

Jules scanned the crowds lining the racecourse. People held signs and noisemakers. She even spotted a cheering squad with megaphones and pompoms. Across the street from them, a small band serenaded passing runners. Jules watched the participants cross the finish line. Shouts and whistles rippled through the crowd as each group came by. The enthusiasm was contagious.

When a lull hit, Jules waved goodbye to her business council friends and hiked back to the Jeep. She threw her purse on the passenger seat and started the engine before she realized there was a flier under her windshield wiper.

Annoyed about having to get out again, she opened the door and retrieved the sheet of white paper. In black marker, the note read, "Stop asking questions. Let it be."

Jules's heart rate increased. She climbed back in the Jeep and stared at the paper. Checking her pocket, she found the folded note. The paper and the writing were similar.

She fired off a text to the sheriff about the pair of notes.

By the time she pulled into her garage, her phone dinged with a response.

You in the office today?

Headed there now, Jules replied.

Be over soon.

Jules popped in the house, grabbed an apple and a granola bar, and leashed up Bijou. "Come on, girl. Let's go see what the sheriff has to say about these notes. Someone's trying to get our attention."

When Jules unlocked the door, Bijou tore through the office looking for people. She yipped at the dividing door until Roxanne came over to greet her. Jules spread the two notes out on her desk and photographed them.

"Hey there, you two. How were the festivities in town?" Roxanne refilled her coffee mug.

"The race was fun. Good turnout. I didn't stop by the school to check on the breakfast with Santa. Elaine and her crew have it all under control."

"I'm relieved I'm not heading any of these committees. I did so much of that when Jack was alive and Max was little. It's nice to be part of the audience now. I don't think I have the patience to keep up with the details and all the volunteers."

"I'm so thrilled to have so many dedicated volunteers who took care of all the details. It made my job easy. Oh, the sheriff is going to stop by soon." Jules wiggled her eyebrows.

A slight smile crossed her aunt's face. "We had dinner last night, but he seemed distracted. We kept getting interrupted by calls and text messages. I guess I should be used to it by now. He's always working."

Right on cue, the store door opened, and Sheriff Hobbs poked his head in. The heels of his motorcycle boots clacked as he strode across the wood floor.

"Morning ladies, what's new?"

"Good to see you, Matt," Roxanne winked.

"It's always good to see you, Rox." The tall man smiled. Then, a serious look crossed his face. "What'd ya find, Jules?"

"These. One was left on Jake's car last night, and this one was on my Jeep this morning when I was in town."

"Any thoughts? Other than somebody's trying to tell y'all something?"

"I'm not sure why Jake got one except that I was with him that night. I think these are all targeting me. We found the one in Jake's car when we were at the high school."

"Do you have an envelope?"

"Matt, you want coffee?" Roxanne asked.

He shook his head, and Jules handed him an oversized mailer. Slipping the notes inside, he said, "Anything else unusual?"

"I talked to Elaine. She's a little concerned." Jules stared at the sheriff.

"About what?"

"She said that you and the state trooper have questioned her several times. She's not sure why. You can't possibly suspect her in Tabbi's death, right?"

Sheriff Hobbs chuckled. "I'll call her later. I thought she understood. We got her statement early on. That was for her role in the altercation and then part of the murder investigation. Then, the victim threatened to file a lawsuit. Tabbi and her partner, Tony Yates, filed a complaint with the town. Trooper Evans was investigating that complaint."

"She'll be relieved. She was beside herself thinking that you all had her in your sights as a murder suspect." Jules let out a puff of air and sank into her chair.

He tried to suppress a grin. "I don't think she has anything to worry about. Thanks for the notes. We'll look into those. Rox, I'll call you later."

"See ya, Sheriff." Her aunt blew him kisses from across the room.

He saluted, and Bijou escorted him to the door.

"Elaine will be so happy." Jules settled in at her desk.

"She's probably been a nervous wreck. Elaine likes everything to go as she planned. But I'm sure did a good job of holding things together," Roxanne added.

"I asked about having folks take over if she needed time, and she insisted that the work kept her mind off of things." Jules turned on her laptop and took a bite of her granola bar.

"I'm concerned about you getting threatening notes, though. Someone is watching you." Her aunt stacked folders on the cabinet.

"Someone's leaving them on windshields. It could be just a prank."

Her aunt cut her eyes at Jules and frowned.

"They're more ominous than threatening. Way too vague. Not sure if it's about Cal, Tabbi, the festival, or something with the resort. I doubt if it's related to the tiny houses."

"You need to still be vigilant even if it's a harmless crackpot. In this day and age, you never know." Roxanne patted her on the shoulder.

"Yes, ma'am."

"Any exciting plans for tonight?" Roxanne asked.

"Nope. What about you?"

"It was supposed to be movie night. But who knows? The sheriff's schedule has been fluid lately. I'll be in early tomorrow to help with the check-outs."

"Tomorrow's the last busy day until New Year's Eve. We'll get a little break. Oh, and we're sold out for the end-of-year celebration. Wooo hooo!"

"We'll all get some time to enjoy the holidays. You and Jake want to come by for brunch on Christmas Day?"

"I'd love to. Let me confirm with him, but I think we can. What should we bring?" Jules asked.

"Just your appetites. Matt and I have it all under control." Roxanne turned and headed to the front counter.

Jules opened her folder and looked at all the names that might be involved with Tabbi's death. She drew circles around the ones that popped up the most and used a thick marker to add connector lines. Her page looked like a spider's web when she finished.

"Mail call." Roxanne dropped a pile of envelopes on Jules's desk.

She thumbed through the pile and recycled the ads. A brown envelope with her name in black marker sat at the bottom of the stack. No postmark or stamps.

Jules slit the flap and opened it. Two sheets of folded white paper fell out. One was blank, and the other said, "Mind your business. Stay out of things that don't concern you."

"Hmm. Got another one." Jules snapped a picture and showed it to her aunt.

Roxanne pulled out her phone and tapped in a message. "It doesn't look like it was mailed. It was on the porch when I came in. I added it to the mailman's stack. Jules, these are directed at you. And the writing looks like a woman did it. Very loopy."

"It almost looks like someone is trying to disguise the handwriting," Jules mused, looking closely at the note.

Roxanne's phone chimed. "Oh, that was quick. Matt responded that he'll pick it up tonight when he comes over. Put it in an envelope for me."

Trying not to touch it any more than necessary, Jules slid the two sheets into a folder and dropped them and the original envelope into a larger one. "Here. Maybe they can find some prints besides mine on it."

"And mine." Roxanne put the envelope in her oversized tan Coach bag. "Like I said. Watch your back. There's a nut job out there."

"I will. But now I'm curious. Who did I bother that much?" She looked down at the spiderweb of connections in her notes and added Mac McAllister, Zac Robinson, and anyone she could remember who was at the wake. None of them seemed to be likely candidates for a killer or an attacker.

They didn't live in the immediate area. It would be a several-hour drive to leave notes around Fern Valley.

Jules emailed Pixel the new list of names. Maybe she'd have some time to do a bit of research. She had a knack for uncovering dirt that wasn't obvious to mere mortals.

Chapter Nineteen

Sunday

Jules and Bijou opened the office as the sun rose over the mountains. She wanted to be ready for check-outs as soon as her guests finished with brunch.

Roxanne breezed in as Jules turned on computers and lights. "Good morning. Ready for a big day?"

"Time to check out the brunch menu. Want me to bring you anything?" Jules asked.

"Nah. I'm going to get settled here. I'll head over after the caffeine has kicked in," her aunt said.

"Be right back." Jules slipped on her coat and headed for the golf cart.

Inside the lodge, the decorations around the grand fireplace and the wall of windows looked festive, and the view of the mountains was stunning. Snow was the only thing missing from what would be the perfect Instagram photo. She should have planned something for family and friends here for Christmas Eve, but she was so wrapped up in the festival that she ran out of time. She'd put it on the calendar for next year to make sure she followed through. It was about time to host a fun party that wasn't for business.

Inside the dining area, Crystal and Mel's spread was a feast for all the senses. Eggnog French toast and candy cane pancakes dominated the buffet table, along with the red and white parfaits and the peppermint hot cocoa. Jules filled a to-go box and waved to Crystal on her way out. "Looks great.

Can't wait to try the French toast."

"Thanks. We had fun with the menu and doing the tabletop decorations. The pancakes with chocolate chips and crushed candy canes taste like dessert."

Jules hustled back to the office to finish breakfast before the guests arrived.

"Mmmmm. That smells good. I'll be right back." Roxanne slipped on her coat.

Jules had finished a slice of turkey bacon and a couple of bites of her French toast when the bells on the front door rang out with their melodic jingle.

She spent the next thirty minutes printing receipts, collecting keys, and talking with guests about their stays. By the time Roxanne returned, she had checked out six parties.

"People get up early on Sundays. I always sleep in when I'm on vacation." Roxanne wiped her hands on a napkin and took a sip of her coffee. "The gals outdid themselves with today's buffet. I won't need lunch."

The screen door slammed, and Jules looked up. Dana strode in. Her puffy pink coat bounced as she clomped across the floor. "Morning. Here are the keys to the two trailers Tabbi rented. We're out of here." She pursed her lips and stared at Roxanne.

"Good morning, Dana. How was your stay this time?" Jules asked.

Dana furrowed her brow. "We've had better weekends. Only the Christmas items did well this time. Our sales were down from the other two times. It's not the same without Tabbi. I think I'm done with all this. It takes too much of my time, and I don't like the path Tony and Sheena want to take with the business. It's so different from Tabbi's philosophy. They want me to be an hourly employee. I'm more than that. I helped Tabbi build her business. I did a lot of marketing and event booking for her. They don't appreciate all I can do. They're trying to cut me out. I mean, Tabbi hasn't been dead a month, and her boyfriend's already moved on. With one of her friends!" Her voice rose an octave.

"We are so sorry for your loss. I know you miss your friend," Jules said in a soothing tone. "It was nice to see you again." Dana tried to bite back the tears, and her face flashed rage. Not knowing what else to say, Jules handed the receipts to Dana, who shoved them in her purse that looked like it had had a former life as a cigar box.

She shook her head and headed for the door. "I can't believe Tabbi's gone, and they're already shacking up. Some people have no couth. I'm done after I tell them what I think. That's no way to treat Tabbi. They better remember to change all the business passwords. I have way more access than they realize." She stomped to the door and slammed it behind her.

Jules looked down at her phone. Pixel had responded to Jules's last request, but before she could read it, the next wave of check-outs arrived.

It was close to one o'clock before Roxanne and Jules caught a break.

"Whew," Roxanne said. "That was a workout. "I'm going to tidy up here and head on out if you don't need me for anything."

"In all the hubbub, I forgot to ask you how your date was." Jules tapped a pen on the counter.

"Fine. After dinner and cleaning up, we watched TV, and he fell asleep on the couch. Very romantic."

"Sounds like a quiet evening."

Her aunt shrugged. "Except for all the snoring. I let him sleep. He's been working night and day. Oh, he said thank you for the notes. He also said for you to be careful."

Before Jules could reply, the back door slammed, and Lester rushed in. "The scanner is buzzing this morning. The sheriff made an arrest in the murder of that gal. A task force went in during the wee hours. It sounded like a full-on raid." Lester grinned and waved his arms around.

"Who, Lester? Who?" Roxanne's eyes widened.

"It was a woman. The wife of that cat guy, Misti." Spots of pink appeared on Lester's cheeks.

"Wow." Jules sank into her office chair. "The sheriff did say that the red purse and gun you found didn't belong to Tabbi. And the handwriting in the notes looked like a woman wrote it."

"I missed the overnight stuff, but there was still a bunch of chatter this morning. The team went to her house and served the warrant. They're holding her here until she can be arraigned. I'm glad the sheriff put this to rest before the holidays. Speaking of that, I'm gonna head out to my niece's house next week for Christmas. I'll have my phone with me if you need me."

"Thanks, Lester. I hope you enjoy Christmas with your family. Don't worry about anything here."

"I'll see y'all before I leave. I couldn't remember if I told you or not about the holidays. I'm gonna grab some lunch and catch some football. I'll let you know if anything comes else comes over the scanner."

Roxanne waved. "I wonder if Matt will still want to go to town for dinner tonight. This will take priority over my personal life again. I guess I should take up knitting or something. Maybe I'll get a cat."

Jules looked at her sideways.

"What? I used to sew and quilt. Maybe I'll drag my sewing machine out again and dust it off. It'll keep me busy while Matt works these long hours or falls asleep on my couch. I'm headed out, too. I'll see you tomorrow."

Remembering Pixel's email, she read, "I didn't find much with a quick search, but I'll dig deeper tonight. Tony Yates has a record. He was arrested a couple of times for drunk and disorderly and assault. Tabbi Morris had several arrests for drunk and disorderly, too, and one for fraud. Misti Collins had an earlier arrest for possession, and then there was that controversy with the dead pageant girl. I didn't see anything on Sheena, Fiona, or the others. I'll keep looking."

Jules thanked her friend and forwarded the office phone to the night attendant. "Come on, Bijou. Let's go see what Jake's up to."

She did a quick walk-through, turning off lights and checking doors.

Jules and Bijou trotted across the field near the tiny houses and around the empty vintage trailers. As they got closer to the cabin, Jules noticed something on the door. They climbed the steps. A white piece of paper, thumbtacked to her door, fluttered in the breeze. "Stay away. This is your last warning! I'm tired of telling you." The message, like the others, contained loopy letters in black marker. Jules's heart felt like it dropped to her stomach. She took a picture of the note and sent it to the sheriff.

After letting Bijou inside, she pulled the tack and note down and dropped them in a gift bag.

An arrest had already been made for the murder. Why would somebody keep leaving notes? *And had this been here a while, and I didn't notice it?*

Jules grabbed a Coke from the fridge. The notes versus the arrest battled for domination in her thoughts. Could Misti really have been the killer? She was angry and mouthy, but a little on the wimpy, whiny side. Did someone not know about the arrest? Or were two things going on?

"Stay here. I'm going back to check something," she said to Bijou, who hopped on the couch and settled in for a pre-dinner nap.

Jules wiggled into her coat, grabbed the bag with the note, and trotted back to the office.

The sun sank behind the mountains as she finished going through the camera feeds for the past few days. She let out a sigh and stretched. She had hoped her security system had caught someone skulking around the property, but she didn't have much luck. The place had been packed with visitors coming and going near the store. She didn't see anyone with anything that looked like a note. Bummed at not finding any new hints as to what was going on, she saved the video in case the sheriff wanted it later and shut everything down. Two notes on cars, one in an envelope and one tacked to her door. With that many notes, someone had to have seen something. *And I guess Roxanne was right. It looks like someone is targeting me.*

On her way out the door, Jake's face popped up on her phone. "Hey, what's up?"

"You hungry?" he asked.

"Yes. Any ideas for dinner?"

"Let's try Nacho Mama's. I'm in the mood for some tacos," he said with a boyish grin.

"Sounds good. I'm wrapping up at the office. I need to go let Bijou out, and then I'll be ready."

"I'll pick you up in thirty minutes or so. See ya."

Jules disconnected and hustled home. She paused at the front door to see if anything was out of place. Not noticing anything, she let herself in. A sense of relief settled over her when she didn't find any more mysterious notes.

By the time she walked the dog, changed outfits twice, and touched up her makeup, she heard Jake's car in the driveway.

"How was your day?" he asked when she met him on the steps.

"Check-out day is always fun," she said. "But it's nice that we had three sold-out weekends in December. New Year's Eve is looking pretty good, too. How's the tiny house coming along?"

"Good. Both parts are framed. I start the walls tomorrow."

"You're getting this down to a science." Jules slid into the seat, and he closed the door behind her.

Jake jogged around to the driver's side. "Lester said they arrested the wife of that cat guy for the murder."

"I was surprised. She was feisty and snippy, but she didn't seem like she'd kill someone. Mostly passive-aggressive."

"I saw a video of her fight with Tabbi on Facebook. She got in several good punches. I'm surprised it didn't make it on some of those *Girls Gone Wild* internet sites."

The pair rode to town in silence. Jules stared out the window. The notes and Misti's arrest seemed unconnected. She'd seen no sign of Misti or Cal on the property this weekend. Jules shook off the morose feeling during the quick walk from where Jake found on-street parking to the restaurant.

The hostess, in a lime and teal dress featuring large red and orange parrots, showed them to a secluded table in the corner.

Jules thumbed through the menu as the waiter dropped off chips and salsa. "I'll be back to take your orders in un momentito," he said.

When the waiter returned, Jake said, "I'll have the fish taco meal with a Coke."

"I'll have a taco salad with chicken and no tomato. And an iced tea, unsweetened. Thanks."

Jake leaned forward and clasped her hands. "So, what's bothering you? You seem like you're somewhere else tonight."

Jules smiled a weak smile. "I was thinking about Misti and the murder. I received three notes after the one you found on your car. One on my car, one mixed in with the mail, and one thumbtacked to my door. None of them are sinister, but I'm curious about who is putting them there."

"Did you tell the sheriff?" Jake's smile faded into a somber stare.

She nodded. "He said he'd look into it. But if these are warnings about the murder, the timing is off. Misti was already in custody when at least the last one was left."

"Any idea where they came from?" he asked.

"Nope. Plain vanilla copy paper and a black marker. The notes are short and look like the one you received. I checked the camera feeds. Nothing stood out. Just lots of guests milling about."

"Here you go," the waiter said. "Let me know if I can get you anything else."

They dug into their dinners. Between bites, she said, "The purse that Lester found had a picture of Tabbi and Cal. Why would Misti be carrying that around?"

Jake shrugged and dipped a chip into the salsa. "Sounds obsessive or weird. Maybe it motivated her. Do you carry photos around of your exes?"

"No, do you?" She looked into his jade-colored eyes.

"No. I don't keep that many pictures. Just on my phone."

"Let me see," she said, waving her hand, palm up.

Jake paused and pulled out his phone. After unlocking it, he handed it to her. She scrolled through dozens of pictures of tiny houses, Bijou, and her. She smiled.

"Satisfied?" he asked.

"Here," she said, handing him her phone. "Turnabout's fair play."

He swiped through her camera roll. "You take a lot of pictures of mystery notes, town events, and Bijou."

"Most of it's for the resort's website or the sheriff. But most of my people's pictures are of you." Jules put her fork on her plate and her cloth napkin on the table.

The waiter swooped in and picked up Jules's half-eaten salad. "May I take any of your plates, sir? Any refills? Dessert?"

Jules shook her head, and Jake handed the waiter the plate. "It was good."

By the time Jake polished off the chips in the plastic basket, the waiter slid the check face down toward Jake, and he grabbed it before Jules could.

"Thanks," she said as Jake handed the waiter his credit card.

When the waiter returned with the receipt, Jake pocketed his card and helped Jules with her coat. She followed him through the seating area to the glass front doors. An icy blast slapped them in the face when they stepped outside.

"Dang. It's cold. Do you want to wait inside while I go get the car?" he asked.

"Nah. We can walk fast. I need the exercise." Jules tucked her chin in her collar, and they hurried down the sidewalk.

Up ahead, a tall man with wavy hair and a light jacket caught Jules's attention. Where was his coat in this weather? When he turned his head, Jules sucked in enough cold air to make her cough. Grabbing Jake's arm, she said, "Get the car and follow me. I want to see where he goes?"

"Who?" Jake looked around and zeroed in on the guy about a block ahead.

"It's Tony," Jules said in a loud whisper.

"You sure?" Jake squinted at the man who hustled away from the pair.

"Get the car, and I'll have a better idea by the time you get back."

Jake hurried to the side street, and Jules caught up to the man in the athletic jacket who continued to lumber down the sidewalk. Tony looked like he was out for an evening stroll despite the frigid temperatures. The streetlights and the dimmed lights from the nearby stores provided a good enough view of the tall man. It was definitely Tabbi's boyfriend.

When Jules was a few feet behind him, she yelled, "Tony, hey, Tony?"

The big man turned and ignored her. He picked up his pace to almost a jog. Jules followed.

Jules heard the growl of a large engine approaching from behind her. A gray blur roared past her and stopped close to Tony. He climbed in the gray Charger, and it tore off before he closed the passenger door. Jules looked up the street, not sure of her next move.

The Mustang screeched to a stop at the curb, and Jules hopped in. "Follow that car. Somebody picked up Tony."

Jake floored it as she snapped her seat belt in place.

"I called his name. He turned and ran off, and then that car picked him up."

"Definitely weird." Jake caught up to the gray muscle car that flew out of town and down a winding backroad. The purply dusk had turned to night. Jake followed the red taillights ahead of him.

They drove in silence for twenty minutes. Jake clicked on his console to see the GPS's map.

"They're headed northwest," he finally said.

"Probably toward their home. Should we keep going or not?"

"I say stop. Unless you want to take a two-hour ride north," he said.

"Nah. I'll text the sheriff and let him know what we saw. Maybe it's nothing, but Tony acted suspiciously. It's odd that he'd be down here for an evening stroll without a coat."

Jake looked for a place to turn around, and the couple headed back to Fern Valley with more missing pieces to the puzzle.

Chapter Twenty

Monday

Jules found a parking space close to the library and walked with purpose to the front doors.

"Small conference room," Gail Matthews yelled with a wave.

"Thanks and good morning." Jules shed her coat and hurried to the back room. Some of the committee members had already gathered. Elaine sifted through her green and red folders while late-comers found seats around the long oak table.

"Good morning, everyone. It's eight-thirty. Let's get started. I know you all have things to get back to, too. Jules, you want to kick us off?"

"Thanks, Elaine. I want to thank you all so much for a wonderful first Christmas festival. We had lots of guests and great events. You all worked so hard, and the council, Fern Valley, and I appreciate all you do. Do we have any firm numbers yet?"

Jules looked up when J. P. Gross slipped in and closed the door behind him. He stood lurking against the wall.

"The sheriff's office is working on traffic and attendance numbers. There were two citations over the three weekends and no arrests related to any of the events. Just the altercation and the..." Elaine stopped abruptly. "Uh, I'll have more details by our next business council meeting. We'll survey of our members to see how they benefited and get their feedback on how things went." She closed her red folder and looked around the table.

"Lula Belle's had great sales all three weekends. This will put us in good shape for our end-of-year totals," Mitch Hill added.

"I think it went well. Foot traffic was up at my shop all three weekends," Darlene Denunzio piped in. "I'm sorry about that woman, but who's to say that the fight and her death were even related to Fern Valley? One gal was the ex-wife, and the other was her ex's new squeeze. Sounds like family drama to me."

There were nods and agreements around the table.

Elaine cleared her throat. "All the supplies have been packed away or returned to the owners who donated them. We raised enough to fund the singing contest prizes and give $3,500 to the school. The Taste of Christmas raised $5,000 for the scholarship fund. The race and the craft show raised $10,500 for the business council's general fund. We'll take suggestions for how to use that at our January meeting. I know you all have lots of good ideas for next year. Oh, and the cruise-in netted over $3,000 in donations for the animal shelter."

"Impressive," Kim Lacy added. "We worked our butts off, and it was worth it."

"Any issues or new business?" Elaine looked around the table.

J. P. cleared his throat. "Any news on the complaint that woman filed against the town? I don't know which is worse, the looming lawsuit or having the town linked to another murder."

Elaine's brow furrowed, and she pursed her lips. "The town is conducting its investigation, and there will be a report out early next year. Any other questions?" Elaine's diction shifted from singsong to clipped.

"I expect a full report, especially about the crimes and what the sheriff is going to do about it," J. P. added.

The satisfied smirk across J. P.'s face irked Jules. She quickly said, "Before we leave, I want to thank everyone again. Please relax and enjoy your holidays. You all deserve it. You are a great team, and Fern Valley is lucky to have all of you. Many thanks from the bottom of my heart. If there are no other items, we're adjourned."

Elaine gathered her folders and pens and dumped them in her bag. She pushed past J. P. and waddled through the stacks.

Jules chatted with the committee members, and the conversation spilled out on the sidewalk.

Twenty minutes later, Jules climbed in her Jeep and blasted the heat to warm up her fingers. Then, on a whim, she shut off the engine and pocketed her keys. Sliding her purse under the seat, she jumped out and headed for the sheriff's office.

The warm, antiseptic-smelling air tickled her nose when she stepped through the glass doors.

"Hi, Jules," Ashley Sharpe called from behind the glass.

"How are you? Congratulations on your big win at the singing contest."

The petite receptionist beamed. "Jake, Red, and I make a good team. I'm trying to get them to record some stuff, but so far, no one's interested. You here to see the Sheriff? If so, he's not here today. He finally took a day off."

"Not today. I was hoping I could pop in and visit with Misti Collins."

"I guess you can see Mrs. Collins. There's nothing in her file that says she can't have visitors. I'll buzz someone to take you back. Have a seat."

"Thanks." Before Jules could settle in one of the hard plastic seats in the waiting room, a deputy, who Jules knew only by sight, popped his head out the oak door and motioned for her to follow him. "Hi, I'm Jules."

"I know. I'm Deputy Hawkins. Right this way. Please put your stuff in that locker, and I need to pat you down. Please don't touch or hand the prisoner anything."

Jules put the key in her pocket and shoved her coat and purse in the locker. The deputy did a quick pat down. "Follow me."

Her boots clicked on the industrial floor with the black and tan squiggly pattern popular in government buildings and schools. She tried to walk slowly to muffle the sound, but the noise seemed to echo through the hallway.

Deputy Hawkins stopped in front of a gray metal door. "You have fifteen minutes." He held the door for her, and it clanked shut behind her. Jules flashed back to her visit with another suspect here last fall. Nothing had changed except the accused.

Misti Collins sat at a scarred wooden table with her wrists handcuffed to

148

two metal rings. As the younger woman looked up, a flash of recognition crossed her face. "Hi. What are you doing here?"

"I came by to see how you are," Jules said.

"Not my best day." The blond rolled her eyes. Mascara and eyeliner streaked her face and gave her a raccoon look. "The cops think I killed Tabbi. Don't get me wrong, I despised her and often wished her dead, but I didn't do it. But now it looks like I did." She rested her head on one arm and sobbed. "That woman continues to ruin my life even after she's dead. And really, why are you so interested?"

Jules shrugged her shoulders. "It happened at my resort, so I'm curious. Did you get any indication of why they think it's you?" Jules leaned against the gray wall.

"They said they had evidence, and it would be easier if I confessed. They found a purse and my gun." She wiped a tear that escaped the corner of her eye with the back of her hand.

"The red purse was yours? Did they say anything about ballistics tests?"

Misti shook her head and wiped her nose on her sleeve. "No, just that it was going to prove that I did it, and I should confess if I knew what was good for me. They said it would save some time. It is my gun, but not my purse."

"How did your gun get in someone else's purse?"

"I have no idea," she sniffed. "I usually keep it in my nightstand or in the glove compartment of the truck."

"When did you last see it?" Jules leaned forward, waiting for Misti to answer.

"I don't know. Probably when we left to go to your place. I threw it in the glove compartment of Cal's Humvee."

"Do you always leave it somewhere?"

Misti frowned at her. "When I'm not near the big cats. We all carry guns when we're near the habitats. Stun or tranq guns don't give you enough time if you're in an emergency situation. We all carry guns. Cal insists on it. You don't want to put yourself in a dangerous situation with wild animals. But I don't carry it around otherwise. Thankfully, I've never had to use it."

Jules nodded. "What about the other stuff in the purse? Was it yours?"

A puzzled look flashed across Misti's face. "No. Only the gun was mine." Misti looked up and wiped her eyes. "I don't wear that brand of cosmetics. It looked like something my grandma would have had."

"What about the picture?"

Misti shrugged her shoulders. "We're entertainers. Everybody wants to take pictures with us or the animals. I can't tell you how many pictures Cal and I have posed for over the years. And she was married to him. The picture could have been old, like the purse." Misti looked up and blinked her damp lashes.

"What about the voodoo doll?"

The younger woman made a face and shook her head. Her curls drooped around her puffy face. "I don't mess with stuff like that. I don't need any bad juju or vibes or whatever you call it. I don't have any dolls with pins in them. How do you know so much?" Misti raised her head and stared at Jules.

"My groundskeeper found the purse on the property. We thought it belonged to Tabbi."

"If it does, she had bad taste. It looked vintage to me, and not in a good way. Why would I carry a picture around of my husband and his ex? That's stupid. I would have burned it." Misti blew her bangs out of her face and stared at Jules. "I heard you've helped the sheriff solve murders around here before."

Jules's brow furrowed. "From whom?"

"People talk. Cal's getting a lawyer, but I don't know if it's going to do any good. I'm still in here, and it's not the nicest place in the world. I'll try anything." Misti tried to push a stray lock out of her face, but her cuffed wrist wouldn't stretch that far. She leaned forward, almost prone on the table, and pushed the hair away.

"Maybe I could help. Start from the beginning," Jules said.

"You'd help me?" Misti suddenly looked like a scared kid with big blue eyes.

"I'll try. But you need to tell me what happened. Everything."

Misti's glance darted around the holding room. She blew out a breath.

"Years ago, I was hired to do a commercial at Cal's Cats. It was for some car dealer, and I got to hang out with the trainers and big cats. It was fun. I went back later, and Cal and I hit it off. He and Tabbi were on the outs by then. She still says I broke up their marriage, but he couldn't stand her. When the divorce was final, we got married the next day. Cal is wonderful. And I get to live at the zoo. Who could ask for anything better?" Misti tried to wave her hand, but the restraint clinked and kept her connected to the table.

"Any reason to think Tabbi was trying to get Cal back?"

Misti rolled her eyes so hard that Jules was afraid she had jarred them loose. "No. Why would he go back to that jalopy? He's moved on. She's old news. She may have tried, but Cal wasn't interested. He traded up."

My camera feed begs to differ. Jules didn't say anything about Cal and Tabbi at the barn. "So, there were no problems with your marriage?"

Misti frowned and paused. "Everyone has problems, but no, we have no issues. I'm happily married. There is no one else if that's what you're asking. And before you ask, the age difference doesn't matter to us."

"You're sure you never noticed that your gun was missing?" Jules probed. Misti nodded.

"And the red purse wasn't yours?" Jules asked.

"It looks like something my mother would have taken to prom in the eighties. No, it's not mine. I didn't have reason to go look for my gun. I wasn't near the animals except for the show, and Cal and Cody were there. I put my gun in the glove box when we left home."

"It sounds like someone is trying to set you up. Any ideas of who or why?"

Misti shook her head. "I'd say Tabbi, but that's not a problem anymore. Her tall, toady friend is always mouthy, but she hides behind Tabbi. I doubt if she would even bother. I really don't know. Maybe it is her..." Her voice trailed off.

"Any disgruntled employees, rivals, or sworn enemies? Any other women from Cal's past?"

She shook her head again. "No. Everyone loves Cal and the cats. He's friendly and outgoing. People naturally flock to him. They like to be near him."

"Anything else you can think of? Any problems with the business? Anyone you've had conflicts with?"

"Cal? Why do you keep asking about him? Our relationship is fine." Misti's face reddened, and she stared at Jules.

"Just thought I'd check," Jules said.

"Cal and me are fine." Misti squinted. "I did have this one girl when I was modeling that was so jealous of me. She would do anything to sabotage me. Her name was Nikki Nicely. Other than that, I can't think of anything else."

"What about Lizzie Edmonds?" Jules asked.

"What?" Misti sucked in air and paused. "How did you know about that?" It looked like a dark cloud descended on Misti. Her gaze turned steely, and she pursed her lips.

"I'm good at research."

"That has nothing to do with this," Misti snapped. "I'd appreciate it if you kept it to yourself. I don't need people spreading rumors. That was a tragic accident. We'll never know."

"If I can find it, the police can, too." Jules stared back at the woman whose face hardened instantly.

"I can't see how it would be relevant," she snapped back.

"A pattern of behavior."

Misti made a face. "The two situations have nothing to do with each other. It was a long time ago. I was on the pageant circuit with her. We were friends." Misti clenched her teeth. "We roomed together sometimes. Then everything changed."

After a long pause, Misti continued. "We were extremely competitive. Lizzie started sabotaging my stuff. It was little things at first. Like an earring disappeared right before going on stage, then someone cut the cord on my curling iron, and if I hadn't noticed it, I would have gotten a shock. Then there was a stain on my white, satin shoes. I knew it was Lizzie. She wanted to win. She'd do anything to be the best."

"How did you know it was Lizzie?"

Misti blinked several times like she didn't understand the question.

"I dunno. I knew it. I found my lipstick in her bag. After that, we kept harassing each other. We kept upping the ante. I cut the strap on one of her evening dresses, and another time, I hid her Spanx. She put a tuna sandwich in a side pocket of my suitcase, and I didn't find it for weeks. She also put a roach in my take-out."

"Sounds juvenile."

"It was. But we were young. It felt good at the time." A slight smile crossed Misti's lips. "Looking back on it, it was stupid, and it went too far. But she needed to be taught a lesson. She had no right to come after me. Then things changed. We found out at a pageant that she had died of an accidental overdose. She took gobs of pills to keep her weight down. It was tragic, but I had nothing to do with it. Anyway, her sister knew of the feud we had, and she accused me of killing Lizzie. I was sad that she died so young. I did harmless little pranks to annoy her. I didn't kill her."

"It didn't escalate to something more serious?" Jules challenged. "Like a prank with the pills? A prank that went wrong?"

"You've got to believe me. I had nothing to do with her death. The timing was bad. It happened when everyone knew we were going at each other. Back then, people were either Team Misti or Team Lizzie." She sat up straight in the metal chair. "Plus, the police never charged me. They didn't find enough evidence." Misti made a harrumphing sound and sat back in her chair hard enough to make it skid on the industrial floor. "I may have done some childish pranks, but I didn't kill anyone then or now. Hey, could you tell them out there that I'm hungry? The food and the service in this place are terrible."

Jules stared at her for a moment and then nodded. She banged on the door, and the door squeaked open.

"Call me if you think of anything else," Jules said over her shoulder.

"Yep. Hey, policeman, what's it take to get food around here?" Misti yelled as Deputy Hawkins closed the door.

"She said to tell you that she's hungry," Jules said to the deputy as she followed him back to the locker.

"She's always hungry. And she thinks we have room service."

Jules grinned and retrieved her belongings.

Once inside the Jeep, Jules rummaged through her purse and called Pixel. "Hey, there. How are you?"

"Good. Work's been busy. But I always have time to talk to you. You have the most interesting things happen around you."

Jules heard Pixel tapping. "I'm still looking into the dead woman's story, and I was wondering if you could check on a few things for me. Cal Collins, his business, and Misti Collins. The sheriff arrested the wife for the ex-wife's murder. Misti said she didn't do it. I asked her about Lizzie Edmonds. She said they had a rivalry that turned nasty, but she didn't kill anyone. When I asked if she had any enemies, she mentioned some model named Nikki Nicely."

"Sounds like a stripper."

Jules stifled a laugh. "Misti didn't offer much new information except her denials about almost everything."

Pixel cleared her throat. "I'll see what I can find on Misti and her inner circle. You don't think she did it?"

"She might have. The evidence points to her, but something's not right with all of this. Cal left Tabbi for her, so there's definitely no love lost between the two women. And then I have Cal and Tabbi in a dalliance at the resort. Lester found a red purse on my property with a gun and a photo of Tabbi and Cal. Misti claims the gun, but not the rest of the stuff. It's odd."

"I'll dig around. Let's have lunch this week." Pixel said.

"Sounds fun. I appreciate all of your help. You have a knack for finding stuff that the rest of us don't have access to."

Pixel laughed. "I'll send you what I come across. I like helping you with your quests."

Jules ended the call and headed back to her office. She had hit a roadblock with this one. Maybe if she cleared her head and looked over all her notes later, something would pop out. But first, she needed to see what was in her fridge for lunch.

After half of a ham and swiss sandwich and some apple sauce, Jules spread her notes across the kitchen table. Sheriff Hobbs had reason to believe Misti was the killer, but something about the whole situation was nagging at the back of Jules's brain. She couldn't quite put her finger on it.

She taped three pieces of paper together and drew a timeline of events. Then, at the bottom, she transferred all the names. She found a red pen and started drawing lines to connect all the players again. The thing that jumped out was all the multiple lines for the romantic relationships, and they were the same connections she had jotted down earlier. She'd hit a brick wall. Jules packed her Tabbi files and whistled for Bijou. "Come on. Let's go see what's going on in the office."

Bijou sniffed everything around the golf cart and the back steps. The dog was reluctant to go inside. She returned to the edge of the golf cart to sniff. Jules paused when she reached for the door. Another note, thumbtacked to the wooden door, fluttered in the chilly breeze. She let out a sigh and yanked it down.

Today's message in black marker was like the rest and read, "I told you to stop asking questions. You'll be sorry. Pay attention and heed the warning."

"What is going on here?" Jules asked as she opened the door.

"I'm updating our end-of-year books," Roxanne said, looking up from her computer screen.

"Has anyone been through this door today?"

Her aunt shook her head.

"I found another note tacked to it." Jules booted her laptop to check the camera feeds. "Someone is really concerned that I've been looking into Tabbi's murder. Why do the notes keep coming?"

"That's curious."

Jules started the long slog of scanning camera feeds to see if her security cameras caught the mysterious person. Jules looked through hours of footage in fast-forward.

Nothing looked out of place. Jules stretched and yawned. The screen tipped, and the feed went dark.

Jules sat up straight and reversed the feed. She froze the scene when a figure in a dark hoodie crept into the picture. She'd missed that before. The person was fairly tall, but the shadowy figure stepped out of the camera's range, and she couldn't see the face. Then she saw a gloved hand reach up, and the camera jerked. The feed went black.

She paused the video and stepped outside. The camera hung limply under the carport's eave. "Great. That'll need to be fixed or replaced," Jules muttered, sending Jake a text on her way inside.

She set her phone on the edge of the desk, and it chimed. **I'm on it**, Jake replied.

"Well, rats," her aunt exclaimed, and Jules jumped. "I thought I was packing up to meet Matt for dinner, but he got called to a scene. They found a body over behind the high school." Roxanne set her phone down on her desk.

"What?" Jules's eyes widened.

"That's all the text says. I'll see what I can find out." Her aunt tapped on her phone's screen and sent a flurry of texts.

While Roxanne mined the Fern Valley gossip mill, Jules picked up her phone and called Lester.

After about the fourth ring, she heard, "What's up, Jules?"

"Hi, Lester. Sorry to bother you. I heard someone found a body at the school."

"Oh, yes. The scanner is on fire again today. Sawyer Kelley was jogging on the track and spotted something weird near the dumpster. The sheriff, forensics, and the state boys are over there now working on the crime scene."

"Any idea who the victim was?"

"No, but they say 'she' every once in a while instead of the victim. They're acting like it's related to the other murder. I'll let you know if I hear anything juicy."

"Thanks, Lester," Jules said, disconnecting.

"It's a woman," Roxanne said, looking up from her phone. "No one local. I heard it was that friend of Tabbi's."

"Dana?" Jules stared at her aunt.

"Yep, the one who came in here yesterday. The one who always looked like she was wearing throwback costumes." Roxanne's voice trailed off.

"Lester's got his headphones on. He'll let us know if anything else comes across the airwaves."

"Well, I'm out. I'll see what I can find for dinner for one. I'll let you know if I hear anything else from Matt. You do the same if you get some good four-one-one."

Jules nodded. A somber mood clouded her thoughts as she gathered her things.

First Tabbi, and now her friend, Dana. And still more weird notes. And Misti's sitting in Sheriff Hobbs's jail.

Chapter Twenty-One

Tuesday

Jules spent the next morning trying to concentrate. She surfed through hundreds of internet pages, not finding anything new about Dana or Tabbi. Frustrated, Jules left Bijou with Roxanne to mind the office, and she hopped in the Jeep for a trip to Verona. Maybe a change of scenery would help clear her head. She plugged in Cal's address in the GPS and took a swig of her espresso. From the map, his facility was north of Staunton. She cranked up the tunes and the heater and decided not to contact Cal ahead of time. Maybe the element of surprise would lead to some new information.

The ride felt quick to Jules. She was in Staunton, home to President Woodrow Wilson's presidential library, in no time. She located the exit to Quick's Mill Road and followed its curves until she spotted Cal's trademark signs with the red slash and the glowing tiger eyes.

An asphalt driveway led to a graveled lot. Jules parked next to two sedans and walked to the gate. A young blond in a tight safari suit worked the ticket booth behind a large glass window. She slid the pane open slightly to hear Jules's request.

"Hi, I'm Jules Keene. Is Cal around today? He stayed at my resort a few weeks ago, and he invited me up to see his place."

The girl raised one eyebrow. "Let me see. He was doing the feeding rounds earlier." She clicked a walkie-talkie. Her voice went up an octave. "Cal, Come in, Cal."

"What's up, Chelsea?"

"There's a redhead here at the gate who said she met you last weekend at her place."

Cal muttered something that Jules didn't catch. Then she heard, "Oh, I know who it is. Be up in a few."

"You can wait over there," Chelsea pointed to the sidewalk on the other side of the gate.

"I appreciate it," Jules said as Chelsea pushed the window closed hard enough for it to rattle. The young woman returned to her phone, but she did cast a sideways glance at Jules every once in a while.

Jules stepped through the wooden gate and pulled her coat closer. She wished she had worn a hat. The breeze caused her ears and nose to tingle. The longer she waited, the more frozen her feet felt. She stomped and moved around to get the blood flowing.

Finally, a desert-camouflaged ATV pulled up and skidded to a stop next to her. "Hey, I remember you," Cal shouted. "Hop in. I'll give you the tour. You picked one of the coldest days to visit."

Jules had barely gotten situated in the seat before Cal slammed it into gear and kicked up a cloud of dust and gravel.

"What brings you out this way?" He flew past fenced-in areas with small wooden buildings the size of sheds. "This is where we let some of the cats out to lounge and play on sunny days. The apes are over there." He pointed in front of her.

"I wanted to stop by and see how you all were doing. I heard about Misti."

He scowled for a moment and then returned to his showman persona. "We've hired a lawyer. He's doing his best to get her out of there. So far, that sheriff is being stubborn. He insists that his case is rock solid. He doesn't know Misti like I do. She's incapable of killing anything, including a bug."

Jules turned her head and gave her best confused-puppy look.

He kept talking, "It was her gun. But she was set up. They found it in a purse with a picture of me and Tabbi. I have my picture taken with thousands of people each year. That doesn't prove anything. Plus, Tabbi was part of the team for a while. I'm sure there are tons of pictures out there. Misti wouldn't hurt a fly."

But she would sabotage another beauty pageant contestant.

He stopped the vehicle suddenly. "This is the tiger area. Right now, we have about thirty tigers in these cement buildings. They all have access to the runs and play areas. He hopped out and whistled.

A white tiger and a large orange male trotted over to the fence area. This is Snowball and Khan. The orange tiger rubbed against the fencing. Cal jumped over the barrier and rubbed the side of the big cat, who purred like the domesticated variety.

"They are beautiful. I enjoyed your show and seeing the cubs. They were a hit in Fern Valley."

"We have five to six cubs born here each season as part of our successful breeding program. We're proud to help endangered species."

"Do you keep all of them? That's a lot of animals."

"Can't. It's a fortune to feed and care for so many grown cats. We can sell and trade them with zoos and other reserves. But we have to make sure they go to good homes. We've also adopted some through the years because they were confiscated from private individuals who had no business keeping a big cat. Our shows bankroll the operation, and we have the cat rescue charity as part of our umbrella of offerings. Donations help for the care of our beauties." He scratched the tiger behind the ears, and it yawned.

"The rescue cats live out their lives here. Not a bad gig for animals who were in roadside zoos or in cramped cages. We give them lots of space and try to keep the habitats as natural as possible." Cal hopped over the barrier. "Come on. I'll show you the lions."

They drove around the corner and down a path. Five lions lounged on rocks near a small pond. "We ended up with some circus lions when the company went under. They sleep most of the time during the day."

He continued down the path around a large wooden stage with bench seating. On the other side, zebras and antelope grazed in a field. A pair of camels watched them drive by. "The cheetahs and leopards are back there. On that side, we have feeding and educational rooms. We do podcasts and classes, and we have a medical center and a massive kitchen."

Two blond women in safari outfits hauled buckets inside the zebra enclosure. The animals stormed the area for breakfast when the women neared the trough. Jules hadn't seen any men on the property except Cal. *Interesting.*

"Oh, I forgot the reptile house," Cal said.

Jules shuddered.

"I guess you don't want a tour of that. How about we feed the bears?"

Jules smiled. "I would love to see the bears. You have a nice place. The open-space designs are wonderful. It doesn't look like the small cages of the zoos I remember."

"Our mission is to let them live as close to natural as they can." He put the vehicle and in gear and drove to the back of the facility. "This is where Raj and Freeda live. They were part of a traveling show that did the fair circuit until their owner couldn't take care of them anymore." He whistled, and two large black bears lumbered toward the fence. Cal exited and pulled out an orange bucket from the cargo area. "Hey, lovelies. Who wants a snack?"

Raj raised his paw. Then Freeda copied him.

Cal climbed over the barrier and held something up for Raj. He took it, and then it was Freeda's turn. "They've got an entire act. The crowds love them."

"They're adorable. I've always been fond of bears." Jules watched as the pair waited for more treats. Raj stood and danced. Freeda rolled over on her back.

Cal handed over the snacks to the delight of the giant mammals.

When the treats stopped, the bears lost interest and ambled back to the building.

"Thank you so much for showing me around."

"You should come back in the summer. I offer weekend and vacation packages for people who want to get up close and work with the animals. Might be right up your alley." Cal winked and sped down another path that led through a wooded area.

Jules stiffened and sat up on high alert. It looked like a scene out of every murder movie she had ever seen. The path, surrounded by trees, looked like the entrance to the forest. It would have been darker and spookier if the trees had had their full canopy.

Her heartbeat jumped into overdrive. *Where were we going?*

A few yards later, the path opened up to a manicured yard. Jules exhaled. A large farmhouse with a detached triple garage and a white picket fence appeared out of nowhere at the end of the driveway. A blond with a laundry basket opened the side door to the garage. Cal waved, and she saluted on her way inside. *Definitely lots of blonds around.*

They drove past two smaller houses on the property. Around the next corner, several cinder block buildings appeared. "Those are the backs of our kitchen and clinic. There's also a reptile and creatures of the night exhibit in that building." Cal pointed over his shoulder as they sped by the buildings.

"The grounds are huge," Jules said.

"Size is everything in this business. You should really think about coming back for our big cat retreat. I think you'd really enjoy it." Cal chuckled at his comment.

"I'll see if my boyfriend is interested. That might be something fun we can do for our anniversary."

Cal nodded and sped up. He skidded to a stop near the ticket booth and concession stand. "Back safe and sound. No boogie monsters." Like he could read her thoughts.

"Thank you so much for the tour. I'll check in on Misti when I get back. If I can help with anything, please let me know." Jules jumped out of the ATV.

Cal nodded and sped off.

Jules wandered into the gift shop before she headed home. The amount of big cat merchandise crammed in such a small area was overwhelming. It looked like a firetrap.

"May I help you?" a petite blond in a leopard-print catsuit asked.

"I'm looking for a souvenir for my boyfriend." Jules wandered past stuffed animals to a wall of T-shirts. "It must be fun to be at the zoo all day."

"We're primarily a big cat rescue. We have exhibits and shows to educate the public about endangered species," she said like she was reading off a cue card.

"This is such a cool place. I'm gonna come back when it's warmer. How long have you worked here? By the way, I'm Jules."

"I'm Jess." She pointed to her big cat paw name tag. "I've been here since high school. Cal and his team are the best. In fact, he's my brother-in-law."

"You're Misti's sister?"

The girl raised one overly manicured eyebrow. "Uh, no. Not that wife. My sister was Tabbi."

"Oh, I'm so sorry for your loss." Jules hoped she hid her surprise.

The girl shrugged. "She's really my half-sister, so her death didn't ruin my life. We didn't grow up together." Jess twirled a strand of her hair. "We weren't that close. Big age difference and all that."

"Our sheriff thinks Misti killed Tabbi. Do you know if Misti had a gun?" Jules whispered.

"They all do. Cal gives all his girls who work with the big cats a gun and a knife for emergencies. When you're in an enclosure with a wild predator, you never know what will happen. They're not domesticated. The cats, I mean."

Jules leaned closer. "Have there been accidents?"

"Uh-uh. Not that I know of. Cal's real big on following safety protocols. We get quizzed on procedures all the time. But if you search the internet, you'll see all kinds of gruesome videos of animal attacks in other places. You know, like Siegfried and Roy."

Jules frowned and picked up a bear T-shirt and a mug for Jake. "I'll take these. Oh, and this." She handed the woman a zebra-striped dog collar. She paid and took the bag. "Do you think Misti really did it?"

Jess shrugged again. "They didn't like each other, but I can't see Misti as a killer. She's all talk. If you confronted her, she'd run crying to Cal. A little weaselly, if you ask me. The team liked Tabbi better, but we didn't have much say. Cal makes the decisions."

Jules chewed on her bottom lip. "So, you stayed even after Tabbi left?"

Jess looked up like she was bored. "It wasn't my fight. Like I said, Tabbi and I weren't exactly buds. I like working here. I get to play with all kinds of animals. It's a cool place, and I get material for my video channel. I can't help it that Tabbi couldn't go with the flow. She always had to nag. No wonder Cal moved on." She shrugged her shoulder.

Sensing the conversation was over, Jules said, "Thanks. I'm gonna come back for one of your weekend gigs in the spring."

"You may like it so much you'll want to stay," Jess said, not looking up from her phone.

Jules hightailed it to the Jeep. For all appearances, the zoo was a happy place, but something bothered her. Jules didn't really relax until she made it to the interstate. She had a little more information to add to her suspect diagram. Everyone affiliated with Cal's Cats seemed to be related or young and blond.

Chapter Twenty-Two

Wednesday

Jules flopped around in bed for hours. The whole Tabbi and Misti thing bothered her. Now Tabbi's friend was dead. Around one-thirty, she pulled on her fluffy bathrobe and moved to her couch with her laptop and a mug of tea. Bijou, whose snores echoed through the quiet living room, had no trouble sleeping on the lap blanket.

Ticking through the facts again in her head, Jules looked at her notes and suspect diagram for anything she missed the first twenty times. Tabbi was murdered. Misti was arrested. Then Dana was murdered. They found a purse with Misti's gun. Someone was leaving warning notes for Jules even after Misti's arrest. There had to be a connection between the two murders, but Misti couldn't have murdered Dana.

She read Cal's entire website and jotted down any name she could find. All the staff listed were female and blond, except for Cal's son. *Very odd. You'd think there would be some guys on the team.* Jules couldn't find any reference to Cal's other child. Didn't Pixel say Cody had a brother or sister? And her conversation with Tabbi's half-sister was odd. At the wake, Fiona didn't mention anything about Tabbi having a sister. Jules didn't remember seeing Jess there, but it was crowded.

Not having any a-ha moments, Jules pulled up the camera feeds, starting with the date of the first note. She spent hours watching each recording to see if she had missed anything.

When her shoulders ached and her eyes burned, she padded to the kitchen for more hot tea. She stifled a yawn and returned to the couch. So far, she had scoured two days of camera footage with nothing to show for her efforts except watching hours of clips of her guests and her team coming and going.

At the point she was ready to give up, something flashed across the screen from the camera near the store. She backed it up and slowed it down. A grayish-colored car zoomed in the parking lot after midnight. She jotted down the date and time. A muscle car? About twenty minutes later, the car sped down the resort's entrance. *Could it be?* She checked all the other cameras for the same date and time stamp. One captured a big guy with dark hair jogging toward the parking lot at twelve twenty. Bingo. She caught Tabbi's Tony skulking around her property in the wee hours. She missed this on her last search.

Now wide awake, Jules searched every camera feed for that time frame. The other trace of him was in the parking lot. He jumped into his Charger and flew down the entrance road with no lights on. Jules copied both of the film clips and sent an email to the sheriff.

Tony had been leaving warnings even after Misti had been arrested. So either he didn't know about Misti, or he had other reasons. Too antsy to go back to bed, she poured over all of her notes on Tony and Tabbi. He worked at the Rock Bodies Gym in Berryville. On their site, there was a cheesy photo of the trainer, and a bio that touted all his competition wins. Jules jotted down the address and headed down the hall for a quick shower.

After a banana and another espresso to ward off the yawns, she filled Bijou's bowls and patted the dog on the head. "I'll be back soon."

Jules texted Jake and Roxanne that she had some errands to do and that she'd be in later in the afternoon. She refilled her coffee and headed off to Berryville.

About an hour from her destination, the sun peaked over the mountain ridge, painting the sky in a swirl of orangey pink. Jules found a rest stop, where she pulled off to stretch her legs and snap some pictures of the sunrise. She checked the gym's web page again. It opened at five. Jules cranked up a classic rock station and settled in for the final leg of her road trip.

166

At about the point she started to feel squirmy, the sign for the exit to Berryville appeared. Jules followed the voice on her GPS to a strip mall. The gym sat as the anchor store location that might have been a supermarket in a past life. Teal and purple LED lights outlined the large glass windows and pulsed to create a disco look from another decade.

Jules put her keys and phone in her coat pocket and hid her purse from view inside the Jeep. She hiked to the front door.

"Good morning. It's a great day for fitness," the tall brunette at the reception desk said as Jules fumbled with the huge door. "I'm Kaycee. How can I help you?"

"Hi, I'm Jules. I was hoping to talk to Tony briefly about some personal training. He gave me his card a while back and said to stop in if I needed his services."

"Sure. I think he's with a client right now, but if you have a seat over there, I'll let him know you're here."

Jules smiled sweetly and sat in one of the oval chairs by the front window.

After checking her email four times, scanning Instagram, and counting people coming and going through the door, she spotted Tony as he trudged to the lobby area in a black muscle shirt and shiny cycling pants. With a red towel draped over his shoulders, he glanced around as he walked, checking out who was watching him.

"Hi, Jules. It's good to see you." He cranked up his kilowatt smile, but his eyes made her doubt his sincerity. *At least he remembered my name this time.*

"Hi, Tony. Do you have a minute to talk? I wanted to check on things and see the wonderful gym that everyone talked about at Tabbi's wake. And since I had an errand nearby, I decided to stop in."

The bodybuilder flinched but recovered quickly, never losing the smarmy smile. "Sure. Welcome. Come on back, and I'll show you what we offer. We have a great facility here. It's well worth your investment. Uh, and think of it as an investment in yourself."

As they walked through the rows and rows of cardio machines and treadmills, Tony rambled on about the importance of exercise and what their program had to offer. Jules noticed that there were more women on

167

the exercise equipment while most of the men congregated in the area with the weight machines.

Tony paused in front of the tiny café in the back and leaned against the bar. "So, what brings you all the way out here? You interested in personal training?"

Jules smiled. "I am, but I'm here to check in with you all. I was concerned after the wake, and I wanted to make sure everything was okay. A tragic and sudden death can be such a shock."

Tony looked puzzled for a moment. "Thanks. We're fine. Getting back to our normal lives."

"I was so sorry to hear about Dana, too."

Tony shrugged, and his gaze darted around the room.

"How's Sheena?"

"She's good. She'll be in later before her shift tonight starts. She's serious about her fitness routine. She comes in every day that I'm here."

"That's good. Hey, while I've got you, we're planning to have a spring festival in Fern Valley with lots of vendors. How do I get in contact with y'all now? I have Tabbi's card."

"Sheena and I are planning to keep the business. Here's my card. You can use this contact information until I get the business switched over to us. We're gonna change it to something like Tony's Tees." He laughed like it was an incredibly original idea.

Jules pocketed the card. "Thanks. I hope you all had good sales at the Christmas festival."

"Pretty good. It would have been better if all the events were in one place. We didn't benefit when the crowds were not in town."

"Good point. All the spring events will be around the town square. We heard that feedback from several of the vendors. Other than that, was everything else okay?"

"Yup. Sheena and I liked your resort. We plan to come back in the summer for a vacation. The spring thing will be good for us. Do you have the dates? I want to get it on our calendar."

"They haven't been finalized yet, but I'll email you as soon as I have the info. I met Tabbi's sister. I didn't remember seeing her at Amigos that night."

He frowned. "What? She didn't have a sister. Uh, you mean Jess? She's not her real sister. Tabbi's dad left when she was a kid. They weren't close. Jess thinks somehow working at Cal's is going to propel her into some kind of showbiz career."

"She was working in the gift shop when I met her."

"She's trying to worm her way into Cal's shows. She thinks she's about to be discovered."

Jules nodded. "Could I ask you something?" Jules lowered her voice. "Do you know if Tabbi had a gun? We found one at my resort."

Tony's eyes widened. "You still have it?"

Jules shook her head. "I turned it over to the sheriff. I'm sure they're doing fingerprinting and ballistics on it."

"No, Tabbi didn't have a gun. She hated them."

"That's interesting. We found it in a purse with a picture of her and Cal."

Tony winced. "Who knows? I couldn't keep up with all her purses, shoes, and things. It's going to take months to clean out her closet. She wasn't the most organized. The business records are a mess, too." His voice trailed off.

"Hey, did I see you Sunday night in Fern Valley?"

"Uh, no. Why would I be there? We checked out that morning. I had to work that day."

"You must have a twin then. I saw this guy who looked like you. Anyway, I'll make sure we notify you as soon as we start taking vendor applications for the spring. Will you and Sheena have the same kind of merchandise?"

"Uh, probably, and then some new stuff. Sheena has ideas to rebrand us. Something hip and fresh. We'll still do T-shirts. Sheena wants more flair and modern stuff. Not sure if we'll do the big cat thing anymore. That was Tabbi's idea. I have lots of plans."

Two women in tight workout outfits sidled up. "Hey, Tony," the taller of the two women purred. "You ready for us?"

"Hey, Terri and Patrice. This is Jules. We're wrapping up here. Go over and start your warm-up stretches, and I'll be there in a sec. And no skimping."

"I don't want to keep you. See you at the spring fling." Jules did a slight wave as Tony turned his attention to Terri and Patrice in their shiny purple and pink outfits.

On her way out, Jules stopped at the desk and waited for Kaycee to finish her call. "Hi. I was thinking about scheduling some personal training with Tony. Does he work every day? I'm trying to figure out my schedule."

"He usually works six days a week. But he was out a lot last week, so we're playing catch-up with his regular appointments. If you tell me what day you're interested in, I can check the calendar."

"Let me check my boyfriend's schedule, and I'll give you a call. Thanks."

Jules hurried out the door. Her stomach rumbled, so she did a quick drive-through for a snack and an iced tea at a Sonics before she headed home.

Tony had lied about being in Fern Valley on Sunday. She caught him on camera, and he sounded pretty confident about taking over and rebranding Tabbi's business. Would that be a strong enough motive to want her out of the picture? Does he know that the police have a suspect in custody?

Chapter Twenty-Three

Thursday

J ules spent the morning wrapping presents at her kitchen table. Her plan was to take it easy this week. Work was slow, and she wouldn't have to put in full days in the office until New Year's Eve. A much-needed break.

She even baked several kinds of Christmas cookies. The cabin smelled like sugar and cinnamon, and Bijou, suddenly interested in all of the action in the kitchen, was constantly underfoot in case anything good hit the floor.

Jules looked forward to this evening. Jake was coming over for dinner and to help her decorate her Christmas tree. She hadn't pulled out her decorations since her dad passed away. It was time to rekindle some of her family's traditions. She missed her parents most at the holidays.

Jules prepped a lasagna and put it in the fridge to heat up later. She dusted her hands on her jeans and said, "Well, I'm about ready for tonight. Let me run the vacuum, and we should be good to go." At the sight of the vroom broom, Bijou hightailed it to the bedroom.

She finished and unplugged Bijou's sworn enemy and surveyed her place. There was enough space for the artificial tree in the corner by the window.

Jules had an idea to add to her holiday collection. She picked up her coat and keys and slipped out before Bijou noticed. Jules's mom had always liked Christmas. She promised herself that it was time to make new memories.

Jules opened the office's back door and flipped on the lights as she walked through to the store. She perused the peach baskets at the bottom of the tree and selected some of the Virginia ornaments to add to her collection.

Jules made a list of the ones she chose for the cost of inventory reconciliation next week. She shut off all the lights and made her way through the darkened store, and let herself out the front.

As she turned the knob to check the lock, something white caught her eye. Another note.

She let out a heavy sigh and yanked on the paper with its message, "I warned you before. Something bad is going to happen if you keep this up."

Jules ran home to check the camera feeds. If it were Tony, why would he drive two hours to leave her a message? It seemed a little over the top. What else was going on here?

About twenty minutes later, Jules yelled, "A-ha!" and startled Bijou. Jules spotted Tony on last night's camera feed creeping across the parking lot to the store. He pulled something out of his pocket and looked around. He tacked up the note and ran back to his car. On another camera, she caught a good shot of his car. Someone waited in the passenger seat. In the next shot, Tony jogged over, hesitated, and looked around before climbing into the car like he heard something. The pair sat in the car for a while. She couldn't tell what was going on inside. Then, several minutes later, the car rolled out of the lot and exited without headlights.

Jules backed up that camera feed to catch the pair pulling into the resort. Again, they sat in the car awhile before Tony climbed out. When he opened the car door, there was enough light that she could identify his passenger, Sheena.

She sent the clips to the sheriff with a photo of the latest note. It was odd that the two would drive all the way down here to leave notes. The mail would have been easier.

Jules shook off the weird feeling. Time to put the lasagna in the oven. She'd worry about Tony and Sheena later.

She set the table and found goblets and her red tablecloth. A knock interrupted her decorating. Jake arrived with a stack of red and green boxes.

"What are all these?" she asked, taking his coat.

"I found some decorations if you need them."

"How sweet. I haven't pulled mine out in a while. I had a few of my own, and then there were boxes of what mom and dad had. This is the first Christmas that I've felt like decorating."

"Where's the tree?"

"In the back bedroom. I bought it because it was already pre-lit. I got tired of untangling the balls of light strings. Dinner will be ready in about fifteen minutes."

"Plenty of time. I'll have the tree up by then. We'll race. Go."

Jules laughed pulled out the salad, and put the garlic bread on a cookie tray.

As the oven timer beeped, Jake yelled, "Taa-dah!" as he plugged in the tree. The lights came on and started to twinkle.

"Beautiful. And just in time. Dinner's ready." She dimmed the lights, and they ate by Christmas lights.

"This is good," Jake said, reaching for the garlic bread. "You outdid yourself."

"Family recipe. What have you been up to today?"

"The house is framed and roofed. I did the two sections, so we'll have to move them in and attach them on-site. I hope to have it drywalled next week, but that means I have to have all the plumbing and wiring done. We'll see. I'm gonna need more guys to help me move this one in place. The others were small enough to handle with two people."

"Hey, Roxanne wants to know if we want to come by her house for Christmas Day brunch."

"Sounds good. I haven't celebrated with family since I went to Los Angeles to see my sister and her kids. Lately, it's been Zoom." He grinned. "I binge-watched Bruce Lee movies and had left-over pizza last year."

"Always a holiday favorite. I watched the Hallmark Channel last Christmas." She pushed a stray curl behind her ear. "I'm glad we'll be celebrating together this year." She stared at Jake and felt the flutter of butterflies in her core. "The lodge looks beautiful with all the decorations. The guests loved them and the roaring fireplace. I was feeling a little guilty about not hosting anything there this year. Next year, we'll have a big bash."

Jake winked and added salad to his bowl.

"Time got away from me this with all the festival events, and well, you know. Maybe some peace on earth would be nice for a change."

"And we can make our own first Christmas tradition."

The butterflies changed into a charge of excitement that coursed through Jules. She smiled. "That would be nice. What'd you have in mind?"

"Dinner's a good start. Let's get your tree decorated."

"And watch Christmas movies." Jules cleared the table.

"Does *Die Hard* count?" he asked.

Jules rolled her eyes. "Sure. As long as I get to see *A Christmas Story*."

"Not a problem. That's a classic. Let me help you clean up in here."

Jules stowed the leftovers and put everything away while Jake stacked the dishwasher.

"Done," she said. She turned on the TV and found *A Charlie Brown Christmas*.

"You didn't tell me what you've been up to lately?" Jake placed the blond angel on the top of the tree. Any ideas for our beach trip?"

Jules grinned. "There are a lot of places to stop to see stuff on our winter beach extravaganza. First, are you okay with stopping, or are you one of those people who want to get to the destination in record time?"

"It's not a race. I haven't driven to Florida in a long time. I was a kid when we drove to Disney World. Let's see stuff."

"I'm thinking Charleston, Savannah, St. Augustine, Daytona, and Miami. We can see some on the way down and the others on the trip back."

"Sounds like a plan, but we have to stop at South of the Border. My parents always stopped there on all our trips south."

Jules laughed. "Definitely. I loved all the funny billboards. We stopped there and at every Stuckey's we passed."

The pair fell silent as they decorated the tree. A napping Bijou opened her eyes from time to time to make sure she wasn't missing anything.

"You look lost in thought," Jake said as Jules stared at the tree.

"Want something to drink?" she asked.

Jake shook his head, and Jules continued, "I was thinking about Tabbi and Dana. The sheriff has Misti in custody for the murder of Tabbi. It's plausible, but there was the second murder and the warning notes that happened while she was in jail. So, if Misti committed the first one, then there has to be a second killer."

"Sounds like you're not convinced of that scenario."

Nope. My Spidey sense keeps tingling. We know Cal is doing something shady with the sales of some of his big cats. And don't get me started on all the relationships and affairs. I need a dance card to keep up with all of them," Jules said.

"Your hypotheses, Miss Marple?"

"Tony and Sheena, who are a thing now, have been leaving the notes. I caught them on camera." She caught the worried look in his eye. "And yes, I let the sheriff know. I'm stumped about Dana's death. I haven't heard too many details. When I talked to her last week, she said she missed Tabbi and that she didn't think she'd work with Tony and Sheena because she didn't like what they were doing to Tabbi's business."

"I ran into Bubba when I was in town yesterday. He said that the woman was shot to death and left behind the school. It was definitely foul play," Jake added.

"Then there has to be a second gun. Two killers doesn't seem plausible. And what was Dana doing at the school?" Jules looked through a box of homemade decorations and pulled out some snowflakes her grandmother had tatted.

"Who knows? It's doubtful that she was there to jog. She could have been lured there or maybe she was planning to meet someone. Or she could have been killed somewhere else and dumped there," Jake said, reaching for another box of ornaments.

"She's a tall woman. It would have taken a strong someone or several someones to move her. I'm guessing that the two murders are related because the women knew each other. That's more reasonable than some random killer running around."

"Was Dana seeing anyone?" Jake hooked Jules's Hallmark ornaments on smaller branches near the top of the tree.

"I don't know. Maybe she was meeting someone behind the high school. It's kinda secluded back there. We've got too many missing pieces in this puzzle. So much disparate information that doesn't seem to go together. It's giving me a headache."

"Maybe if you concentrate on something else, it'll come to you," Jake said.

The pair spent the rest of the evening decorating the tree and watching movies. Jules felt nostalgic looking at all the decorations that triggered memories of her parents and Christmases past. Jake added his ornaments from his collection. She enjoyed listening to him talk about his own past holiday celebrations and happy times with family. Good memories and hope for the future. But Tabbi and Dana's murders kept worming their way into her thoughts.

Chapter Twenty-Four

Friday

Jules's phone buzzed. **Found some stuff. Have time 4 lunch?**
Definitely. Where? Jules answered.
Pizza at Pie in the Sky?
Perfect. 12? Jules smiled at the alliteration.

Pixel responded with a check mark and a string of pizza emojis.

Jules had enough time to make her bed, straighten the kitchen, and find her shoes. She paused and smiled when she caught a glimpse of the Christmas tree.

She didn't pass anyone on the ride to the edge of town, and she guessed people were home getting ready for the holidays. Jules did a quick mental check of her task list to make sure she didn't need any last-minute gifts or food. Satisfied that she was ready for Christmas and could relax, she found a parking spot at the edge of the strip mall that the pizza place shared with an art supply store and a small gallery.

Jules glanced around the parking lot for Pixel's Prius. Not seeing it, she hurried inside and found a table away from the glass doors and their constant blast of arctic air.

Pixel bustled in with her parka and black messenger bag. "I got a call on the way over, and it took longer than expected. I hope you haven't been waiting long."

"Nope. Just got here." Jules handed her friend a menu.

"Good afternoon. What can I get y'all?" The tallish waiter who sported tattoos on his fingers and hands asked.

"I'll have thin crust personal cheese pizza with unsweetened tea." Jules put her menu back behind the napkin container next to the parmesan and spices.

"I'll have a personal veggie pizza with water. Can you put a lime in it?"

"Not a problem. Be right back with your drinks," he said.

"Are you all ready for Christmas?" Jules asked.

"Not yet. It kinda snuck up on me this year. I'm headed to my brother's house on Christmas Day to have dinner with him, his wife, and kids. What about you?"

The waiter returned and dropped off their drinks. Pixel squeezed her lime wedge in the water.

"I think I'm ready, but I always feel like I'm forgetting something." Jules played with the straw wrapper. "I'm doing a New Year's Eve special at the resort, so I have a short break before the next wave of guests arrive."

"That's good. You deserve some time off." She rummaged through her bag for her tablet. "Okay, I was able to find a little more about Tabbi's business. She owns four trailers and her SUV. She rents her condo, and she has a loan on another SUV. She's got a lot of personal and business credit card debt. She received some money from her divorce, but that was about the time she bought the trailers, so I'm guessing she blew through that. She had a will, and her beneficiary is her cousin Fiona."

"Interesting. Sheena said something about Tony owning some of the trailers and inventory."

"Not sure. Everything I found is titled to Tabbi." Pixel took a sip of her drink and squeezed the lime wedge into the glass again.

"Anything on how the business was doing?" Jules asked.

"She's got a savings account and a couple of checking accounts. The business is registered, and she files sales tax. She lists the business's address as a storage unit near her home."

"Sounds like she's doing okay."

Pixel smirked. "She's making a living and paying her staff. She does the seasonal county fair and festival circuit. It looks like she's customizing T-shirts for large orders during the rest of the year. Her internet reviews are mixed. They're either over-the-top and gushing or at the bottom of the barrel."

"Polarizing, just like in life. She was abrasive and brash, so that's not surprising. She always seemed to be in the middle of plenty of altercations with different people while she was in Fern Valley. No other day job for her?"

"Nope. Not since she worked for Cal," Pixel added.

The waiter returned with their lunches. "Anything else I can get you all?"

Both women shook their heads and dug into their pizzas.

After a few bites, Pixel pulled out a couple of paper napkins from the dispenser and wiped her hands. "I couldn't find much on Dana Taylor. She's twice divorced and rents a condo near Tabbi's. She had a grown daughter from her first marriage. During the day, Dana's a receptionist, and from her Facebook feed, she hangs out a lot in bars with Tabbi and a bunch of other women. Her dream was to open a vintage clothing shop. She also had tons of credit card debt, and her daughter and ex-husband are her beneficiaries."

"I got the sense when she checked out of the resort last weekend that she didn't like that Tony and Sheena had made their relationship public so quickly. She was still defending Tabbi."

"Tabbi and Dana were all over each other's social media feeds. Tony was on Tabbi's feed a lot, and he was also in a bunch of posts on Sheena's page. Then there were tons of Tony pictures on Tony's page." Pixel made a face.

"Interesting." Jules picked up another piece of her tiny pizza.

"I didn't find out much more than I already told you about Tony and Sheena. Other than Tony moved into Sheena's apartment recently. It seems he was living with Tabbi prior to that. I couldn't find a previous address. Oh, wait. There is something. He declared bankruptcy a couple of years ago. It seems he was pushing a pyramid scheme of vitamins and energy supplements. The FDA shut down the company for false claims, and Tony got stuck with lots of merchandise he couldn't move because of all the bad publicity."

"I appreciate you checking into this. Something keeps nagging at me that these two murders are related. But the sheriff has Misti Collins in custody. The gun that killed Tabbi was hers."

"That doesn't mean there weren't two guns. I'll see what I can find out about your cast of characters and their gun habits." Pixel tapped on her screen.

Jules took another bite of her pizza and pushed the plate away. "Any word on the FBI?"

"I have a meeting the first week of January in Quantico. Hopefully, they'll make me an offer, and it's not another series of interviews or tests. This is the longest job interview process I've ever been through."

"Fingers crossed. I'm so excited for you."

"The last thing I had that I wanted to tell you is kinda big. Cal and Tabbi were sued several times by different animal rights groups over their practices. They settled out of court on two of the cases, and one was dismissed by a sympathetic judge."

"Interesting. What were the suits?"

"The two that they settled had to do with animal welfare. They were using their big cats as breeders and selling off the cubs."

Jules raised her eyebrows, and Pixel continued, "The one that was dismissed was about overinflated claims of supporting animal charities with profits from his shows. Cal has had more than a few employees sue him for various things over the years. He's won some and lost some. I looked into Tabbi, too. She had filed multiple lawsuits since her divorce against festivals, carnivals, and event sponsors when she didn't feel she was treated fairly. Most of those were also settled out of court. It sounds like she's a frequent court visitor."

"Hmmmm. That makes sense. I think Cal's still dealing cubs under the radar. Tabbi threatened to sue the business council and town over that altercation. She filed an official complaint."

"That shouldn't be a concern now, right?"

"Well, our town manager said that her heirs could still sue if they saw fit. I'm hoping her estate drops the whole thing. I'm not sure the case was that strong to begin with."

"She seemed to make money by filing flimsy lawsuits and settling them before they went to trial. Dana was involved in most of these. Her name showed up frequently as a witness. By my count, there were fifteen lawsuits in the past six years. I skimmed some of the case information. Several of the judges scolded her side for being petty and frivolous and wasting the court's time."

"She and Dana had quite the business arrangement. Did Dana profit from any of the cases?"

"From what I could see, she had a steady stream of income from Tabbi's Tees, and sometimes, the checks were bigger than her receptionist's salary." Pixel wiped her mouth on a paper napkin and finished her drink. "I hate to eat and run, but I have an eye appointment of all things this afternoon. I hope you have a great holiday."

Jules motioned for the waiter.

"What else can I get for you all today?" he asked as he approached their table.

"Just the check." Jules rummaged through her purse for her wallet.

The waiter pulled a plastic folder from his back pocket and slid it to her. After he had her card, he sauntered over to the counter with a swagger that caught Pixel's attention. Jules raised an eyebrow, and Pixel shrugged, but continued to steal glances at the waiter.

"I hope you have a great Christmas and a really good meeting with the FBI. I can't wait to hear all about it." Jules retrieved her card and receipt from the waiter and followed Pixel out the door.

Fiddling with the radio and the heat, Jules checked the mirror and turned around in the parking lot to head back through town. At the stoplight on Main, a gray Charger with a red hood stripe sped past in the opposite direction. Can it be Tony and Sheena again? When the light changed, she whipped a turn in the nearest driveway and followed the pair from several car lengths.

They drove through town in the opposite direction for at least ten miles and jumped on the interstate, heading west. Not wanting to make another trip to Berryville, Jules made a U-turn and headed to the resort.

Why do these two keep showing up in town? The festival is over. They don't live close enough for day trips. Why are they so interested in Fern Valley?

Chapter Twenty-Five

Saturday

Jules's bed was so warm and comfy, and her cabin looked so festive that she didn't really want to go into the office on Christmas Eve. But she needed to check on the food delivery and to see if any other reservations had come in for New Year's Eve. Next week, she and Roxanne would assemble baskets for all the guests who purchased her End of the Year Extravaganza package. Pleased that the vintage trailers had been reserved for the big night, Jules was excited about her numbers for this quarter. Her planning and special events had paid off, and she was looking forward to her beach adventure with Jake. Tonight, she'd find more things that they should see and do on their road trip. She wanted this vacation to be memorable.

As she wandered over to the coffee machine for a vanilla latte, Bijou followed her with her eyes. She chose to stay in her puffy bed since no snacks were in plain view.

Jules's phone dinged from across the room.

What are you doing? Roxanne texted.

Checking on stuff. What's up?

Brunch tomorrow at eleven. Just bring Jake. Go home now. It's Christmas Eve.

Jules replied with a Christmas tree and three smiley emojis.

She flipped through photos from the Christmas festival weekends, choosing the best ones for her website and newsletter. She also scheduled

Instagram and Facebook posts for the next three weeks. Then, she made customized gift tags for each reservation. The black and gold paper would go well with the sparkling gold ribbon. Each basket would be filled with gourmet snacks, chocolates, a book about the Blue Ridge Mountains, champagne, resort logo glasses, funny hats, mugs, and party favors. She offered two dinner packages. One was a buffet in the lodge, and the other was a take-out option from the Good Thyme Bistro. Everyone would end the weekend with a champagne brunch on New Year's Day.

Feeling accomplished for completing all her outstanding tasks, she opened her Tabbi/Dana file and unfolded the timeline with all the players. Red arrows pointed to Misti, Cal, Tony, and Sheena. Jules wondered about Cal's son Cody. She didn't know much about him, and he was only at the resort the first weekend for the cat shows. Jules stared at the paper for a long time. Too many missing pieces. Then there was Dana's murder. The sheriff had been pretty tight-lipped about her death. He kept whatever he was investigating to himself.

Jules opened a web browser to see what she could find about Cal's son. A small blurb under a smiling headshot said that he had grown up at the resort with the big cats. There were lots of photos of him through the years with a variety of lions and tigers. From his teen years on, most of the photos were of him with the big cats and a bunch of women who all looked like models. She also found a series of videos he did online. Cody exuded charm with his megawatt smile. He had inherited his dad's showman skills. There was nothing mentioned about his sibling. For a family that posted everything they do online, it was odd that this person wasn't mentioned anywhere. *I wonder if it's even worth having Pixel look into.*

Interrupted by her phone, she glanced down at Jake's text. **Dinner?**

Sure. What are you thinking?

I'll bring the food. Let's start a new tradition. See you at six?

It's a date. Jules set her phone down. Her heart warmed at starting new traditions with Jake. It was nice to have someone to hang out with, especially during the holidays.

Not gleaning much from Cody's social media sites other than the posed candids with wild animals and lots of blond women, Jules packed up and headed home.

She changed clothes three times before she settled on a purple sweater and black leggings. Then, with enough time to make the cabin presentable, she lit a cinnamon candle and turned on the Christmas tree lights. She pulled out a green tablecloth and matching napkins, her mother's go-to Christmas decorations for a holiday table. The white china and crystal candlesticks, wedding presents from a relationship worth forgetting, rounded out the place settings. The dining area looked romantic.

Before she could straighten or rearrange anything else, a knock at the door sent Bijou into full security mode. Jake stepped inside with two large bags and a cheesecake.

"Here, let me help you." Jules grabbed the dessert and led him to the kitchen table.

Jake started unpacking. "I went with chicken. I hope that's okay." He pulled out bread, salad, and their to-go orders.

"Fantastic and perfect timing, too. I'm hungry."

Jules cleared the shopping bag and containers and put the cheesecake in the refrigerator. "Tea, okay? If not, I have coffee, water, or wine."

"Tea's fine." Jake settled in at the table, and Bijou sat at the ready at Jake's feet in case any food rained down from the table.

"I thought we could start a new Christmas tradition. Dinner and gifts," Jake said as she returned to the table with two glasses.

"My kind of evening. What have you been up to today?" she asked.

"I finished the plumbing. I need to do the wiring and the sheetrock. I may do that after I move the pieces in place. I should be ready to paint as soon as I do all that and get the trim installed. Getting close." Jake spooned chicken mixed in some kind of garlic sauce, vegetables, and rice onto his plate.

"You've got a rhythm going now. Construction doesn't take as long as it did in the early days. This looks good." Jules savored the smell of the dinner.

"Let me know the color pallet, and I'll order the paint." Jake took a bite of a bread stick.

"Black and red will be too dark for the main colors, but I have some ideas for accent walls with a little gothic flare."

Bijou kept nudging the shopping bag Jake had left on the floor. He picked up the bag and set it in the chair. "I've got two prospective orders for custom houses. One for a mother-in-law's residence, and the other will be a She Shed."

"That is great news. Your business is taking off."

"Thanks to you, I have your little village to use as model homes. The website's been getting a lot of hits, too."

The twinkle in his eyes made Jules smile. "We make a good team."

"We do." Jake stared at her, and she felt her heat rise in her cheeks. She hoped she looked as good as he did in the soft light. She tucked a curl behind her ear.

The pair dug into their meals, and the conversation faded.

After a long silence, Jules asked, "You done?"

When he nodded, she cleared his place setting. He poured another tea as she loaded the dishwasher.

"Okay, time to open presents," Jake said.

Bijou yipped and ran to the den. Jake grabbed his shopping bag, and Jules set his gifts on the coffee table.

"Merry Christmas," she said.

"You too," he said. "All of this is for me?"

She nodded, and he settled on the couch.

"Open this one first." Jules handed him a large, square package.

"It's heavy." Jake unwrapped the set of carving tools. "Wow. These are nice."

"I thought you could use them on your custom projects."

"They are great. Thanks." He opened the box and fingered several of the chisels.

Jules watched as he unwrapped the sweater and casual shirt she picked out. "One more," she said, handing him a large box with a bright green bow.

He slid his finger under the tape and pulled out a digital radio. "Oh, sweet."

"It comes with a subscription service. I thought you could listen to it in the barn. You can hook your ear things up to it."

"Love it. Thank you for all of this. Now, your turn." He handed Bijou a small package.

It took the terrier a few seconds to destroy the wrapping in her attempt to get to the bag of gourmet dog treats.

"She kept nudging the bag during dinner. I knew she could smell them." Jake smiled.

"Awww," Jules said. "The way to her heart is always with snacks."

Jake winked and opened the bag for Bijou. She took her treat to her puffy bed in the corner. "This is for you." He pulled a red jewelry store box from his pocket.

Jules hoped she didn't have a startled look on her face. She was excited, but then she had panicked thoughts about being too early in the relationship to get serious. She chewed her bottom lip and took the small box he offered.

She opened the lid, and a pear-shaped amethyst ring sparkled. "Jake, it's beautiful." Jules pulled it out and slid it on her right hand.

"This goes with it." He handed her another jewelry box. Inside were matching amethyst studs and a solitaire necklace. "I've never seen you wear your birthstone. And I like purple."

She pointed to her shirt. "Thank you. They're perfect." Jules let out a breath she didn't know she was holding. She loved the jewelry, and a wave of relief washed over her that it wasn't what she first thought it was. After her short marriage to the Idiot, she wasn't sure when she would be ready to even think about long-term plans. Old wounds take a while to heal.

Pushing thoughts of her ex-husband out of her mind, she tried on the earrings and necklace and hopped up to get a glimpse of them in the mirror by the door.

Jake picked up his radio and plugged it in. After fiddling with the settings, smooth jazz filled the cabin. "Wanna dance?"

"I'd love to."

Jake took her hand and rested his other on the small of her back.

The music, the twinkling lights on the tree, and being with Jake made for a magical Christmas Eve. New traditions were a good thing.

Chapter Twenty-Six

Sunday

W hile Jules did her makeup, she kept thinking about Cody Collins. They had only talked briefly. Why did he keep popping up in her thoughts? Was she overlooking something that involved him in his stepmother's death?

She dashed off a quick text to Pixel. **Merry Christmas. Hope you're celebrating. When you get back to work, could you see what you can find on a Cody Collins?**

Not a problem. Always poking around the dark side. Pixel responded as soon as Jules set the phone on the counter.

Jules texted, **Thanks!** Surrounded by Christmas tree emojis. Then she added a tiger one for good measure.

She scrunched her curls with gel and put away her makeup and brushes. A knock on the door sent Bijou into Defcon Four mode.

Jules admitted to Jake, and he kissed her. "Merry Christmas."

"Merry Christmas to you, too. Come in. It's cold out there. Let me get my coat and the bag of gifts."

He held her coat as she wiggled her arms in. Jules patted Bijou and locked the door behind them.

Once inside the warm car, she sunk down in the passenger seat and pushed the button to turn on the heated seats.

"You're awfully quiet," he said as he sped through the gate and headed for

Roxanne's renovated farmhouse.

"Just thinking about Tabbi and Dana. If the murderer was the same, then he or she had two guns. Why kill both of the women? What was Dana's connection besides being Tabbi's best friend? I'm leaning toward Tony or Sheena, but could Cal's son Cody have done it? Maybe he and Misti were in on it?"

Jake shrugged as he navigated through the winding road that led up the mountain.

"There could be two killers," he said.

"That's plausible. But it's too coincidental to think that two friends and co-workers were murdered in the same town where they didn't live by two different killers. There has to be some connection between them that would cause someone to want them both dead. I made a list of all the possible suspects and connected all the relationships with my trusty red pen. The paper was filled with lines and arrows. For Tabbi, there was the whole on-again-off-again romance angle with Cal, Misti's jealousy, and Tony's dalliances. That's enough to keep a soap opera going for months. Dana seemed like the sidekick in all of this."

"Could it have been something related to her business?"

"I heard from several people that Tabbi jumped onboard every get-rich-quick scheme that materialized. She was abrasive and filed many lawsuits over the years. Her business ethics left a lot to be desired. So that's a definite possibility. Pixel discovered that Dana was her witness in many of the lawsuits."

"Maybe they sued or cheated the wrong person." Jake turned into the lane that led to Roxanne's house. The white saltbox farmhouse, perched on the side of the mountain with a panoramic view of the valley, always reminded Jules of the one on *The Waltons*.

Roxanne and her late husband, a doctor who'd sold his established practice to a medical conglomerate in the eighties, had restored the farmhouse to something that jumped off the pages of a designer magazine. For the holidays, her aunt had covered the front porch railing, swing, and rocking chairs with pine and holly bows. A huge pine wreath with gold ribbon framed the brass doorknocker on the red front door.

Jake parked behind Sheriff Hobbs's truck. He retrieved two shopping bags from the trunk while Jules climbed out of the car.

Roxanne opened the door before they knocked. Memories of Christmases past flashed in Jules's mind when she got a whiff of cinnamon and nutmeg. The foyer's interior, with dark pine plank floors and lots of white trim, welcomed them in and surrounded them with country luxury.

"Hey there," her aunt said. "I'm so glad you could come. Let me take your coats, and y'all settle in the den. Matt's got the fire going. I'll have brunch on the table in a few, and we can eat."

"Can I help with anything?" Jules handed her coat to her aunt.

"Nope. Matt and I have it all under control." She patted her beau on the shoulder and trotted down the longish hallway to the kitchen.

Jules followed Jake to the den. He set the shopping bags of gifts next to Roxanne's towering tree, covered with every kind of blown-glass ornament imaginable. The white twinkle lights refracted off of the decorations and sent shards of light in every direction. Faint strains of jazz music wafted through the air, along with scents of bread, cinnamon, and peppermint.

"I think this is the first time I've been to Roxanne's house," Jake said. "It reflects her personality." He picked up a brass kaleidoscope on the mantel and looked through it.

"The house is gorgeous. She's done several upgrade projects since my uncle died, and my cousin Max went off to med school. I love all the little touches. She even turned one of the extra bedrooms into her massive closet."

Before Jules could sit down, Roxanne breezed in through the entryway. "Come and eat. We're almost ready."

The pair followed her across the main hallway to the dining room. Sheriff Hobbs set a casserole dish on an iron trivet and shook his hand.

"It's hot, Matt," Roxanne said softly and patted his shoulder. "Y'all sit, and I'll go get the drinks."

Jules and Jake sat next to each other on one side of the long wooden table. Jules pulled the red cloth napkin out of the wine goblet and put it in her lap.

The sheriff entered with a tray of mimosas in champagne flutes. He set each one on the table like he was dealing cards. Roxanne zipped in behind him and poured iced water into the goblets. "There. Let me get the biscuits and gravy, and we'll be ready."

She returned with another casserole dish. "Oh, I forgot the fruit parfaits. Matt, you mind getting those?"

After another five minutes of adding last-minute touches, the four were ready for brunch.

"Roxanne, you outdid yourself," Jake said.

"I feel like we should take a picture of the table before everyone digs in." Jules pulled out her phone. "Here, Jake, you have longer arms. My selfies always look awkward."

Taking the camera, Jake set up the picture. "Lean in a little, Sheriff. There, that's good. Now, everybody smile." After several clicks, he handed the phone back to Jules.

"Thanks so much for having us over. This is fabulous." Jules said.

"My pleasure. Max couldn't make it home this year, so I'm so glad you all could join me to celebrate. I love having family over for the holidays. And Matt helped with the sausage gravy and the spinach quiches."

"A man of many talents," Jake added.

The sheriff grinned slightly and heaped biscuits and gravy on his plate.

Jules sampled a little bit of everything while Jake joined the sheriff in adding hefty portions to his plate.

The only sounds were munching and the clinking of the silverware on the china. Roxanne interrupted the lull with, "So, Matt. We were so busy getting everything ready, you didn't tell me what you and your team have been up to lately. I heard through the grapevine that you all have been locked in a war room pouring over evidence and clues." She winked at her niece.

Sheriff Hobbs took another bite of his biscuits and gravy and chewed determinedly. After a swallow and a long pause, he looked up to see the three of them staring at him. "We are investigating the two deaths as related. We have a suspect for the first one. Misti made bail on Friday, so she has returned to her home. My team continues to investigate all leads and possible suspects."

Jules tried not to look surprised. She was glad to hear that his team was looking at people other than Misti for the murders. Was one of them Cody? Or what about Tabbi's half-sister?

Roxanne's smile turned into a straight line. Before she could say anything, Jules added, "This one has a bunch of tentacles. Jake and I went to the wake. From talking to the folks there, we got the gist that Tabbi had angered a lot of people over the years and was involved in countless lawsuits. Settling out of court seemed to be a revenue stream for her."

The sheriff cut his eyes at Jules but didn't reply.

"So, Misti is home for Christmas," Roxanne added. "I'm sure she's thrilled."

The sheriff nodded, wiped his chin with his napkin, and took a swig of water.

"Anything on Dana's murder?" Jules asked, watching the sheriff's facial expressions intently.

"Nothing new. We're waiting on the final autopsy results. From the crime scene evidence, she was killed near the parking lot of the school and moved to the back near the track and the dumpster."

"What was she doing at the school? The vendor events were over. Did she go to meet someone?" Jules took a bite of her quiche and glanced around the table.

"Don't know." He took several bites of his parfait and stared out the window.

When no one commented, Jules popped a sausage ball in her mouth and savored the spicy cheese flavor. "Yum. You'll have to give Crystal the recipe. I like the hint of cayenne pepper."

Roxanne paused. "Crystal catered this for me."

Sheriff Hobbs let out a laugh. "And I thought you'd been up all night cooking." He looked relieved at the change in subject.

Roxanne cut her eyes at him. "I like to support my friends. Crystal and Met do a really great job at the resort with the food. And I planned brunch and decorated."

Jake stifled a laugh and helped himself to another slice of quiche.

"Well, it's on your plates," Jules said with a wink. "And it's very good."

192

"If I had to heat it up or stir it, then it's homemade somewhere," Roxanne said with a mischievous grin.

Roxanne stood and cleared the table after she shooed everyone to the den. "I'll clean up later. It's not that much. Time for presents."

Everyone found seats in the country chic den decorated in deep burgundy and plaids. Roxanne breezed in and handed out gifts. Jules and Jake added theirs to the pile. When everyone was seated again, Sheriff Hobbs handed Jake, Jules, and Roxanne each an envelope.

"Thank you, all. This is so nice. I'm excited to rekindle some old traditions this year and make some new ones. It's nice to celebrate the holiday with family. It's been a while," Jules said before the opening began.

Jules made out like a bandit. Her aunt gave her a black Coach bag and perfume, and Sheriff Hobbs gave her a gift card for Between the Covers. Bijou scored a red sweater and a bag of gourmet doggie treats. "Thank you, both. These are so nice."

"I'm glad you like it," Sheriff Hobbs said. "Thanks for the pen set, funny mug, and the coffee accessories. They'll go well on my desk."

Roxanne opened the envelope and gasped. "Matt, this is fabulous. I can't wait." She jumped up and hugged him.

"I'll take some time off in the new year, and we'll spend a week in Barbados. We both could use a change of scenery."

"You both deserve a vacation," Jules said, thinking of the sugar-sand beaches and palm trees. Thoughts of her winter road trip with Jake pinged around in her thoughts. It would be a nice getaway. *I can't remember the last not-for-work trip I took.* All she seemed to do was work at the resort or for the business council.

"I never seem to get to take time off," Sheriff Hobbs said. "Something always comes up. This time, we're going. Fern Valley will still be here when we get back."

"Definitely," Jake said. "Thanks for all the wonderful gifts. You guys know me well." Jake stacked boxes that contained a parka vest, cologne, and gift cards next to Jules's purse.

"Time for dessert," Roxanne exclaimed, hopping up and heading to the kitchen. The sheriff followed.

Roxanne and Matt laid out a platter of gooey brownies and shot-glass desserts. "Anyone want coffee?" Roxanne asked. "I have soft drinks, tea, water, or hot cocoa."

"Coffee for me, please," the sheriff said.

"You're the help," Roxanne said over her shoulder. "I'm putting you in charge of the beverages."

The sheriff leaned over and whispered something in her ear that made her burst out laughing. She stood on her tiptoes to kiss his cheek. "Okay, but get on that coffee service. I'll have one while you're at it."

"Jules? Jake?" the sheriff asked.

"Water's good," Jules replied, and Jake nodded.

Jules smiled at her aunt and the sheriff. She was happy that they got along so well. Roxanne hadn't had anyone steady in her life in a long time. Jules loved how the big sheriff did all kinds of things, even ones out of his comfort zone, for her aunt.

After everyone had sampled the desserts, Jules and Jake cleared the table.

The sheriff yawned and pushed back his chair. "It feels like nap time after so much rich food."

"We've got to be going soon," Jules said from the kitchen. "Thanks so much for the brunch and festivities. You all made this Christmas special."

Roxanne hugged Jules and then Jake. "Thank you all for coming. This has been a fun Christmas." After gathering coats and gifts and more conversation that spilled out on the porch, Jake finally closed the passenger door and jogged around to his side.

Jules leaned over and kissed him on the cheek. "Thanks for coming with me. I enjoyed it. This has been the best Christmas in a long time."

Chapter Twenty-Seven

Monday

Jules settled in at her desk and listened to the office sounds that she normally ignored. The heat whooshed through the ducts, and the printer's motor hummed in the background. Roxanne had texted her that morning with a reminder that she was headed to Short Pump near Richmond for the after-Christmas shopping deals. With her team off duty, the resort was eerily quiet. She streamed an oldies station on her laptop for company. "Surfin' USA" blasted through her speakers, making her think of beach life. A tingle of excitement jolted through her as she thought of her upcoming excursion to Florida with Jake. She had lived and breathed life at the resort for the last four years. It was time for a much-needed break, and it would give Bijou a chance to hang out at Aunt Roxanne's.

Her phone buzzed and jolted her out of her daydream.

"Hey, Jules. Can you talk?" Pixel asked.

"Sure. What's up? Did you have a nice Christmas?"

"I did, and I'm on my way to Quantico for an afternoon meeting. Fingers crossed that I'll get an offer. They moved my January meeting to today with not much notice. I really want this job. How was your Christmas? You're not engaged or anything, are you?"

"Not hardly," Jules said. "I did get jewelry, but not that kind. Jake's great, but I've sworn off marriage for a long while. I still haven't fully recovered from my ordeal with the Idiot. Enough of that. I am so excited about your thing with the FBI. I want details when you get back."

"Speaking of ordeals. I've lost count of the number of interviews, exams, and reviews I've been through. I hope this job will be worth it. Maybe I'll know something today. The reason I'm calling is I found some stuff on Cody Collins. He's lived on his father's cat reserve all his life. His mother was Cal's first wife. And as far as I can tell, he's Cal's only child. So, there's no other sibling. Cody's been raising big cats since he was a tween. He did almost three years at Virginia Tech in their pre-vet program. I couldn't find anything that said he graduated. He's had a regular spot in Cal's shows since he was a little kid, and he has his own video channel on YouTube. He's got quite a following on Instagram and Twitter or X or whatever it is these days."

"He seemed to know his cats, and he likes to talk."

Pixel sounded like she took a drink of something. "He's also quite the gun collector. I found a site using a dark web browser where he posts photos of his gun collection. Lots of long guns and handguns. From what I could tell, it looks like he's got a side hustle going with online sales."

"Is it legal?"

"Legalish. Maybe? State laws vary, and the Dark Web is the new wild wild west. I counted the sales I could find over the past two years, and he made about a hundred and fifty thousand dollars. If everything you see on the internet is true."

"Very interesting. Thanks so much for all you do to help me."

"Not a problem. You've got a reputation now for sleuthing. I like to think of myself as Nancy Drew's sidekick."

"You're too funny. I do appreciate it. Well, we seem to keep uncovering all these little secrets. I feel like I have a lot of random information but no real leads on who killed Tabbi and Dana."

"Whenever I'm trying to figure something out, I work through the rings," Pixel said.

"Huh?"

"If you drop a pebble in a lake, you get a bunch of concentric circles. When you don't know much, you're on the outer, bigger rings with not many leads. You need to keep narrowing down your options, moving toward the smaller center. Keep looking. Keep asking questions. Keep moving. You know, it's all about focus."

"I thought I had a knack for that, but so far, it hasn't done much good this time." Jules sighed.

"Keep at it. Let me know if I can help. My exit's coming up, so I'm going to have to jump off this call. See ya."

"Good luck! Let me know what happens." Jules disconnected and put her head on her desk. *There were so many bits of information that didn't point to anything. Maybe I should plan our beach vacation and let the sheriff's team take care of this.*

Jules texted the sheriff with what she found out about Cal's son. Not sure if it had anything to do with either murder, but it was something that he needed to check on if he didn't know about it already.

Jules stood and stretched, and that turned into fifteen minutes of yoga before she returned to her desk, determined to find something in her notes. *Focus, girl.* Grabbing a clean piece of paper, Jules made a list of the things that bothered her. There were two dead women who had been guests of her resort. Abrasive Tabbi made a steady income off of filing lawsuits and settling. The police felt they had enough to charge Misti, the angry new wife. Cal had a side business in the sketchy big cat trade, while his son also had ties to some shady gun sales. Then there was Tony and his new girlfriend, who kept leaving threatening notes for Jules. It was enough to make her head spin.

She clicked on her reservation application and looked for Cal and Misti's contact information. Maybe the number they provided at registration belonged to her. Jules couldn't remember who made the reservation.

After three rings, she heard a gruff "Hello."

"Cal, this is Jules Keene from the Fern Valley Luxury Camping Resort. I was trying to get in touch with Misti."

"Oh, hey. She's up at the house. Call her at 540-222-8778. She'll be glad to hear from you." Jules hoped she captured the number correctly. He clicked off kind of abruptly.

Short and sweet. Jules dialed Misti's number.

A singsong voice answered on the first ring. "Hellloooo."

"Hi, Misti, this is Jules Keene. How are you? The sheriff said you had been released, and I wanted to check on you."

"I'm fine. Glad to be back home. Have you found anything on your end? My lawyer keeps saying not to worry, but it feels like the police have a giant file with a big red arrow that points to me as Tabbi's killer."

"But not Dana's," Jules added.

"I guess that's something to be glad about." Misti let out a heavy sigh.

"Any idea about who could have taken your gun?" Jules asked.

"No, and I've spent countless hours wracking my little brain over that one. I know I put it in Cal's glove compartment. I never thought to check on it while we were at your place. It could have been taken at any time during our stay."

"Was the truck locked?"

"Not while we're working. Anyone on the team or anyone walking by could have opened the door," Misti said with a sigh.

Like Cody? What could he have against Tabbi or Misti?

"What about the cage doors? How vigilant are you all with those?" Jules was glad Misti couldn't see the face she made.

"We double and triple-check those. You don't want to be in a bad situation with a loose cat," Misti quickly responded.

Interesting. They pay close attention to the locks for the animals but not the guns. "How are you doing?" she added when she realized there had been a lull in the conversation.

"Oh, much better since I'm at home in my own bed. It was a Christmas miracle. Cal got me out before the holidays. I'm praying that I don't have to go back. I can't go back. I am such a mess. That's where you come in. Jules, I'm counting on you. You said you'd help me. You've got to figure out who did this." She sounded almost breathless in her delivery.

"I have talked to so many people and heard so many stories. Hopefully, I'll be able to narrow it down. Does your lawyer have anyone on his team working on your case?"

"He keeps telling me not to worry about it. But that makes me worry more.

I want to believe him, but I don't want to spend my thirties locked away in jail. Cal will forget about me. I'll be old when I get out after a murder charge," she wailed. "Jules, promise me you'll call me the second you hear something. I know that you'll be able to figure this all out. I don't get the warm and fuzzies from my lawyer. He's always harping on the bad stuff."

"Will do," Jules said reluctantly. *I hope I don't disappoint you.* She let out a breath. "The purse thing is bothering me. Who would have a red evening purse at the resort, and why are they trying to frame you? Where would they get a clutch like that?"

"Who knows? A vintage clothing shop? It looked like a prom accessory that my Mom would have bought. Back when they dyed their purses to match their shoes."

"I wonder," Jules said.

"What?"

"Just a thought I need to check out. Anything else you can think of?"

"No. Not really. I'm still catching up on my sleep. I lost ten pounds in that place. I guess that was something good that came out of this mess. It felt like I was in there for months, but I have a panic attack every time I think about going back to jail."

"Talk to your lawyer. He can provide solid advice about what's next with your case. If you think of anything, you have my number. I'm glad you're home. I'll let you know what I find," Jules said.

After disconnecting, Jules checked her registration application again. *Shazam!* Sheena bunked with Dana when they stayed at the resort, and Sheena filled out the visitor card with her phone number.

Jules cleared her throat and dialed the number, hoping it was late enough in the afternoon for the waitress to be awake.

After three rings, she heard a groggy, "Hello? Who's this?"

"Hi, Sheena. This is Jules Keene in Fern Valley. How are you?"

"Getting up to get ready for work. What's up?"

"This is a weird question. I hope you can help me. I know that Dana had a lot of vintage clothing and jewelry. She showed me some when she was here. Do you know what happened to her things? I mean, was there someone cleaning out her place that maybe I could talk to? I had an interest in some of her fifties stuff."

"Uh, how would I know?" the woman slurred.

"I'm sorry to bother you. I thought y'all were friends and you'd know. I'd be willing to buy some stuff if the price was right."

"She was closer to Tabbi than me. I think she had a kid, though. A daughter. I'm guessing she would be the person to talk to if you can find her. I have no idea what her name is. Sorry, can't help you. I didn't even go to the funeral. We weren't buds if you get my drift." Sheena's giggle sounded almost maniacal.

"Thanks for your time. It was a long shot, but I thought I'd ask. Sorry to have bothered you."

The other woman clicked off without saying anything else.

"So sorry to have bothered you," she repeated to dead air. Bijou's ears shot up and made Jules laugh. "Well, it was a hunch. Maybe I was right about the red satin purse."

Chapter Twenty-Eight

Tuesday

J ules's tried to shake the gloomies. A foggy mist hung over the mountains and her thoughts. If it had been colder, she would have predicted snow. She had so many bits of information but no neon arrows pointing at the guilty party. Something tickled the back of her mind, and she couldn't quite put her finger on it.

Thinking that if she focused on something other than the murders, her mind would relax, and her thoughts could better coalesce into something that made sense. Jules spent the morning dusting and vacuuming the house. She emptied the dishwasher, changed the sheets, and did a load of laundry.

Jules plopped down on the couch next to Bijou. Housecleaning hadn't stimulated any eureka moments, but the cabin looked nice. "Okay, I'm headed to the office for a little while to check on things. I'll be back before you know it."

Outside, everything was as quiet as the mist that hovered over the mountains. The clouds cast a gray pallor on everything and didn't help her disposition.

Jules sat down at her desk. After taking care of a handful of resort emails, she pulled out her Tabbi/Dana folder and read through her notes. Nothing new yet again. Maybe this time wasn't like the others. She seemed to have a knack for uncovering information that solved four murders in the past. Maybe it was a fluke, and she should leave the sleuthing to the professionals.

Jules stuffed her notes in the folder and shut down the office. She'd try a walk in the chilly temperatures to get her out of this funk. Or maybe she would take a ride into town.

After checking all the doors in the office and flipping off the lights, she traipsed past the empty amphitheater and the shuttered barn. No one was stirring near the cabins or the lodge. The vintage trailers stood empty, too, waiting for the New Year's Eve revelers to arrive later in the week. Jules decided to finish the circuit of the resort and head home. *Maybe it was time to admit defeat. I'm not a detective, after all. Maybe I should stick with what I'm good at and leave the crime-solving to Sheriff Hobbs.*

Jules let out a heavy sigh as she strolled through the tiny house village. The new Bram Stoker house would be a popular addition to the collection that already featured houses named after Beatrix Potter, J. K. Rowling, and L. Frank Baum. She enjoyed decorating them to represent their namesake's writings, and they'd had steady bookings since they opened.

Pausing at the entrance to the neighborhood, Roxanne's idea of creating a tiny, free library popped into her head. Jake could build her a miniature house on a post to hold the books. If they put it here, anyone at the resort could access it. She had seen some online in all kinds of locations. The idea was perfect for the resort. She'd see if the council would want to add a couple more around town. Gail from the library and Elizabeth from the bookstore would help her with this project. Ideas about design contests bounced around her head.

Jules felt a charge of excitement about the tiny library project. She'd head home and look for some ideas to show Jake. It wouldn't take him long to make a little container that looked like a dollhouse. Inside, it could have some shelves to hold books people donate. She wanted something that looked like a cottage, or maybe this could be the model for her Great Gatsby mansion idea.

She picked up her pace between the Baum and Rowling houses, excited to get home and sketch out some ideas when something caught her eye, something moving. A light flashed. Jules searched the space ahead and spotted movement near the window of the Potter tiny house. Her heart started to pound.

Jules wandered around the side. Behind her, she heard something crunch. Footsteps? Before she could turn, she felt a rush of air behind her and then searing pain as something hit the back of her head. Her vision blurred, and dizziness swept over her like a wave. Darkness closed in like an old TV shutting down, and her eyelids drifted shut.

Jules woke up in the dark. She blinked but could make out faint shadows in the gloom. The air smelled of wood and linen and something she couldn't place. Lifting her head, the room swam, and she lay down again. Forcing herself to take a deep breath, she stretched out her hands. There were pillows on each side of her and a rough carpet under her fingers. When her queasiness had subsided, Jules raised her head a second time and then rolled onto her side. She waited. Only her head ached. Squinting, she could make out a sliver of light under what she hoped was a door. She crawled forward, closer to the light.

At the door, she pulled herself to her feet, listening. There was only quiet. She reached for the doorknob. It didn't budget. Panic welled up in her throat. She leaned her head against the door and forced herself to breathe again.

Jules patted her coat pockets. She found her gloves and a tissue. No phone. She slammed her shoulder into the door. Then she pulled on the knob again. It moved slightly.

Tired and dizzy, she plopped down on the floor near the pillows. Harry Potter flashed in her thoughts. Why Hogwarts, Quidditch, and the Dursleys? Harry's aunt and uncle popped in her head. Peering through the dark, Jules recognized her surroundings as the reading nook under the staircase of the Rowling tiny house. She rubbed the back of her head. When she pulled her hand back, it was covered in something sticky. She wiped her hands on her jeans. Edging closer to the door, Jules fought off another wave of nausea.

She didn't know how long she had been out or how long she had been trapped in this room. Jules strained to hear anything around her. All was quiet except for the occasional rumble of the heating unit. It sounded like she was alone and locked under the stairs. Now she knew how Harry Potter felt.

She wiggled out of her coat and checked the inside and outside pockets again. She patted down her jeans. Still no phone. A charge of panic made her pulse race.

Breathing deeply, she tried to quell the wave of fear. She had to be smart about this and figure a way out. Nobody knew where she was. Her head ached, but the nausea had abated slightly. She hoped she wasn't concussed.

She tried the door again, but it wouldn't budge. Nothing under the staircase to pry the door open with. Waiting quietly and seeing who her attacker was another option, but she'd rather do something. She made a mental note to have the lock removed from the door. *Wait a minute. This was supposed to be a fun room for kids and Potter fans. There wasn't a lock on the door.*

She stood up and tugged on the knob again. Then she counted to three and shoved the door with her shoulder. The shock wave rippled through her head and neck. Resting her head on the door frame, she forced herself to visualize the door. *This door opens inward. I've got to shake the cobwebs from my head and think clearly. I can do this. Focus, girl.*

Jules turned the knob. The door shifted slightly. *What am I missing?* Taking a deep breath and mustering her gumption, she yanked on the door. It made a creaking sound and opened. The brightness on the other side of the door caused her to blink until her eyes adjusted. Outside the doorway, a five-shelf bookcase blocked her exit.

She let out a heavy sigh. Nothing today was going to be easy. She pulled on the side. The heavy piece of furniture moved several inches. *Desperate times call for desperate measures.* Putting both hands on the back, she shoved, and the bookcase teetered forward and landed with a crash. She paused and listened.

Jules heard the air from the heater. Cautiously stepping over the shelf and the books splayed all over the floor, she picked her way through the house's tiny living room.

Something creaked. Jules froze. Searching for a hiding place, her glance darted around the first floor of the tiny house. Not too many places to hide.

Ducking behind the loveseat, she heard noises on the porch. Someone jiggled the doorknob. She heard muffled voices that she couldn't discern. Then, retreating footsteps. Jules held her breath.

Jules had to get out of here. What if whoever was out there was near the front door? The bedroom had a large window that Jake used to move in the big furniture. That could be plan B. She'd slip out the back and hide in the woods.

She crab-walked to the bedroom and pulled back the purple drapes and the white sheers. Not seeing anyone outside, she opened the window and climbed out. Jules landed with a thud that was louder than she wanted. She froze and listened for footsteps. Hugging the side of the tiny house, she crept to the corner. Not hearing anything except her own heartbeat pounding in her ears, she stuck her head round the corner.

Something cracked behind her. She turned as someone taller than she threw something over her head. She clawed at the cloth while the person grabbed her and pulled her toward the front of the house. The person, definitely a man, half-picked her up and dragged her up the porch and back inside. Jules kicked and tried to scream, but a beefy hand covered her mouth. She tried to bite a finger, but the man's grip tightened, one thick arm around her neck and another around her waist. Her breathing came in spasms.

Bile welled up in her throat. Nobody knew she was out here, and they wouldn't miss her for a while during a holiday week. It could be hours or days. She had to get out of this house.

The guy pulled the cloth, which turned out to be a wool scarf, tighter around her head. He shoved her onto the couch. "Be quiet," he snarled. The itchy fabric caused her nose to twitch.

Jules waved her hands frantically and started moaning. She couldn't tell if he noticed, so she moaned louder, gagged, and fell over onto her side. Jules didn't move a muscle. Playing dead, or at least passed out, might buy her some time.

Someone neared the couch and yanked the scarf off her head. She moved her head slightly and opened her eyes a crack. Tony! Her heartbeat raced.

"She's breathing. She's okay," a female voice said. "Tie her up. We can leave her here for now and come back later. You worry too much."

Jules lifted her lids. Sheena stood to one side, her legs wide, feet planted on the carpet. With the gun in her outstretched hand, her stance looked like something out of *Charlie's Angels*. Closing her eyes tight, Jules moaned for good measure.

"I think she passed out," Tony said. "Maybe she's dying. We should do something."

"Nah, she's still breathing. We need something to tie her up with. Hurry up. Go find a cord or tape," Sheena ordered. "We've gotta get out of here and come up with a plan."

"It's not like I brought rope with me. Sheesh. Who knew we'd need it on the fly? I wasn't prepared to tie someone up today," Tony muttered and moved around the room. "Maybe I can find something in the kitchen. There's got to be something in there."

"If not, use your shoelaces," Sheena yelled.

"My shoelaces? Are you nuts? They are limited editions. I don't want to ruin the set," he whined. "I'm sure there is something around here. Just keep an eye on her." Tony stepped into the other room and slammed drawers and cabinets.

"She doesn't look like she's going anywhere, but hurry up anyway." Sheena snapped. The woman pulled out her phone and balanced it in one hand. Sheena concentrated on scrolling with her thumb while the gun bobbled in her other hand.

Jules opened one eye wider. She needed another diversion. Maybe she could surprise Sheena while Tony was preoccupied. *It was now or never.*

Jules took a deep breath and prepared herself for the pain. She knew she had to get out of there before they tied her up or worse. She launched herself off the couch with a screech that rivaled an angry three-year-old.

Sheena startled and dropped her phone. For a moment that seemed to play out in slow motion, Sheena pointed her gun. Then she looked at her phone. When Tony's girlfriend stooped to reach for the phone, she froze in mid-bend. Jules, taking advantage of Sheena's distraction, landed on top of her and knocked the gun from her other hand. The two scrapped on the floor, and Sheena grabbed Jules's hair and didn't let go until Jules punched her in the arm. The tussle turned into scratching, and then Sheena tried to bite Jules, who landed several punches to the younger woman's face and stomach. Sheena curled up in the fetal position, holding her head and moaning.

Jules scrambled for the gun. When she reached for it, someone grabbed her around the waist and swung her into the air. Tony hoisted her ceilingward and over his shoulder. She kicked him in the back until he hit her lower back. More pain shot through her back and hips.

"Sit still and be quiet," Tony roared. "I need to think. This wasn't supposed to happen."

Sheena picked up the gun and crawled to the couch. "Tie her up so she doesn't get loose. Gimme your shoes."

"No. I'll be right back." Tony strode into the kitchen and rummaged through the cabinets. When he didn't find anything, he lumbered back into the living room. "All I could find were bread ties and a dishcloth. Maybe I can make these work." He looked at the scene on the floor, and a puzzled look crossed his dark countenance. They had knocked over the coffee table, and the contents were strewn across the floor.

"Wait," Tony said, yanking the blinds off the wall. He wound the cord around his beefy hand and then wrapped it around Jules's ankles and wrists. He tied the scarf around her neck and stuffed one end in her mouth.

Panic caused Jules to freeze. Tony tied her wrists and ankles so tightly that she could barely move. It was hard to breathe with the scarf around her face and neck. Sheena wiped blood off her face with the back of her hand and waved the gun at Tony and then toward the front door. "Come on. I don't have all day. Now I have to get cleaned up."

He shoved Jules on the couch face down and followed Sheena out the front door. Jules strained to listen for footsteps.

"We need to go do something. And you don't get any smart ideas. We'll be back in a little while. We'll take care of you then," Sheena said, slamming the door.

Jules waited for what seemed like an hour, but it was hard to track time.

Would they really come back? Her head throbbed constantly. When she was sure they had left, she rolled off the couch. The thud made her head and back hurt more. Jules wiggled and writhed, trying to loosen the bindings. She managed to get the scarf to slide down her face so she could spit out the part in her mouth. She gulped in air.

Then Jules bucked like a bronco until the cord loosened enough to free a leg and an arm. Minutes later, she kicked the blinds off and stood up. The room spun around again, and Jules plopped down on the couch. She had to stay awake and get out of this mess, but she needed to rest. She'd only close her eyes for a minute.

A noise registered in the fuzzy part of her brain. She opened one eye and then the other. It was hard to tell where she was in the semi-dark room. Jules blinked several times and remembered she was in the Rowland tiny house. Panic welled up in her throat. She had to get out of there before Tony and Sheena returned. *Why would they come back if they had already escaped? None of this made sense.* Thinking made her head pound again.

She stood and gingerly made her way across the sitting room to the door. Opening the door a crack, she peeked outside. Twilight slowly turned into night, and the only sound was an occasional frog or bird. Not seeing any lights, Jules tiptoed down the steps.

A twig snapped, and Jules froze. She heard footsteps. Jules turned and ran into the house. She locked the door and scooted the couch over to block the entrance.

Someone climbed the steps and stomped on the porch. The doorknob jiggled.

"I thought you left it unlocked," Tony said.

"I did," Sheena hissed. "Keep trying, Maybe it's stuck. I can't see in any of the windows. It's too dark. Hurry up."

The door shook. Tony did everything but huff and puff. Then he banged on the door. Jules moved behind the couch and edged closer to the back of the room. The floor creaked.

Jules turned, and Sheena popped in from the bedroom with her gun cocked sideways. Jules suppressed a panicked squeak. Sheena took a couple of steps in the dark and tripped, landing with a thud. The gun flew out of her hand, and Sheena swore loudly.

Jules scurried for the weapon and grabbed it. Standing up, she held the gun on Sheena. "Stay where you are."

Tony continued to rattle the front door. Jules used the moment to catch her breath and assess the situation. Shoving the couch, she flipped on the lights and unlocked the door. Tony yanked, and the door flew open. He stumbled and steadied himself with the door jamb.

Jules pointed the gun at him. "Get in here and sit on that ottoman. Don't move. I'm a little twitchy right now, so don't give me an excuse to shoot you," Jules said. "What are you two doing on my property anyway? If you got away, why did you come back?"

Tony blinked several times. "This is our hideout. And we tried to warn you, but you wouldn't listen. You had to keep poking around in our business."

"But why Tabbi? You could have walked away." Jules said.

"Sheena wanted Tabbi out of the picture. You couldn't leave well enough alone. It had nothing to do with you. But now it's your problem. Look at all this you've caused. Sheena, what are we going to do?" Tony blubbered.

"Shut up," Sheena screeched. "You don't have to say anything. It's none of her business what we're doing. Just shut your mouth."

When Sheena moved toward her, Jules kicked her in the side, and the woman groaned.

"But she asked me a question," Tony replied.

"That doesn't mean you have to answer," Sheena winced.

"So you killed Tabbi?" Jules added, egging him on.

"Uh-uh. She did. Because Tabbi was ruining our lives. We needed a clean start." Tony leaned forward and covered his head with his arms. "She controlled all the money and everything. I couldn't do anything without asking her first," he whined. "Plus, Sheena and I want to get married and have kids."

"You could have left. Why go to these extremes?" Jules asked.

Tony shrugged his shoulders. "Sheena said Tabbi was ruining everyone's life, and we'd never be rid of her. We all live in the same town. She'd always be there, making her rude remarks and bothering us. Knowing her, she'd stalk us or sue us. We, I mean she, decided it was better if she wasn't around." His voice trailed off to almost a whisper as he pointed to Sheena.

He made a gasping sound, and Jules looked to see if he was crying.

"I said shut up," Sheena snarled.

Tony hung his head.

"What about Dana? How was she involved?" Jules prodded.

"She's annoying. She started asking too many questions. Sheena said she had to go, too." Tony's voice drifted off again.

"Enough, stupid!" Sheena yelled. "She doesn't need to know what you know. Just be quiet. How many times do I have to tell you?"

Jules cocked the gun and kicked the woman in the ribs. "I said don't move. Now, don't talk. If you do it again, I will shoot you and tell the officers how you both attacked me."

Jules took several deep breaths. "Whose idea was it to frame Misti?" Jules stared at Tony.

"Hers," he smirked. "It was all her idea. She killed Tabbi and Dana. It was perfect. Everyone suspected the ex-husband and his new wife. It was too easy. Misti left the gun in the truck, and Tabbi and Dana left their stuff everywhere. Plus, Cal and Cody had a lot of guns." His lips turned into a half smile. "Then you got involved." His mood soured quickly, and he looked down at his red basketball shoes.

"Just shut up, Tony." Sheena sighed and stared daggers at her boyfriend. "Close your mouth. We'll all be better off." A look of panic flashed across her face as she waited for Jules to kick her again.

"What about the voodoo doll? What was that about?" Jules looked from Sheena to Tony.

Tony laughed. "That was our little joke. It was something stupid that Tabbi and Dana always did when they hated someone. They made a bunch of those dolls, and they'd sit around drinking and sticking pins in their enemies. Sheena found some in Dana's trailer and picked two that looked like Tabbi. It was brilliant."

Sheena groaned but didn't reply.

Jules reached down and picked up Sheena's phone. The lock screen popped up when she touched it. "Password."

"Like I'm going to help you," Sheena hissed.

Jules pulled her leg back in mid-kick. Sheena flinched but kept her teeth clinched.

"It's eight, six, six, nine," Tony said. "It spells Tony on the keypad." He chuckled again.

Jules hoped she didn't roll her eyes as she tapped the code in. She looked up the direct number for the sheriff's office on the website and dialed.

"This is Jules Keene at the Fern Valley Luxury Resort. I need you to send the sheriff over to our tiny houses now. I was attacked by the two people who killed those two women. You may want to send an ambulance, too. There was a fight."

"Are you safe?" The dispatcher asked.

"Yes," Jules said. She cut her eyes at Sheena and Tony to make sure they didn't try anything. "I have their gun. It's the tiny house with the purple door."

"Okay. Stay on the line with me until the police arrive. I've notified them of the situation. Several units are responding, including the sheriff."

Jules took a few deep breaths to calm down the adrenaline. She was positive that Tony and Sheena could hear the rat-a-tat-tat of her heartbeat.

"The first unit is about five minutes out. Is everything still okay there," the dispatcher asked.

"Yes. We're waiting patiently and having a good chat. Tell the officers that I will give them the gun when they arrive. We're in the front room of the house."

"Will do. They know there is a weapon on site. The ambulance is also en route."

Faint sirens echoed in the distance. Their whine grew louder as seconds passed. Tony fidgeted on the ottoman that looked like a child's seat under the bodybuilder.

Vehicles roared and slowed to a stop outside as Jules backed slowly toward the door and pushed the couch further out of the way. Tony and Sheena didn't move.

The sheriff and three deputies with riot helmets and bulletproof vests stormed the tiny house's porch and entered.

Jules felt the walls closing in on her in the small living room with six people. She handed Sheriff Hobbs the gun and resisted the urge to hug him.

"You okay?" he asked.

Jules nodded and stepped out on the porch. Her head started pounding again, and she felt woozy. The cold air helped for a moment. She sat down on the top step and rested her head on the railing.

The two deputies handcuffed Sheena and Tony and waved for the EMTs to come in and check them out. They left the gurney next to the porch.

Sheriff Hobbs joined Jules on the porch. "A little too tiny in there for me, too," he said. "You wanna tell me what happened?"

"I was walking around the resort, and something caught my eye. I remember getting hit on the head. Then I woke up in the cubby under the stairs. When I snuck out, I bumped into these two, and she had a gun. Then we got into it, and I got the gun." Jules managed a half smile.

He wrote furiously in his notebook. "Then what?"

"Then Tony overpowered me and tied me up with the miniblinds. They left, and I wiggled out. When they came back, there was another fight, but I did better this time."

The sheriff smiled faintly and continued to scratch notes in his book. "Tony accused Sheena of killing Tabbi and Dana?"

"He did. She kept telling him to shut up."

The sheriff nodded. "They'll both face charges. I'll need to get a formal statement from you, but this is good for now. The EMTs need to check you out next. I texted Roxanne. She'll be here any minute. They were worried sick when they couldn't find you. Jake said Bijou was barking her head off at your cabin."

The EMTs guided Sheena to the porch steps and onto the gurney, and Deputy Mario Caswell leaned over and handcuffed her to the metal rail. He climbed in his cruiser and followed the ambulance down the maintenance road. The other officer led a handcuffed Tony down the stairs and into the back of his patrol car.

"Your turn," Sheriff Hobbs said.

The EMT who stayed behind motioned for Jules to follow her inside the house. "Sit here, please." She pointed to the ottoman. Jules surveyed the damage in the room. Only the blinds were broken. It wouldn't take that much to right this place before the holiday guests arrived.

The EMT checked Jules's pupils, temperature, and blood pressure. Then she looked at the back of her head. "You're going to need stitches. I want them to check you out for a concussion. Your temperature and color are off."

Jules sighed. All she wanted was to get home and take a hot shower. "I'm always this pale."

"I still want to have you checked out." Before the EMT could radio for an ambulance, the sheriff said, "Deputy Dempsey can transport you. I'm sure you can catch up to your rig at the hospital."

Jules stood as the EMT packed her equipment. Charles, who will always be Bubba to Jules, stepped forward and took hold of her elbow, guiding her to the door. "This way. I'll get you to the hospital in no time, and you can ride up front with me," he said to the svelte EMT. "I'm Deputy Charles Dempsey." His grin showed all of his teeth.

"Nice to meet you," the EMT said, picking up her bag. "I'm Margot Stephens." She followed the pair out the door to the deputy's cruiser.

Charles fell all over himself, trying to impress Margot. Jules tried hard not to giggle at his schoolboy antics. *Bubba and his priorities. I'm glad I'm not dying here.*

Margot held the door for Jules and got her situated in the backseat. The hard vinyl seat felt like she was sitting on a board, and Plexiglas walled her in from the occupants in the front seat. No door or window handles. *There's nothing comfortable about the backseat of a patrol car, and it had a funky odor.* Jules's head throbbed so bad that she didn't even care if people saw her driving through town in the back seat of Bubba's car.

Charles chatted up the lovely Margot. The constant banter rattled around in Jules's head and made her feel queasier. She leaned her head back and closed her eyes.

"Hey, hey, Jules," Margot said, turning in her seat. "Don't go to sleep on me. Are you okay?" She tapped on the Plexiglas with her knuckle.

"I'm fine," Jules muttered, opening her eyes.

Charles took that as an invitation to use all of his deputy tools. He flipped on the siren and lights and floored it. Jules bumped around in the back seat and had to steady herself with both hands on the barrier in front of her.

The deputy pulled up to the emergency room entrance, and Jules fought back another wave of dizziness as the orderly arrived with a wheelchair and whisked her inside.

It felt like hours between the barrage of tests and long periods of waiting. Roxanne and Jake popped in, but all she could manage to tell them was to take care of Bijou and the resort emails. Then darkness descended. Her thoughts of Roxanne, Jake, Bijou, Tony, and Sheena banged into each other and merged into a weird dream where they were all at the beach.

Chapter Twenty-Nine

Wednesday

Jules woke up in a semi-dark room. She blinked several times and stared at a machine with a series of green and red lights. She inhaled deeply. Her head felt slightly better than yesterday, and a flood of thoughts about Tony, Sheena, a gun, and Harry Potter flashed in her head. *That's why I'm here in the hospital.*

Before Jules could fall back asleep, a nurse opened the door and tip-toed in.

"What time is it?" Jules asked.

"It's a little after four on Wednesday. Do you want some water?"

Jules nodded without jarring her head too much.

The nurse poured water from a pitcher into a sports bottle with a long straw. "So, can you tell me what happened?" The nurse leaned over to check the monitor next to the bed.

"I was going to ask you the same thing," Jules said faintly. "I remember being attacked at my resort. I managed to get away, but not before I got conked on the head and in a fight. A lot of the other parts are a little blurry."

"Speaking of that, how's your vision?" The nurse held up a pen for Jules to follow with her eyes.

"Fine. The headache's better, too. I feel very groggy." Jules yawned. "And tired."

"They'll be by around six-thirty or seven with breakfast. The doctors should be in after that. If he clears you, you can check out and go home."

"That's a relief. I didn't sleep very well here." Jules tried her best to smile.

"Well, your vitals check out. You should try to get some sleep before we wake you again." The nurse patted her arm. "Can I get you anything?"

"I'm fine. I'm going to try to go back to sleep. I am so tired."

"Press that red button if you need anything." She pulled the door behind her, and Jules rolled over and stared at the wall.

Jules woke up when the breakfast cart clattered down the hallway. She passed on the runny eggs but ate the fruit and yogurt with orange juice. No caffeine anywhere on the tray. She needed to get out of here.

Mid-way through a cooking demonstration on TV of raspberry crepes that looked interesting, Roxanne rushed in. Jake strode in behind her, his usual collected self.

"Oh, my stars, Jules. Are you okay? You scared me to death yesterday when we couldn't reach you. Even Mr. Calm and Cool here was on edge. He found your phone in the field." Roxanne dropped a shopping bag on the guest chair.

"I'm okay. Thanks for finding my phone. I was walking around, and someone, either Tony or Sheena, hit me in the back of the head with something hard. I woke up in the reading nook in the Potter house. I climbed out the bedroom window but ran into the pair outside. Sheena was waving a gun around. It's a little blurry, but Tony said Sheena killed Tabbi and Dana. Sheena was a screaming banshee and wanted him to keep quiet."

Jake sat on the edge of her bed and held her hand. "You had us worried. All you kept mumbling last night was check on Bijou and the resort. And for me to fix the Baum house before the guests arrive."

"We've got it covered. It's all under control. Bijou stayed with Jake," Roxanne said.

"How'd you get in?" Jules asked.

"We found your purse near the tiny houses. Your keys were inside," Roxanne added.

"No lock picking or broken windows this time." Jake grinned.

"I'm going to go check with the nurses to see when we can take you home." Roxanne zipped out the door and down the hallway.

"I'm glad you're okay." Jake kissed her on the top of her head.

"Me too. I had no idea they were on the property. Tony said he kept leaving me notes to scare me off. They wanted it to look like Misti killed Tabbi, but the pieces didn't fit together. They didn't think through their plan."

Before Jake could comment, a thin man with thick, black glasses stepped in the room. "Good morning. I'm Dr. Acharya. Jules, how are you doing?"

Jake hopped off the bed and stepped in the doorway.

"I'm fine. Hoping I can go home."

"Did you eat? No nausea?" The doctor looked at her pupils.

"I feel okay. Just tired. I ate everything but the eggs," she said.

"Okay, I'd like you to stand up for me." The doctor lowered the bed rail.

Jules swung her feet over the side and stood. She got her balance and took a couple tentative steps forward. She moved around the tight space.

"Everything looks right this morning. I think you're ready to go home. You have five stitches in the back of your head. It may be sore. Take acetaminophen every four hours. You have a mild concussion. No exercise, housework, or heavy lifting for about five days. If you experience dizziness, headaches, or nausea, come back in to get checked out."

"I will." Jules sat on the edge of the bed.

"An aide will be by soon to discharge you. You're free to go after that."

"Roxanne brought your clothes and shoes." Jake pointed to the red shopping bag in the guest chair.

Jules headed to the closet of a bathroom to change. Her hair was hopeless. With no brush or makeup, this was the best that it was going to get.

It took almost an hour to get the correct paperwork and check out. Jules left with a pile of papers and a shopping bag.

Jake helped her into the backseat of Roxanne's white Mercedes.

"You need anything before I take you home?" Roxanne asked, looking over her sunglasses in the rearview mirror.

"I'm good. I need a nap and a shower," Jules said.

Jake closed the car door, and Roxanne zoomed off toward the resort.

In what felt like an instant, Roxanne braked in front of Jules's cabin, and Jake hopped out, unlocked the cabin door, and handed her the key.

"Thanks, y'all. I appreciate everything you've done for me," Jules said.

"Go inside and get some rest. Do you want me to bring you dinner?" Roxanne asked.

"I'm fine. I didn't sleep well."

"All right then. I'll leave you in good hands with Jake. Call me if you need me." Roxanne waved and hopped in her car. She backed down the driveway before anyone spoke.

When the door opened, Bijou bolted out and jumped on Jules. She picked up the terrier and snuggled her. "I know, baby. I missed you too."

"Let's get you inside and settled, and I'll take Bijou for a walk," Jake guided her in the house.

"It's time for a much-needed shower," Jules said, heading toward her bedroom.

"Come on, Bijou. We'll take a long walk to burn off some of that energy while she's busy."

Jules heard the door slam as she stepped into the shower. The warm water pulsed on her and made her sore muscles relax. She gingerly washed her hair, careful not to get too close to the stitches. The back of her head was still tender from whatever the pair clobbered her with.

Feeling much better after the shower and being in her own pajamas, Jules grabbed a pillow, her tablet, and the remote and settled on the couch with her fuzzy blanket.

About ten minutes later, Bijou bounced through the front door and landed on the couch.

"Did you have a nice walk?" Jules asked.

The terrier danced around on the blanket and finally settled in a spot for a cuddle and a nap.

"What can I get you?" Jake asked, putting Bijou's gear on the coffee table.

"I'm good for now. I'm going to binge-watch what's on my DVR until I fall asleep."

"I'm headed over to the barn. Call me if you need me. I'll bring dinner.

Any requests?" Concern showed on his face. His longish brown hair and green eyes made Jules's heart flutter.

"Thanks. Nope. Anything but sushi or fish."

"Be back later." Jake locked the door and pulled it behind him.

She settled on the couch, and thoughts of Tabbi, Tony, and Sheena banged around Jules's brain like bowling balls until she finally drifted off to sleep.

Chapter Thirty

Thursday

Jules stretched, despite the aches, and tried to double-time her morning routine. "Come on, Bijou. We've got to play catch up today." She picked up her laptop, and the pair headed out for a walk around the resort before the start of their work day.

Once inside the office, she turned on all the lights and equipment while the coffee maker chugged away to make her espresso. The caffeine and the sugar made the dull headache go away.

The night before, Jake had brought creamy tomato soup and sandwiches from the Good Thyme Bistro for dinner. The TLC and the rest had done wonders. He'd hung out for a while and showed her pictures of his progress on the Stoker house. It would be ready for transport and installation soon if the weather holds.

Jules plowed through the reservation emails and checked to see if there was anything pressing for this weekend's New Year's Eve check-ins. Roxanne had taken care of the last-minute questions. They'd work on the gift basket assembly later.

While adding creamer to her second cup of coffee, Jules heard the bells jingle on the front door. Heavy footsteps echoed in the store.

"Good morning, Sheriff," Jules said when he popped his head in the door. Bijou yipped and jumped up to greet him.

"Howdy. Just checking in on you. Roxanne said you were glad to get home."

"I feel much better after a rest and some soup."

The sheriff smiled. "I need to get a statement from you, but I can come back if I caught you at a bad time."

"Nope. Just catching up on things here. Have a seat. Would you like some coffee?"

"Yes, please." Sheriff Hobbs settled in Roxanne's chair. He smiled and picked up a framed photo of them at a local winery. He pulled out his notebook and pen. "Okay, start from your walk and your encounter with Tony and Sheena."

Jules set a mug under the coffee machine and pressed the blue button. "I left the office and was walking around. Something caught my eye at the tiny houses. Wasn't sure what it was, but it was enough to make me check it out. Then I woke up in the reading nook. It took me a bit to realize where I was with no lights and phone. I was able to climb out of the house's bedroom window, and I ran into Tony and Sheena. She had a gun, and they hustled me back inside the house. When Tony was in the kitchen, Sheena and I had a wrestling match. Then they left and returned. Then I called you all."

"How were they when you were with them?" he asked.

"Tony liked to talk. He said that they had to get Tabbi out of the way and kill Dana because she had figured it out. He blabbered on and on, and Sheena tried a couple of times to get him to be quiet. Sheena was more agitated than he was. And she kept saying that he wasn't going to pin the murders on her."

"Anything else?"

"Nope. That's about it. Then you guys arrived and took me to the hospital."

"How's your head?" he asked.

"Still a little sore, but I feel better. I'll be ready to celebrate on New Year's Eve." She smiled faintly.

"Good. Good. We have them both in custody, and right now, they're both proclaiming their innocence and blaming the other. Both of their prints and yours were on Tony's gun."

Jules raised her eyebrows. "It sounded like a love triangle gone bad. They wanted Tabbi out of the picture. My hunch is Sheena is the brains of the operation, and she goaded Tony into helping her. Sheena wanted out from under both of the domineering women. For some reason, she thought Tony would get the business. When Dana started asking questions, they killed her to keep her quiet. Tony said that they had tried to warn me with notes."

"You're lucky that's all they did. They panicked with Dana. It could have gotten much uglier for you. I'm glad you had the wits and the opportunity to fight back," he said.

"I think Sheena thought that they could throw suspicion off themselves by making it look like Tabbi's issues were with her ex-husband and his new wife," Jules said.

"It might have worked if no one had asked questions or they hadn't killed Dana." The sheriff looked up from his notebook and paused.

"Using Dana's purse and Misti's gun was a clever ruse. Elaine and the business council will be relieved that this is all wrapped up. Maybe Tom Berryman and his legal team can persuade Tabbi's family to drop the lawsuit," Jules said.

"That's his plan. I think they're going to point out the number of frivolous lawsuits that Tabbi had filed over the years. I don't think Elaine or the town has anything to worry about."

Jules smiled. "But you know Elaine. There is always something to worry about. I give her a couple of days after New Year's for her to get rolling on plans for our Spring Fling."

The sheriff took a swig of his coffee. "Oh, I did talk to Sam at Game and Inland Fisheries. They're actively looking into the Cal's big cat sales. So, you can add that to your list of credits, too. You're good at finding stuff, but I worry about you getting yourself hurt and in dangerous situations."

"Thank you for your concern. Trust me. It's not a hobby that I'm going to pursue, but I need to find out about things that happen at my resort." Jules shrugged her shoulder. "People like to talk. Maybe being a resort owner is like being a bartender or hairdresser. I listen, and folks tell me their stories. Sometimes more than I want to hear."

"Maybe I should deputize you," he said, putting his notebook away.

"I'll keep that in mind in case I ever want a career change. But for now,

I'm happy here at the resort. We've come a long way since that old seventies campground that my parents started with."

Ooey Gooey Chocolate Brownies

Ingredients

- ½ cup of melted, unsalted butter
- 1 tablespoon cooking oil
- 1 and 1/8 cup of white, granulated sugar
- 2 large eggs
- 2 teaspoons of vanilla extract
- ½ cup of all-purpose flour
- ½ cup of unsweetened cocoa powder
- ¼ teaspoon salt
- Chocolate chips

Instructions

1. Preheat your oven to 350 degrees Fahrenheit. Grease an 8-inch square baking pan and line it with baking or parchment paper.
2. Combine the hot butter, oil, and sugar in a medium bowl. Whisk well. Add the eggs and vanilla. Mix until the batter's color lightens.
3. Add the flour, cocoa powder, and salt. Mix well. Pour the batter in your pan and even it out. For extra gooeyness, add chocolate chips to the top.
4. Bake for 25 minutes. Test with a toothpick. It is done when the center the toothpick is dry.
5. Cool, slice, and enjoy. Also great with vanilla ice cream.

Jules's Cheesy Chicken Pasta Bake

Ingredients

- 12 ounces of uncooked penne pasta
- 12 ounces of Velveeta
- 2 cups of shredded Colby-Monterey-Jack
- 1 cup milk
- 3 cups of cooked, shredded chicken
- 1 can of enchilada sauce
- 1 can of chopped green chiles
- 4 tablespoons of melted butter
- 1 package of taco seasoning mix
- 2 tablespoons of sliced green onions

Instructions

1. Heat the oven to 375 degrees F. Spray a 3-quart glass baking dish with cooking spray. Cook the pasta, drain it, and set it aside.
2. In a large microwavable bowl, mix the Velveeta, one cup of cheese, and milk. Microwave for four minutes on high. Stir. Continue to microwave until the cheese melts. Stir in pasta and pour into the baking dish.
3. Mix the chicken, enchilada sauce, green chiles, butter, and seasoning mix. Pour over the pasta mixture.
4. Bake for 30 minutes. Cover the top with the remaining cheese and let stand for five minutes.
5. Top with green onions and garnish with cheese or sour cream.

Pop's Coca-Cola Cake

Ingredients

- 2 cups of all-purpose flour
- 2 cups of sugar
- 1 teaspoon baking soda
- ½ teaspoon salt
- ½ teaspoon ground cinnamon
- 1 (12 oz.) can of Coke
- 1 cup butter (cubed)
- ¼ c. baking cocoa
- 2 large eggs
- ½ cup buttermilk
- 1 teaspoon vanilla extract

Icing/Glaze

- 1 (12 oz.) can of Coke
- ½ cup butter (cubed)
- ¼ cup baking cocoa
- 4 cups sifted confectioner's sugar

Instructions

1. Preheat your oven to 350 degrees. Grease a 13x9 baking pan.
2. In a large bowl, mix the first five ingredients. In a small saucepan, combine the Coke, butter, and cocoa. Bring the mixture to a boil. Stir

as needed. Add flour.

3. In a small bowl, whisk the eggs, buttermilk, and vanilla. Add to the flour mixture. Stir well.

4. Transfer the batter to the pan and bake for 30 minutes.

5. Prepare the glaze in a small saucepan. Bring the Coke to boil. Cook for 15 minutes. Stir in butter and cocoa. Add the confectioner's sugar and stir until smooth. Pour mixture over the hot cake. Serve with vanilla ice cream or whipped cream.

Crystal's Eggnog French Toast

Ingredients

- 2 eggs, beaten
- 1 ½ cups eggnog
- 1 ½ tablespoons of ground cinnamon
- 1 teaspoon pumpkin pie spice
- 12 slices of French bread (or any thick bread)

Instructions

1. Mix the eggs, eggnog, cinnamon, and pumpkin spice in a mixing bowl. Blend and pour the mixture into a shallow dish.
2. Grease and preheat your electric skillet to 300 degrees F.
3. Dip each piece of bread (one at a time) in the mixture. Coat each side of the bread completely.
4. Put the bread on the skillet. Turn, so each side is golden brown.
5. Garnish with powdered sugar, warm syrup, whipped cream, or fruit.

Lula Belle's Pecan Pie Muffins

Ingredients

Muffins:

- 2 cups all-purpose flour 1 egg
- ¾ cup sugar ¾ cup heavy cream
- 1 tablespoon baking powder 5 tablespoons of melted, unsalted butter
- 1 teaspoon cinnamon ½ teaspoon salt
- ¾ cup milk

Crumble:

- 1/3 cup flour ¼ cup brown sugar
- Pinch of salt ½ teaspoon cinnamon
- 3 tablespoons of cold butter, chopped ½ cup chopped pecans

Instructions

1. Line a 12-cup muffin container or butter the tin. Preheat the over to 400 degrees F.
2. In a large bowl, stir the flour, sugar, baking powder, cinnamon, and salt.
3. In another smaller bowl, whisk together the egg, cream, milk, and butter. Blend well. Mix this with the flour mixture. Pour the mixture in the individual muffin tins.
4. In a small bowl, combine 1/3 cup of flour, brown sugar, and a pinch

of salt. Add the cold butter and chopped pecans. Mix well and then sprinkle on the top of the muffin batter.

5. Bake for 20 minutes. Set the muffins on a cooling rack.

Kissy Peanut Butter Cookies

Ingredients

- 1 stick of unsalted butter
- 1 cup of light brown sugar
- ¾ cup of creamy peanut butter (Jif is my favorite.)
- 1 egg
- ½ teaspoon of vanilla extract
- 1 ¼ cups of flour
- ½ teaspoon of baking powder
- ½ teaspoon of baking soda
- ¼ teaspoon of salt
- Granulated sugar
- 1 bag of Hershey's Kisses

Directions:

1. Preheat the oven to 350 degrees F. In a large bowl, mix the butter, brown sugar, and peanut butter. Make sure it's blended well. Add the egg, vanilla extract. Then mix in the flour, baking powder, baking soda, and salt. Roll the dough into small balls. Roll in granulated sugar and place them on an ungreased cookie sheet.
2. Use a fork to flatten the balls. Then press the fork in again to create cross marks. Bake about 9 minutes until they are a light brown.
3. While they are still warm, firmly place an unwrapped Hershey's Kiss in the center of each.

Crystal's Cheesy Sausage Balls

Ingredients

- 1 pound spicy sausage, uncooked
- 8 ounces of cream cheese, softened
- 1 ¼ cups of Bisquick
- 4 ounces of shredded cheddar cheese

Directions:

1. Preheat the oven to 400 degrees F.
2. Mix all of the ingredients well.
3. Roll the dough into 1-inch balls.
4. Bake for 20 minutes or until browned.

Triple-layer Peanut Butter Brownies

Ingredients

- 1 package of brownie mix (20 ounces)
- 1 cup of cold milk
- 1 cup of creamy peanut butter
- 1 ½ cups of Cool Whip
- ½ cup of dry roasted peanuts, chopped
- 1 package of vanilla instant pudding
- ½ cup of powdered sugar
- 3 squares of semi-sweet chocolate

Directions:

1. Bake brownies in 13x9-inch pan. Follow the package directions.
2. Beat milk and pudding mix with a whisk for 2 minutes.
3. Add peanut butter and sugar. Mix well.
4. Refrigerate until brownies are completely cooled.
5. Spread pudding mixture over brownies.
6. Microwave Cool Whip and chocolate on high for 1 minute. Stir every 30 seconds. Spread over pudding. Sprinkle with nuts.
7. Refrigerate for 1 hour.

Acknowledgements

I want to thank my family and friends who support me along this path. Stan Weidner, thanks for always being there, my parents who instilled in me a lifelong love of reading, Cortney Cain for being my sounding board, Meagan and Jocelyn Cain, my social media gurus, and Bill Cain for always keeping everyone in stitches. And I appreciate all the encouragement, love, and support from my Bethia UMC family.

Many, many thanks to my fabulous agent, Dawn Dowdle for all her help and hard work. And a huge thank you to Shawn Reilly Simmons and her team at Level Best Books for letting me share Fern Valley with you. Thank you to Joy Pfister and her wonderful crew at Studio FBJ for making me look good.

I am so grateful for my talented Sisters in Crime, Guppy, International Thriller Writers, and James River Writer friends. Your support is invaluable!

And most of all, many thanks to all the wonderful readers, reviewers, book bloggers, and podcasters who are the reason for all of this.

About the Author

Through the years, Heather Weidner has been a cop's kid, technical writer, editor, college professor, software tester, and IT manager. *Christmas Lights and Cat Fights* is the third in her cozy mystery series, the Jules Keene Glamping Mysteries. She also writes the Delanie Fitzgerald mystery series and the Mermaid Bay Christmas Shoppe Mysteries (2023).

Her short stories appear in the *Virginia is for Mysteries* series, *50 Shades of Cabernet, Deadly Southern Charm,* and *Murder by the Glass,* and her novellas appear in The Mutt Mysteries series.

She is a member of Sisters in Crime and active in Central Virginia, Chessie, and Guppies Chapters, International Thriller Writers, and James River Writers.

Originally from Virginia Beach, Heather has been a mystery fan since Scooby-Doo and Nancy Drew. She lives in Central Virginia with her husband and a pair of Jack Russell terriers.

SOCIAL MEDIA HANDLES:
Website and Blog: http://www.heatherweidner.com
Twitter: https://twitter.com/HeatherWeidner1
Facebook: https://www.facebook.com/HeatherWeidnerAuthor

Instagram: https://www.instagram.com/heather_mystery_writer/

Goodreads: https://www.goodreads.com/author/show/8121854.Heather_Weidner

Amazon Authors: http://www.amazon.com/-/e/B00HOYR0MQ

Pinterest: https://www.pinterest.com/HeatherBWeidner/

LinkedIn:
https://www.linkedin.com/in/heather-weidner-0064b233?trk=hp-identity-name

BookBub:
https://www.bookbub.com/authors/heather-weidner-d6430278-c5c9-4b10-b911-340828fc7003

AllAuthor: https://allauthor.com/profile/heatherweidner/

YouTube:
https://www.youtube.com/channel/UCyBjyB0zz-M1DaM-rU1bXGA?view_as=subscriber

AUTHOR WEBSITE:

http://HeatherWeidner.com

Also by Heather Weidner

The Mermaid Bay Christmas Shoppe Mysteries
Sticks and Stones and a Bag of Bones

The Delanie Fitzgerald Mysteries
Secret Lives and Private Eyes
The Tulip Shirt Murders
Glitter, Glam, and Contraband
Male Revues and Subterfuge

Short Stories in *Murder by the Glass, Deadly Southern Charm, 50 Shades of Cabernet, Virginia is for Mysteries, Virginia is for Mysteries II*

Novellas in the Mutt Mysteries series
To Fetch a Thief
To Fetch a Scoundrel
To Fetch a Villain
To Fetch a Killer

Printed in the USA
CPSIA information can be obtained
at www.ICGtesting.com
LVHW091747021123
762909LV00038B/432